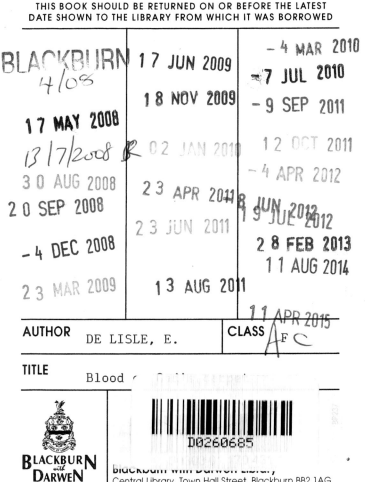

BLACKBURN 1 7 JUN 2009   - 4 MAR 2010

4/08   1 8 NOV 2009   -7 JUL 2010

17 MAY 2008   - 9 SEP 2011

13/7/2008   02 JAN 2010   1 2 OCT 2011

30 AUG 2008   2 3 APR 2011   - 4 APR 2012

2 0 SEP 2008   2 3 JUN 2011   1 9 JUL 2012

- 4 DEC 2008   2 8 FEB 2013

23 MAR 2009   1 3 AUG 2011   1 1 AUG 2014

1 1 APR 2015

| AUTHOR | DE LISLE, E. | CLASS | AF C |

TITLE   Blood

BLOOD ON GOD'S CARPET

After the death of her mother, timorous, downtrodden Gertrude Simms resigns herself to living alone. Until she meets Bill Reed, the man of her dreams — or so she thinks . . . Determined to take charge of her own life at long last, she rechristens herself Jenny and, assisted by her best friend Tamara Watson, is transformed into a modern-day woman. But whilst the new Jenny is enjoying wedded bliss, the other residents of Woodfield are rocked by rape and murder in the community. Does the ghostly apparition in the white suit hold the key to the deaths, and can she help catch the killer from beyond the grave?

Books by Eileen de Lisle
Published by The House of Ulverscroft:

NINE BETTS LANE
INHERITED FEAR

EILEEN DE LISLE

BLOOD ON GOD'S CARPET

Complete and Unabridged

ULVERSCROFT
Leicester

First published in Great Britain in 2006 by
Beagle Publications
Southampton

First Large Print Edition
published 2007
by arrangement with
Beagle Publications
Southampton

British Library CIP Data

De Lisle, Eileen
  Blood on God's carpet.—Large print ed.—
Ulverscroft large print series: crime
  1. Detective and mystery stories
  2. Large type books
  I. Title
  823.9′2 [F]

  ISBN 978–1–84782–018–1

01 170 431 1

Published by
F. A. Thorpe (Publishing)
Anstey, Leicestershire

Set by Words & Graphics Ltd.
Anstey, Leicestershire
Printed and bound in Great Britain by
T. J. International Ltd., Padstow, Cornwall

This book is printed on acid-free paper

For my family

1

Gertrude Simms stood in the park with her little Yorkie dog Pepper. Glad of the respite from her overbearing mother. She treasured this lunchtime hour of peace and contemplation. Each day at one o'clock, regular as clockwork, she would take Pepper out for his walk. It was a grey cold November day, but she didn't care. This was her time, her hour of peace away from the old dragon. She sat on the park bench wondering what the future held for her. Here she was, forty five years old and still an old maid, as her mother would constantly remind her. *I was married to your father at the age of twenty you know, and here you are over twice that age and still unclaimed.* It was times like this when her mother was at her worst, complaining, nagging, criticizing, that she could quite cheerfully have put a pillow over her head and smothered her.

What had she done with her life? Nothing, absolutely nothing! Unlike her friend Tamara Watson, who had everything, brains, beauty, a career, men falling at her feet. She had never even had so much as a date. No man would ever fancy her. She was deep in thought when she was suddenly startled by a magpie which flew down and landed on the grass in front of her. She looked around, only one magpie, the messenger of death. She knew in that instant her mother had died. She looked at her watch, she was only twenty minutes into the walk and was determined to have the whole hour. She reasoned with herself: If I rush home and she is alright then she will have won yet again. Dragging me away from the only pleasure I have, being alone with my dog and having time to myself. If on the other hand she is dead, then she isn't going anywhere so she can wait. Eventually at two o'clock she thought she had better head back home and face the consequences. Suddenly Pepper started barking furiously at a clump of bushes.

'Pepper, shut up and come here at once.' The dog continued barking, determined to draw her attention to what he could see. I suppose it's teenagers from the college up to no good as usual. Disgraceful behaviour, they need a good caning. As she looked towards the bushes she caught sight of something blue. Someone was in there. She felt slightly uneasy and decided to head for home. Suddenly her path was barred by a man who stepped out from the bushes. Now she was really scared. A young girl had been murdered six months earlier and no one had been charged with her murder. The police called on everyone in the immediate vicinity telling them not to walk alone in the park. The ladies especially should walk their dogs in pairs at least, or better still in a large group. They advised that they should all meet at a prearranged time at the park entrance and complete the walk together. Gertrude ignored this piece of advice; she preferred her own company, and anyway, who would walk with her? She had no friends.

'I'm sorry, I didn't mean to startle you. A call of nature you know, so sorry.'

Out from the bushes scurried a very indignant looking young couple, clothes in disarray, school bags slung over their shoulders. They glared at the couple standing on the path and hurried off towards the park gate, calling from a safe distance, 'Filthy old perv! Weirdo! Loser!' A thought occurred to Gertrude that perhaps the man had been watching the young couple. Then she dismissed the thought as nonsense. It was probably as he said a call of nature. He probably didn't know the young couple were there and was as surprised as me when they came out from the bushes.

'I don't know, young people today! My

father would have taken a leather belt to me if he found out I'd behaved in any way like they do today.'

'Yes, my mother was very strict with me.' She suddenly realized she had used the word in the past tense. Something about the man seemed vaguely familiar. 'Do I know you?'

'No but I know you. I've seen you every day dead on one o'clock walking your little dog around the park.'

Gertrude experienced mixed emotions at this statement. She didn't know whether to be pleased that at last someone — a man — had actually noticed her, or to be frightened that someone had been watching her without her knowledge.

'Bill Reed.'

The man extended his hand to shake hers. She accepted it rather reluctantly. It was hot and sweaty. She looked at his face and there were beads of sweat on his brow. She wondered why he should be sweating on such a freezing cold day. Perhaps it was embarrassment. Yes, that must be it. He was embarrassed.

'And your name?'

'Ger . . . Jenny Simms.' She just stopped herself from saying Gertrude. A horrible old-fashioned name. She had never liked it. From now on she would be known as Jenny.

'Perhaps I'll see you the same time tomorrow Jenny.'

'Perhaps, we'll see. Goodbye.'

She glanced over her shoulder as she was leaving the park. He was still standing on the path watching her. She glanced at her watch. Heavens, it's two-thirty, I'm half an hour late. Mother will go mad. Then she remembered her earlier premonition of her mother's death. No she won't, she'll never be able to moan or complain about me ever again.

She entered the house, it was silent as the grave. No screeching voice from her mother's bedroom. *'Is that you Gertrude, you were a long time. How long does it take to walk thatstupid little dog?'* Slowly she took off her coat and scarf and hung them on the hallstand. She started to climb the stairs. She took a deep breath and said aloud, 'Here we go.' Standing outside her mother's door she stood and listened for a moment. Silence! Looking around the door she called loudly.

'Mother, I'm back. Is there anything you want?'

She kept up the daily ritual, knowing as she glanced down at the deathly white still figure, it would be the last time she would perform it. Taking hold of her mother's hand she felt for a pulse but none was there. Sitting on the bed she thought, what's next. I suppose the doctor is the first one to call.

★ ★ ★

Doctor Powell was at the house within twenty minutes of Gertrude ringing him.

'Gertrude my dear. I'm very sorry she's gone. I know how much she meant to you.'

You don't you silly old fool. No one does, at last I'm free to do as I please. Travel, do a hundred and one things before it's too late.

'The years of devotion and love that you lavished on her . . . but she was eighty-six, a good age, and her heart was very weak, as I told you before she could have gone at any time.' Gertrude managed a little sniff and a dab of imaginary tears from her eyes. Playing the part of a dutiful daughter till the last.

'Would you like me to give you anything to help you sleep my dear?'

'No, no thank you,' gulped Gertrude.

'Have you anyone you could call to come and stay with you tonight?'

'Yes, my friend Tamara.'

'Ah good, you do that my dear and try not to get too upset. You were a wonderful daughter to her. No mother could have asked for better.'

You can say that again. Sanctimonious old

twit. As soon as the doctor had gone she began to relax, humming softly to herself as she set about making her tea. I'll give Tamara a call as soon as she gets in from work.

She sat in her favourite armchair mulling over her life, while she sipped her mug of tea. Mother always made me use cups, she said mugs were so common and only for building workers. Well all that is going to change from now on. I'm going to try and emulate Tamara. I wish I could have led the life she has, on her third man and I haven't even had one. At school she was my saviour standing up to anyone bullying me, always taking my side against others. No one frightened her. The girls use to call us beauty and ugly. I pretended not to hear their cruel comments but I did. Things are definitely going to change from now on. I'm going to have some excitement in my life. Perhaps Tamara will help me to create a new image. I may even get a job. She put her mug down and dozed off to sleep.

A noise in the street suddenly roused her. My God, it's six o'clock, I'd better ring Tamara and the few people in mother's family that are still alive.

'Hello Tamara, it's me, Gertrude. Mother passed away this afternoon.'

'Oh you poor love. I'll be over right away.'

7

'Are you sure?'

'Yes of course I am. I'll be with you in about fifteen to twenty minutes.' This was the time it took her to drive from her flat at Ocean Village in Southampton to Gertrude's home at Woodfield in the New Forest.

*   *   *

'I know you're very efficient Gertie, but is there anything you'd like me to do? Did your mother want to be buried or cremated?'

'Cremated.'

'I always thought she preferred a burial.'

'She did once, but changed her mind towards the end.' I'm not burying her and having the responsibility of tending a grave. It would be like she's still alive lording it over me.

'There is one thing you could do for me.'

'Yes anything, you name it and it shall be done.'

'Well, could you please call me Jenny from now on? I've always hated Gertrude or even Gertie. I want a new life, a new start from now on. Please help me Tamara?'

'Of course I will.'

The two women hugged each other. As usual Tamara felt protective towards her friend and would have done anything to ease her pain. Completely unaware of her friend's

8

true feelings towards her mother.

Gertrude proceeded to tell her about Bill, the man she had met in the park that day.

'Be careful Jenny, picking up strange men in the park. See, I've started calling you Jenny already. As soon as the funeral is over and everything settled, I'll take you to a beauty salon for a makeover.'

★ ★ ★

A week after the funeral, Tamara was as good as her word and arranged various beauty appointments for Jenny.

'The first stop my girl is the hairdresser's. You're sure you want your long hair cut off and dyed another colour?'

'Yes, definitely. I want it completely different. Cut very short like yours and an almost black colour, instead of mousy brown.'

The transformation complete, Jenny walked down the road, head held high, and was amazed that for the first time in her life she attracted admiring glances from the opposite sex. Neighbours walked past without recognizing her. She was elated. What do the Yanks say — this is the first day of the rest of my life? She could hear her mother saying to her, *Yanks! Don't you mean Americans, I do hate all this modern day slang.* Well tough, mother,

I'm going to talk any way I like from now on, so go away to wherever you are supposed to be, with the angels or somewhere, or would it be with the other lot in the hot place. She giggled, and then suddenly realized people were looking at her; she composed herself and walked to the bus stop. Her mind immediately focused on the clothes she was going to buy in the Shopping Centre.

★ ★ ★

She had not seen Bill in the park since the day her mother died, so she decided to walk Pepper at different times of the day in the hope of bumping into him. As she approached her house, a terrible row was raging three doors away at the Rickman's, everyone in the road must have heard it, even with their windows shut. Judy and Roy Rickman had inherited the house from a maiden aunt and had been living there for the past six months with their three teenage children.

Liam was seventeen and had already been in trouble with the police over drug related crimes. His twin sisters Kendra and Danya were a year younger but looked twenty with their bleached hair and a cigarette permanently protruding from their mouths.

Martha Simms had said many times that the tone of the road had been lowered the day they moved in. As Jenny passed their door the row had spilled out into the front garden with the twins screeching obscenities back at their mother. Normally Jenny would have been annoyed by the nuisance being caused by the family, but not today — she had other things on her mind.

Muttering to herself, dysfunctional family, she passed by their house without a second glance. On reaching her front door she decided to collect Pepper and go straight to the park in the hope of bumping into Bill, only pausing momentarily to change into a pair of suitable shoes. It was three o'clock and she knew the park would be crowded with youngsters. The local college and comprehensive all finished at three, and most of the pupils made their way home through the park. She was ahead of the throng of young people, so decided to let Pepper off the lead before they all appeared. The minute Pepper was let off the lead, he made a beeline for some bushes barking furiously and totally ignoring Jenny's call to come back to her. She approached the bushes apprehensively knowing that someone was sure to be there. Pepper didn't bark without reason. Then she saw the same flash of blue as before and knew it was

Bill. Surely not another call of nature. He should really use his bathroom before leaving home. It makes him no better than the teenagers who use the bushes as a public convenience. A slightly disgusted Jenny called out.

'Bill, is that you?'

A very red faced Bill emerged from the bushes.

'Je . . . Je . . . Jenny?'

For the first time she noticed Bill suffered from a stammer when he was nervous. She concluded that he was embarrassed being caught for a second time lurking in the bushes.

'What's happened to you? You look lovely.'

A warm glow spread over her face at the compliment.

'I hope you don't mind me saying Bill, but it's not showing a very good example to the teenagers using the bushes as a toilet. That's just the sort of thing they get up to.'

'Oh dear me no. You've got it all wrong. I went into the bushes after a cat to see if it was alright. A dog chased it and I thought it had hurt its paw, but it was too quick for me and escaped into that garden.'

'Bill, I'm sorry. I feel an absolute fool. Will you forgive me? To make it up to you I'd like to invite you over for a meal tomorrow night.

Please say you'll come.'

'Of course I will, and there's nothing to forgive, an easy mistake to make.' The next evening Bill Reed was ringing Jenny's doorbell sharp at seven o'clock. And so began a strange relationship between the two which was to last a lifetime.

★　★　★

Jenny couldn't wait to tell Tamara all the details, of how she lost her virginity at the age of forty-five.

'Please Jenny, spare me the details, too much information. I thought I was a fast worker, but on your first date ever! Well, that's going some even for me. I hope you won't get hurt and he's not just using you.'

'Don't worry about me. I know he's a good man.'

'How do you know, Jenny? You've had very little experience with men. In fact you've had none up till now. Please be careful.'

Tamara felt a little apprehensive on her friend's behalf. She did not know why, but she had this feeling of uneasiness, that Bill Reed was not all he appeared to be. I must keep a close eye on her without spoiling things. She has had so little happiness in her life and deserves to have some.

13

'What is it Tamara? You look anxious.'

'It's nothing. Nothing at all. I was just wondering when I'm going to meet this gorgeous man of yours.'

'Well, how about coming for Sunday lunch? I could ask Bill to come, providing he's not got anything else on.'

'That would be great Jenny, thanks.'

★   ★   ★

As Tamara got out of her sports car, the first sound she heard was the harsh shrill voice of Judy Rickman.

'Whores, the pair of you. You're nothing but dirty little whores. Get out of our house and back to the streets where you both belong.'

'Don't talk to my sisters like that you fat old bag.' Liam responded on his sisters' behalf.

Tamara, not wishing to hear any more, was relieved to see a beaming Jenny had opened the front door and was waiting for her.

'Come on in Tamara. Bill's already here. Thank God for double glazing.'

As soon as Tamara and Bill clapped eyes on one another there was an instant mutual dislike. The evening did not go as Jenny had planned. There were times throughout the evening when there were long frosty silences and Tamara and Bill sat glaring at one another.

What a creep! How could Jenny fancy someone like that? Still, if I say anything I'll get accused of interfering.

Stuck up cow. She needs taking down a peg or two and I'm just the one to do it.

Jenny interrupted their thoughts.

'Anyone want anything else to eat or drink?'

Before they could answer Tamara's mobile phone rang.

'I'm so sorry Jenny, I thought I'd turned it off.'

'It doesn't matter, really. Go on, take your call, I expect it's Gary.' Tamara nodded that it was.

'Hello darling. When did you get back?'

'I can't abide mobile phones. The worst thing ever invented. Everywhere you go someone's phone rings. You can't escape them. You'd never catch me with one in a million years.'

'Ssh . . . .She'll hear you.' Jenny tried to silence Bill, but he persisted.

'I don't care if she does. I think it's really rude to bring one to your home like that. Who does she think she is? Some sort of celebrity that needs to be in touch at all times?'

Tamara had finished her call and was seething. She couldn't stay a moment longer, she knew that if she did, she might say things she would regret, and she didn't want to hurt Jenny's feelings, when she had worked so hard to make the evening a success but had failed miserably.

'I must go now Jenny. Gary is back from the States and waiting at the flat. Thank you so much for a lovely meal. You always were a superb cook. I'll be in touch. Give me a call if you need anything. Here's my new mobile number. I lost the old one. I just can't think where I left it.'

She handed Jenny a piece of paper with her new number. Jenny put it down by the phone on the hall table, and went to the front door to see her off. Bill remained inside and quick as a flash he had written down the number and returned to the armchair, to pick up the evening paper.

The two women walked down the garden path towards the front gate, when suddenly the row that had started earlier in the evening at the Rickmans' house just erupted all over again, with the arrival of the twins the worse for drink.

'I don't know how you can put up with that sort of thing all the time. Have you thought of moving? Perhaps a lovely little flat on the waterfront near me.'

'Oh I don't know. I'm settled here and it's near the park for walking Pepper — and Bill too of course. Did you like him? Tell me honestly what you thought of him.' Tamara immediately felt uncomfortable. She didn't want to lie to her friend and on the other hand she didn't want to hurt her feelings.

'Well, to be perfectly honest Jen, I'm not really sure.' She glanced at her watch.

'Heavens, is that the time? I really must get back to Gary. Thank you for a lovely evening. We'll speak again soon. You have my new number. Bye for now.'

Jenny turned and walked up the garden path with the distinct feeling that the two people who meant the most to her in the world hated each other.

2

Gary Stevens was becoming increasingly worried about his girlfriend. She had suddenly become very subdued and nervy, on edge all the time and would jump every time the phone rang, not making any effort to answer it.

'Can you get the phone Tam please? I'm just about to have a shower.' Tamara got to her feet slowly, praying that whoever it was would have rung off before she reached the other side of the room. She was not in luck. She lifted the receiver, her voice barely above a whisper.

'Hello.' There was silence. 'Who's there? Can I help you?'

'For Christ's sake Tam you're not at work. Can I help you?' Gary mimicked her voice.

'Who the hell was it? What did they want at this time of night? It's eleven thirty for God's sake.'

Suddenly everything became too much for her and she broke down unable to control the tears and emotions she had kept bottled up for weeks. It was like the floodgates had opened and she sobbed in Gary's arms for a good five minutes before he could get any sense out of her. Gary offered her a tissue from the box on the coffee table. She blew her nose and cleared her throat ready to confide all her fears to Gary.

'Now Tam what is it? You haven't been yourself for ages.'

'I've been getting these threatening phone calls. At first I didn't take too much notice. It was just somebody calling and then hanging up. I thought it was children messing about. Then there was heavy breathing and now he's started to threaten me, saying he's going to kill me.'

'Do you recognize the voice? Is it someone at work having a laugh?'

'No. He sounds older than the people I work with and his voice is muffled and distorted. I am really scared Gary. What am I going to do? He's calling on both phones my mobile and home phone.'

'Stay calm for one thing. You're playing right into his hands by being frightened. The first thing to do in the morning is get onto the phone company and see if they can trace who is making the calls. Then we'll take a walk to the Civic Centre police station and report the death threats.'

'Walk.' Tamara was quite horrified by this suggestion; she never walked anywhere, she went everywhere in her sports car.

'Yes walk. It'll do you good and put some colour back in your cheeks. You look like death warmed up. Oh sorry Tam, I didn't mean to upset you.'

'It's alright, I'm not that sensitive. Now I've got you to look after me I'll be fine. Come on, bed, it's nearly twelve-thirty. We have been talking for nearly an hour.'

For the first time in ages she felt safe and snuggled close to Gary. He's so good for me, always taking charge and knows exactly what to do in a bad situation. I love him so much and don't know what I'd do if he ever left me.

* * *

Bill Reed had spent yet another weekend with Jenny and was spending more time at her house than his own. She was more than happy with this arrangement. He was so attentive to her needs, never in her life had she received such attention from anyone. Tamara was the only person who had cared about her, but a man's affection was different from a best friend's.

'I'm just off for the morning paper my sweet. You stay in bed a bit longer and when I get back I'll bring you breakfast.'

'I'll come with you if you like.'

'No, I insist you stay where you are and give me a chance to spoil you. It makes my heart bleed when I think of all the years you were at your mother's beck and call with never a word of thanks or kindness uttered from her mouth.'

Jenny smiled and agreed to stay in bed and wait for her breakfast. She thought, at last this must be payback time for all she had suffered at the hands of her mother. Perhaps it's true we all get our reward in the end.

'I'll slip out the back way darling, I won't be long.'

'Alright, bye.' Jenny snuggled back down in bed to await his return.

Bill Reed had another reason for slipping out the back way. The Rickman girls a few doors down slept in the back bedroom and never closed their curtains. At night when he'd take the rubbish out for Jenny he'd see them strutting about their bedroom with next to nothing on. I hope there're up and it's not too early for them. I may catch a glimpse of one or both of them. A young lad was walking towards him along the path at the back of the houses and called out to the girls. Danya leant out of the window wearing a very revealing top. He dodged behind a bush hoping to watch her for a while unnoticed. Too late — he was spotted by Danya.

'What you looking at you old perv?'

The youth swung round and looked menacingly at Bill.

'How'd you like my fist in your face old man?'

'Don't be so ridiculous. I'm looking for my keys. I must have dropped them somewhere along here and if you had any decency at all you'd help me look for them.'

'Blind as well as pervie, are you? Here they are.'

The youth bent down and picked up Bill's keys and handed them to him.

'Now shove off old man before I hang one on you, and if I catch you sniffing around my girlfriend again I'll have you.'

Bill scurried away thanking his lucky stars he had had the presence of mind to drop his keys when confronted by the lad, and that having landed on the leaves, they had made no sound. He was not sure whether his story was believed or not. He breathed a sigh of relief as he entered Jenny's back garden and quickly locked the gate behind him.

'You were a long time Bill.'

'I was accosted by one of those Rickman girls' boyfriends. Obnoxious yob.'

'Are you alright?'

'Yes, he doesn't frighten me. Let's not talk about them, we have the rest of the day to enjoy ourselves.'

'I thought we might invite Tamara and Gary over next weekend. I haven't seen much of her lately. Promise me you'll be nice to her, please . . .'

'But of course my sweet. You know I don't think much of her and her swanky ways, but she's your friend and I respect that.'

'Oh thank you.' Jenny threw her arms around his neck and kissed him.

* * *

The following weekend Tamara and Gary arrived for their Sunday lunch. It took a lot of persuasion to get Gary to agree to come along. He thought Jenny most odd, but as Tam had been so down lately he didn't want to upset her further by making excuses. Anyway it will be interesting to meet the wonderful Bill who she bangs on about for hours on the phone to Tam. Still while she's on the phone for an hour it stops the phone pest getting through.

Jenny was at the door waiting to greet them as soon as she saw their car pull up.

'How lovely to see you both.' She flung her arms around Tamara and kissed her.

'Tamara, whatever's the matter? You look so pale, and you have lost even more weight. Are you ill?'

'No, I'm alright Jen. I haven't been sleeping too well lately.'

'You work far too hard you know. Try to relax more and enjoy yourself. It makes a change for me to be giving you advice, it's usually the other way round.'

Bill stood behind Jenny with a sneer on his face; he was highly delighted with his handy work. That's taken her ladyship down a peg or two, she's not so high and mighty now. I must think of the next step in my plans for her. Rape perhaps! Jenny's voice broke in on his thoughts.

'Bill! A penny for them, you were miles away.'

'So sorry, I was just relaxing in the charming company. I very nearly drifted off to sleep.'

He's a smarmy git, thought Gary. Tam was right about him. I don't suppose he has anything to do with all the phone calls. No, he doesn't seem capable, but still there is something odd about him. I can't quite put my finger on it.

'Are you off on any more trips abroad Gary?'

Bill was instantly interested in his answer.

24

'Well Jen, I'm supposed to go on a trip to the States again next week, but I'm not at all sure that I should go, with things as they are with Tam at the moment.'

'What do you mean Gary, what things? Is there something you're both not telling me? You're not ill are you Tamara?'

'No of course not. Gary's just being silly. I've been getting a few nuisance calls, that's all. Nothing I can't handle.'

'How long will you be away for, Gary? Tamara can come and stay here if she feels worried. I'll look after her for a change, she always looked out for me at school, now it'll be my turn.'

'About a week. Not long really.'

'Will you stop discussing me like I'm some sort of silly scared child? I'll stay in my own home where I belong. Thank you for your offer Jenny, but I'll be alright, really I will.'

Bill could hardly contain his excitement that Tamara was going to be totally alone for a whole week. He could take his plans for her a step further.

'May I suggest something? I could call every evening when she gets in from work to check all is well, spend a little time with her and then come home to my other charming lady.'

Tamara shuddered at the thought and was

about to protest when Gary answered for her.

'That's really decent of you mate. I'll see you're not out of pocket. I'll pay your bus fares into town.'

'You certainly will not. Tamara is Jenny's best friend and any friend of Jenny's I regard as a friend of mine. Jenny is the love of my life and I fully understand your concern for Tamara. If the boot was on the other foot I'm sure you'd be only too pleased to help me out.'

Tamara wanted to be sick. How could Gary lumber me with that creep for a week? Wait till I get him home, I'll give him a piece of my mind.

★ ★ ★

The week of Gary's departure came around all too quickly for Tamara; with dread in her heart she waved him goodbye.

'See you soon darling, and don't worry, I'll be fine with creepy Bill looking after me.'

The next evening when she arrived home from work her heart sank when she saw Bill waiting on her doorstep.

'Hello Bill. I didn't expect to see you just yet.'

'I'm just keeping my promise to your beloved. I'll come in and see your flat is

26

alright and have a quick cuppa with you, then I'll be off.'

'Come on up then.' My God, how am I going to put up with this for a whole week? I'll die of boredom. Gary has a lot to answer for.

'What a lovely place you have here, very expensive tastes you have my dear.'

'Well there's just the two of us and it's only money, so we might as well spend it.'

'True, very true. Some of us are not so lucky as to be in that position.'

Tamara didn't like his tone, and felt he was invading her space. I must try and get rid of him as soon as possible; have I got to endure him every single night?

'Tea or coffee Bill?'

'Tea please my dear.'

I wish he'd stop calling me dear, like we're the best of pals. I don't know which is worse, the phone calls or him. At least they have stopped for the time being.

'I don't know too much about you Bill.'

'I'm sure by the end of the week we'll know a lot more about each other.'

Tamara shuddered at this thought. I really don't want to know, but I suppose I must keep up the pretence of being friendly if only for Jenny's sake. Dear Jenny, I really don't know what she sees in him.

'Where do you work Bill? Jenny has never said.'

'Oh, I don't work. I have been signed off because of my back trouble and will never work again. I'm a slave to pain, but I don't like to make a fuss.' Another skiver. I bet there's nothing wrong with his back. He's just working the system like all the other bad back brigade.

'Where did you work before you were incapacitated?'

'For the Council.'

'Really! What did you do?'

'A refuse collector'

'Oh, a bin man.'

Bill glared at her. She could see he was annoyed at being called a bin man; she had a job to hide her amusement and turned away quickly so he couldn't see the smile on her face.

'Would you like a biscuit, a sandwich or something Bill?'

'No thank you. I will be eating with Jenny shortly, and don't want to spoil my appetite.'

I bet he doesn't offer a penny to help pay for all the food he eats at Jenny's. A sponger as well as a skiver.

'Look, don't let me keep you Bill, you can see I'm fine. You get on back to Jenny and have a nice evening, and thank you for coming.'

28

Tamara moved towards the door to open it. Bill was close behind and made a movement as if to kiss her on the cheek, but she moved away swiftly and avoided contact with him. This enraged Bill. I'm not good enough for a friendly kiss on the cheek. Right, we'll see about that. The calls will resume this evening, maybe one or two through the night. You won't mess with me lady. Sneering about my job. You think you're so high and mighty, we'll soon see how high and mighty you are by tomorrow.

Tamara breathed a sigh of relief as she shut the door behind him. Now for a nice long soak in a hot bath. She had no sooner got into the bath when the phone rang. Oh hell, I'd better answer it. It's probably Gary ringing early this evening. Perfect timing Gary.

'Hello darling. You're a bit early ringing tonight — I had just got into the bath.' There was silence from the other end of the line.

'Gary, is that you? Stop messing about, you're not funny. Say something for God's sake. Who is this?'

Fear began to grip her as she realized it wasn't Gary.

'Speak, whoever you are. I'm not frightened of you.'

A muffled voice on the end of the phone

29

began to answer her.

'Are you nude then? Not a pretty sight. Too skinny for my liking.'

Then there was a spine-chilling, hideous laugh, she dropped the phone and ran screaming from the room. She ran into the bedroom and threw herself on the bed sobbing uncontrollably. What am I going to do? I can't stand it. I think I'm going mad. She lay there for what seemed like hours, till eventually she pulled herself together. She looked at the clock on the bedside table. Nine o'clock and Gary still hadn't rung. He usually rang at eight-thirty on the dot every evening. Then she realized the phone was still off the hook. She picked it up and replaced the receiver. Within minutes the phone was ringing.

'Tam, it's me, Gary. Whoever have you been talking to for the past half hour?'

'Hello Gary. Sorry, the phone wasn't put back on the receiver.'

'Are you alright? You sound really weird and distant. Have you had another phone call from the weirdo?'

'Yes I have. What I don't understand, Gary, is how he got my new number, only a few people have it. A lot of good that was changing it.'

'Do you want me to come home? I could

get the next flight back if you want.'

'No, of course not. I'll be fine, really I will. I'll speak to you again tomorrow. Bye darling. Love you.'

She replaced the receiver and thought, what next?

3

On the flight home Gary pondered over the situation and wondered what further developments there had been since yesterday evening. Tam had said all was well and nothing further had happened since the start of the week, but he could not be sure she was speaking the truth. He was not expecting the sight that greeted him when he put his key in the lock and opened the door. Tamara was standing there like some ghostly apparition, pale, even thinner than when he went away, and wearing a white long dressing gown. Her hair, usually styled so beautifully, was straight and lacked lustre. There were dark circles under her eyes like she hadn't slept in days.

'What the hell has been happening?' Gary exploded. 'You look like some washed-out old hag.'

With these harsh words Tamara burst into tears. How could he be so cruel? Gary the love of her life speaking to her in such an angry, heartless tone. He used to be so proud of her and couldn't wait to show her off to all his mates, introducing her as his beautiful girlfriend.

'Stop the waterworks Tam and tell me what's been going on.'

'Look!' Tamara screeched back at him, throwing a pile of letters down on the table.

'That's what's been going on. Death threats! I've had one every day for the past four days.'

Gary picked up one of the letters and read the words neatly cut out from old newspapers and pasted on the paper. **DIE YOU BITCH.** Another said **NOT LONG NOW & IT WILL BE ALL OVER.** Gary wanted to laugh, but dared not for fear of upsetting her. This can't be serious. It's like something out of an old black and white movie. Someone's having a laugh. I've thought all along it must be a joke.

'Have you told the police?'

'No . . . I was waiting to hear what you said about it,' Tamara wailed and then burst into tears.

'For Christ's sake Tam, get a grip.'

For the first time in their relationship Gary felt repulsion towards this quivering wreck of a woman. This was a side of her he had never seen before, vulnerable, clingy, depending on him. Where was the strong beautiful woman he was about to marry? She was acting like a silly, snivelling teenager, not a mature woman. If things don't improve pretty damn quick I'm out of here.

'Have you been to work this week?'

'Not for the past few days. I rang in sick.'

'Well you'd better get straight back to work on Monday while you still have a job to go to.'

She still couldn't take in the tone in which he was speaking to her. It was so hard and severe. Something had changed him while he was away. He's met someone else.

'Gary, is there someone else?'

'Don't be so bloody stupid. I'm going to have a shower then get to bed, and I don't want to be disturbed. If that sodding phone is going to ring all night take it off the hook!'

He slammed the door behind him as he headed for the bathroom. Monday morning was cold, damp and grey, which matched her mood. It had been a terrible weekend. Gary was in a foul mood from the moment he set foot inside the flat. I had better make a really big effort or I'm going to lose him. She sat in front of the mirror applying her makeup with a shaking hand.

'I'm off now Tam. You'd better take those stupid letters to the police in your lunch hour.'

'I thought we might meet up for lunch.'

'No. I'm too busy, a lot of catching up to do from last week. See you.'

The door slammed and he was gone. She looked at the time. He's left half an hour before he needs to. Something is not right. I'm sure he's got someone else. I feel tempted to stay home and wallow in misery. I suppose I had better get to work, at least the girls are a good laugh and might be able to cheer me up.

As she entered the office there was a chorus of 'Hi Tam.'

'Are you feeling better, you still look a bit peaky?' queried Barbara.

'I'm fine now.'

Barbara Smith was the one person in the office that she could relate to. She was kind, a good listener and could keep a confidence. She pondered over telling her the truth about what was really going on in her life, but decided against it and settled down to a pile of paperwork that had accumulated in her absence. It would be nice if someone actually took over my job while I was away instead of just leaving it all till I got back. It's the same when I go on holidays. I dread coming back to it all. I'm just so fed up.

'Coffee or tea Tam?'

'Coffee please Barbara.'

'Come on, cheer up. You seem really down. Are you meeting Gary for lunch today? He usually cheers you up.'

'No. I've got something else I need to do and he's having a working lunch in his office.'

At lunch time Barbara set off for the shops, planning to buy a few things for her holiday in a few weeks' time. After half an hour's shopping she wondered if she had time to get a quick sandwich before heading back to work. She was walking towards the escalators in the shopping centre when a young couple coming towards her caught her attention. The girl, in her early twenties, had long blonde hair and wore lots of make-up. Barbara thought she looked quite attractive in a common sort of way. There seemed to be a lot of banter between the pair, then the girl suddenly became aware Barbara had been watching them. She immediately pulled the man to her and kissed him full on the lips. He kissed her back then gently pushed her away.

'Jodie we're in a public place. People are looking at us.'

'I don't care.' She looked defiantly at Barbara.

She's one of those girls that likes to get attention by shocking people. Well she's not getting a reaction out of me. As she looked towards her male companion she couldn't believe her eyes.

'Gary!' Guilt written all over his face, he answered her in a subdued voice.

'Hello Barbara, how are you?'

'Very well thank you.' She fixed him with a disapproving stare and walked on.

'Who was that old bag?'

'For once in your life be quiet Jodie, you don't know how much trouble you've landed me in. If this gets back to Tam we could be finished.'

'Good, it's about time you ditched your precious Tam. I don't know what you see in her anyway. She's twice as old as me and so boring.'

'Shut up and let me think.'

How the hell am I going to explain this one to Tam? Barbara is bound to tell her. He approached the flat that evening with trepidation, took a deep breath and put the key in the lock, and called out from the hall.

'Tam, are you there?'

'Yes. The meal shouldn't be too long. Old man Patterson let me out early. He said I didn't look at all well and appreciated me coming in to work before I had completely recovered, and he wished some of the younger members of staff were more conscientious.'

'I suppose he's being conscientious on the golf course three afternoons a week. Anyway, how did you get on with the police?'

'Well, they can't really do a lot, and said to

keep them posted of any further events. I'm not really sure if they took it seriously or not. Let's not talk about that now. How did your lunch break go? Did you get through a lot of work? My in-tray was piled high.'

'Yes, but I did manage to pop out to the West Quay Centre and grab a baguette to take back to the office. I saw Barbara shopping there. Didn't she tell you?'

'No, she must have forgot to mention it. She's so full of her Greek holiday.'

Thank you Barbara, I owe you one. Inwardly Gary gave a sigh of relief.

★ ★ ★

Jenny thought she would pop out for the evening paper before she started preparing the evening meal for her and Bill. He had been gone all afternoon, saying he had some business to attend to and was then going to check on his house and have a bit of a tidy up, refusing all offers of help from Jenny. As she stepped outside the door a commotion was going on outside the Rickmans' house. A police car was there and Kendra was screaming hysterically, causing quite a few neighbours to come out of their houses to see what was going on.

'Shut your bleeding noise up Kendra

before I give you something to yell about.'

Judy Rickman turned to the crowd of people watching and yelled, 'What you lot looking at?' One of the policeman remonstrated with her.

'Mrs. Rickman, can we go inside please? Your daughter has been attacked.'

'Attacked my ass! I expect she's been fighting with that druggie lot she hangs out with.'

'Mum I've been raped! Don't you ever listen?'

Kendra screeched at her mother in a high-pitched voice. For the first time in her life Judy Rickman was speechless. Her face was ashen and she continued in a more subdued voice.

'Who did this dreadful thing to my little girl? Answer me. Why aren't you lot out there looking for him?'

'Mrs. Rickman I'm PC Jill Hayward. I've been assigned as Family Liaison Officer to look after Kendra and the rest of the family and keep you informed of events. I can assure you our officers are out there now looking for him.'

When Bill eventually came in for his evening meal Jenny thought he didn't look himself. He had a very high colour and he had a slight stutter, which only happened when he was excited or very nervous.

'Are you alright Bill? You don't seem your usual self. You have a very high colour. I hope you're not sickening for something.'

'No, I'm alright love. I feel a bit exhausted I've been moving heavy furniture around. It really does take it out of me at times.'

'You should have let me come with you. Two pairs of hands are better than one. I'll come next time.'

'No.' He replied rather sharply. 'I can manage on my own. After all you've been through with your mother, slaving for her year in and year out. You'll not be doing the same for me. You're far too precious for that.' Jenny was pleased with the compliment and soon forgot the sharpness of his reply.

'There was some excitement here this afternoon just before you came home. Kendra Rickman was attacked and the police brought her home, all the neighbours came out and Judy Rickman was screaming and shouting at them. You don't seem very surprised.'

'I'm not. It was only a matter of time before it happened. The way those girls dress they're just begging for it. Do you mind if I have a bath and an early night? I really do feel done in.'

'Of course not darling, I'll go and run you one.'

Bill stood up feeling relief that he was going to be away from Jenny's incessant chatter for a while. He needed to collect his thoughts and pull himself together.'

'Bill, what's all that mud on your trousers? You're absolutely covered like you've been rolling around in it.'

'That infernal dog next door knocked me over in the park. I fell straight into a muddy patch and the stupid animal was on top of me licking my face. I had a real struggle to get free of him.'

'Didn't his owner call him off?'

'Yes but he doesn't pay any attention to her. He's completely out of control.'

'She wants reporting. What breed is it?'

'A Doberman, but he's harmless enough. I don't think he would ever bite anyone.'

'What did she say to you?'

'Oh, you know, the usual sort of thing. I'm so sorry Mr. Reed. Benjie is so loving he's showing you how much he likes you. Let me pay for your laundry.' Bill mimicked a woman's voice much to Jenny's amusement. 'I said, no, that's alright, just try to keep him under control in future.'

'Oh well, no harm done I suppose. Let me have your clothes and I'll pop them in the washing machine.'

Bill inwardly sighed with relief. She

swallowed that one hook, line and sinker.

Bill lay in the bath congratulating himself on the day's events. No one would ever suspect him. Upstanding Bill a pillar of society. He laughed to himself. Kendra was his first but not the last by a long way. He thought of the other girl he tried to rape that unfortunately died. He had his hands around her throat and she just went all lifeless on him. She was like a scared rabbit. Unlike Kendra full of spirit and fight. That's how I like them. I wander what Tamara Watson will be like, she'll be the prize one. It's time I resumed the phone calls.

★ ★ ★

Tamara was beginning to feel her old self once more when she glanced at the evening paper, and the headlines gripped her with fear. 'Gary, quick, come and look at this. A local girl has been raped. You don't suppose . . .' her voice tailed off.

'Now, don't start Tam, I'm not in the mood for all that nonsense; and before you say it, no I don't think it's the same person who has been ringing you.'

'But how can you possibly know that?'

'I just do. A rape is hardly along the same lines as a few nuisance phone calls.'

She was appalled at his lack of concern for her. How could he treat it so offhandedly?

'I've had enough of all this. I'm off to the pub to see a few mates and have a quiet game of darts.'

'Gary don't go, please. I'm sorry.'

The flat door slammed and he was gone. She sank down in the chair and began to sob. I must pull myself together before he gets back. I still have this sick feeling in the pit of my stomach that he is seeing someone else. I know, I'll give Barbara a call and confide in her, we couldn't really talk at work today.

She dialled Barbara's number at the same time as Bill was trying to get through to her. He cursed his luck. Jenny was downstairs with the telly on and wouldn't hear him. Knowing women I suppose she'll be on the phone for hours. Still, she'll keep. Another time Tamara, another time.

Tamara felt better after her chat with Barbara and decided to make an effort. She showered and put on her prettiest nightdress and waited for Gary's return. When he eventually returned well after midnight he was drunk and smelling of cheap perfume.

'Right Gary, you can come clean. Who is she?'

'No one.' His words were slurred and he was swaying about until he eventually collapsed on the settee and started snoring loudly. Well, that was a complete waste of time and effort. She was so disgusted with him, she decided he could sleep it off in the lounge and she wouldn't even bother to cover him with a blanket. I hope he freezes to death. She went back to their bedroom slamming the door loudly. Loud enough to wake the dead but not Gary Stevens, she thought.

The next evening she was home from work first and was thankful that she was alone when the evening paper arrived. The rape hasn't made the headlines this evening, she pondered, then quickly flicked through the pages until she came to page seven where there was extensive coverage on it. She quickly read down the page until she came to a paragraph on his description. *A white male, possibly middle-aged, about 5 feet 8 inches tall, dressed in black and wearing a balaclava. Could be a dog owner.* I wonder what they based that on. I suppose some people's dogs do smell. I know Jenny's does; you can smell him as soon as you enter her house, although everywhere is clean and tidy. Still, I don't want to hurt her feelings by telling her. He's all she's got, unless you count creepy Bill. The phone rang and interrupted her thoughts.

'Hello Tamara, it's me, Jenny. Can you spare

a minute? I've loads to tell you. You know the rape that's been in the paper . . .' She paused for effect. 'Well it was Kendra Rickman two doors away from me who was raped.'

'How dreadful! Poor girl. I bet her mother had a lot to say about that.'

'She did. Bill said it was only a matter of time, the way she dresses she was asking for it.'

'Jenny, that's a terrible thing to say. No woman deserves to be raped no matter how they dress. OK she's a bit loud and mouthy but she only dresses like all the other teenagers today.'

'I don't think Bill meant anything by it. It was just an observation on how she dressed. What he meant was if anyone was going to be raped it would probably be someone like her.'

Always quick to defend him. She must really love the guy but I can't think why.

'I must go Jen, I've just heard Gary's key in the lock. We'll speak again soon. Bye.'

Tamara decided not to mention the rape to Gary or what was in the paper.

'Well, what have you got to say for yourself after last night.'

'Shut up Tam please, I've got a bad head and I could do without your sarcasm.'

'I think I deserve an apology at least.'

'Give it a rest will ya.'

'Gary please talk to me and tell me what's wrong.' She moved forward to put her arms around him, but he pushed her away. She began to feel alarmed. He seemed to be confirming her worst nightmare that their relationship was over. Why, what had she done wrong? Nothing! She continued in a more severe tone.

'Gary we have to sort this out. Don't you love me anymore? Is there someone else? Please tell me the truth. After five years of being with you, I deserve that much at least.'

He hesitated for a moment not quite sure what to do or say. His next words were like a knife in her heart.

'It's no good pretending any longer. We're finished Tam, we've come to the end of the road.'

'Then I was right — there is someone else.'

'Why does there have to be someone else? Can't you get it into your head it's over, finished? It's run its course; there's nothing for me anymore. I'll pack my things and get out of here tonight.'

'Where will you go?'

'That's none of your business. Just shut up your incessant talking and let me pack.'

He went into their bedroom, slammed the door, and within fifteen minutes he was packed and gone. Not leaving any trace of having been with her for the past five years. That's it then, all over, nothing's left. What do I do now? She was even too exhausted to cry. Gary Stevens, the love of my life gone forever. She took some sleeping pills and fell into a deep sleep. She slept so soundly that she didn't even hear the sound of the phone ringing every half hour into the early hours of the morning.

The next morning was Saturday and she was still in a state of shock. How could a five-year deep and meaningful relationship be over just like that? Without a reason, or none that she could think of. There must be someone else. She decided she would shut herself away from the rest of the world and not speak to anyone until Monday morning when she had to go to work.

Just as she was getting ready for work the phone rang. Just for a second she hoped it was Gary asking for forgiveness and pleading to take him back. Of course she would. Our relationship is worth saving.

'Hello.' She answered in the most cheerful tone she could muster.

'You sound cheerful. I was just wondering if you and Gary would like to come to tea tonight and spend the evening with me. We have a lot of gossip to catch up on.'

'It'll just be me Jen. I'll explain all when I

see you. Will Bill be there?'

'No, he has some work to do at his house. I don't know why he bothers to keep it on. He practically lives here all the time, he might just as well sell it.'

'OK, see you after work then Jenny, and thanks.' That's a small mercy him not being there. I bet he'll have a jolly good gloat when he finds out about me and Gary.

That morning at work she could hardly concentrate and felt she had to confide in Barbara.

'I don't know what I'm going to do without him Barbara. I love him so much. He's been my whole life for the last five years. I'm hoping he's just having a mad moment and he'll come back home tonight and all will be forgotten.'

'Did you say he took all his things?'

'Yes but that's Gary for you, dramatic.'

'Look, there's something I need to tell you Tam.'

Barbara related the scene she had witnessed in the Shopping Centre. Tamara could bear it no longer and tears began to stream down her cheeks. She sobbed in Barbara's arms till she could sob no more.

'That's it, let it all out love. You'll feel better for it.'

After work she thought she would go home

first and change before going to Jenny's house. She was approaching her flat when she became aware that someone was behind her. She turned around and thought she caught a glimpse of someone darting into a doorway. Her heart began to pound. She was relieved that the block of flats where she lived was close by. She was in the door like a shot, slammed it quickly and ran up the three flights of stairs to her flat. Once inside she sank down in a chair and suddenly the full implications of Gary leaving began to dawn on her. She hadn't taking into consideration the fact that she was totally alone, vulnerable and at the mercy of the phone pest. Her thoughts were interrupted by the ringing of the phone. With a shaking hand she picked up the receiver.

'Yes, who is it?'

'You know who it is Tamara. That was a close one just now, I just missed you. Lucky for you.' There was a horrible cackle of laughter on the other end of the phone. Tamara dropped the receiver and began to scream. As it lay on the floor the voice continued to taunt her with bad language and vile suggestions as to what he might do to her when he got her alone. She slammed her hand down on the base unit cutting him off and leaving the receiver on the carpet so he couldn't call back.

That evening she poured her heart out to Jenny, telling her everything about Gary and the phone pest; she didn't stop talking for nearly an hour. Jenny had never before heard her say so much in one go. Secretly she felt flattered. All through their lives Tamara had been her mainstay. Always sticking up for her, listening to all the problems she had with her mother, helping her change her appearance to look more modern instead of the frump she used to be. Now at last it was her turn to pay back all the kindness she had received in the past.

'Tamara if there is anything at all I can do to help, you know that I will don't you? Would you like to come here and stay with me for a while? Just say the word and I'll sort out the guest room.'

'No, that's really kind of you Jenny. Just being my friend and listening has helped me no end.'

'What about tonight? Would you like to stay the night?'

'No really, I'm fine now. Look at the time, I must go. I didn't realize it was so late.'

'I don't know what's keeping Bill. I think that's him now. Bill, where have you been? I expected you ages ago.'

'Good evening Tamara.'

Tamara shivered slightly at his greeting, she thought it was more like a leer than a friendly smile.

'I've been held up by the police. They are everywhere, apparently another young girl has been attacked in the park. They're stopping everyone and questioning them, I had to come home the long way as no one was allowed through the park.'

'I wish you wouldn't take that short cut late at night Bill, especially with some nutter on the loose.'

'I'm quite safe. I'm not a young girl.'

Jenny thought he looked a bit flushed and was stammering slightly. Still, it's to be expected with the police suddenly pouncing on you.

'I really don't know what this town is coming to. It always used to be such a quiet place with nothing much going on at all. Would you like Bill to see you home?'

'No, really, I've got my car, I'll be fine.'

4

Barbara was shopping with Tamara in their lunch hour when suddenly they came face to face with Gary and the precocious Jodie. For a moment Tamara felt angry and humiliated to see him acting like a teenager with this common looking young girl. She couldn't understand why he had thrown everything away they had, and for what? A common little tart. Her cheeks flamed with indignation. Barbara tried to steer her away from the confrontation.

'Come on love. Just ignore them, don't let them get to you. We'll go into this shop and try on some shoes.'

All Barbara's efforts were in vain. Tamara was determined to stand her ground.

'No, I'm not hiding away from him. I want to hear what he has to say for himself.'

'Hello Gary.' She glared at Jodie.

'Hello Tam. How are you?'

'As if you care. I'm fine. Is this my successor? Really Gary, I thought you had better taste than that. To think I imagined you with some beautiful woman I couldn't compete with and instead all you have

52

replaced me with is the office bike. Well, you're welcome to her. Good luck, you're going to need it.'

She turned and walked away with Jodie screaming obscenities after her. They turned the corner out of sight of the angry lovers and she burst out laughing. Barbara was speechless; she didn't know what to say or do. She wasn't quite sure whether Tamara was hysterical or completely calm, and was expecting her to burst into tears at any moment.

'Tam, I'm so sorry you had to witness that. You must be feeling quite bad. Shall we get a coffee to steady your nerves?'

'It's the best thing that could have happened to me. All this time I was living in a fool's paradise imagining I was madly in love with someone who didn't exist. Today for the first time ever I saw the real Gary Stevens who was nothing like the man I thought I loved. We'll have that coffee but not to steady my nerves, just to relax and talk about the future.'

Barbara was reluctant to believe Tamara had got over Gary so quickly after five years together.

'Are you sure you're alright Tam? You don't have to pretend with me. I know how painful it must be for you and I really admire the brave face you're putting on.'

'I'm alright Barbara, I'm not pretending. It's like I've suddenly had my eyes opened at last and I'm seeing everything in a new light. I'm free to do as I please, when I please. No more waiting around for Mr. Gary Stevens to come home from his trips abroad, putting my life on hold waiting for him. Hoping that one day he would propose and I'd become Mrs. Stevens and be at his beck and call. I must have been really stupid. It has taken a shock like this to bring me to my senses.'

As they strolled back to work together Barbara was not at all sure she meant what she had just said. Any minute she will take it all back and break down again. I just know it. I can't believe she has got over him just like that.

Jenny and Bill were just settling down to their evening meal when the door bell rang.

'Who on earth can that be at this time of the day.' Jenny went out of the room muttering to herself about how inconsiderate people were calling at meal times.

'Bill, it's the police. They want to talk to us about the rape.'

Bill was visibly shaken.

'Good evening sir. I'm DC Woods and this is my colleague DC Harding. We are conducting door to door enquiries and would like to talk to you about the recent attack on a young girl in the area.'

'Why do you want to talk to me? I know nothing.'

Jenny thought Bill was a bit sharp with his reply.

'All males in the vicinity of the crime are being questioned. Would you mind telling me where you were on Friday the 19th of March, sir?'

'I was here all day with my girlfriend Jenny.'

'And you didn't leave the house at all that day?'

'No I didn't.'

Jenny was about to open her mouth and point out that that was the day he was in his own house shifting furniture, when he shot her a warning look. Although puzzled by his deliberate lie she went along with it.

'Can you verify this madam?'

'Yes I can officer, he was with me all day.'

'Right, thank you. That will be all, and sorry for interrupting your meal. We'll see ourselves out.'

'Bill, why did you lie to the police like that? You know very well you weren't here that day.'

'Je— Jenny my sweet, you know the police. I would be easy prey for them having no alibi.

How many miscarriages of justice have we heard about recently on the television?'

She pondered over this last statement and wished he wouldn't get so upset and start stuttering when there is any sort of pressure.

'Yes, I suppose you're right.'

'Jenny, do I honestly look like a rapist? It's ridiculous.'

'Of course you don't darling, don't get so upset. We'll say no more about it.'

Outside in the road the two policemen were discussing the likely suspects.

'What do you reckon to the geezer in number thirty-one, Harry?'

'A bit of a weirdo, but he has an alibi. His woman backed him up, but there is something a bit strange about him. I can't quite put my finger on it.'

'He seems too much of a wimp to be up for anything like that.'

'You'd be surprised Don. He seems just the type to me.'

Bill was secretly panicking and wanted to get away for a while till things had cooled down.

'Jenny, I've been thinking. What would you say to us going away on a little holiday?'

'That would be marvellous Bill. Where to? I've never had a holiday before. Mother didn't believe in wasting money on holidays and when I was old enough to go by myself she was always ill and couldn't be left.'

'You should have put your foot down and insisted on having a break. There are organizations who would have looked after her for you. Didn't anyone tell you about them?'

'Yes I know, but mother always insisted she wouldn't have strangers in her house robbing her and she certainly wasn't going to shift out of her own home for anyone. Besides I had no one to go with, and it wouldn't have been any fun on my own.'

'Where would you like to go my dear?'

'Anywhere, just anywhere. I'm so thrilled. You choose, you've been around a lot more than I have. Where do you think we'd both enjoy?'

'Um, let me see. How about the Lake District? You know how much you enjoy Wordsworth's poetry, especially the one about the daffodils. This is the right time of year to see the daffodils. We'd better get booked up right away before we miss them.'

'Oh, I can't wait.'

She felt like a young girl, excited and nervous, not knowing what to expect. Within three days they were sat on a train on the way to the Lake District. She lay back in her seat watching the countryside roll by. Thinking how lucky she was to have found Bill, and how he was so kind and considerate towards her. She wondered if it would end in a marriage proposal. Bill was also thinking along the same lines but for very different reasons. If I were to marry her I would appear even more respectable.

'Jenny, would you do me the honour of becoming my wife?'

She was shocked out of her day-dreaming. Bill had been thinking along the same lines as her — it was almost as if he read her mind. We really are a compatible couple.

'Oh Bill, yes! I'd be honoured to be Mrs. William Reed.'

'You don't know how happy you've made me, my darling Jenny. I know this is a bit presumptuous of me but I thought we could get married at Gretna Green. What do you think?'

'How romantic. There's only one small detail spoiling the whole thing.'

'What is that my sweet? I'm sure we can iron out any snags we come up against.'

'It's Tamara, she won't be there to share my happiness and she is my best friend.'

'Jenny, I wanted you to have a different romantic wedding with just the two of us. We can celebrate with our friends when we get home. We'll throw a party and you can invite who you like, so no one will really miss out on anything. After all I feel the ceremony of pledging our vows to one another till death do us part is very special and private. Not really for a lot of onlookers who haven't any religious conviction and are only waiting for the ceremony to end so they can get to the food and drink as quickly as possible, and hoping the photographer won't be wasting too much time taking photographs. But of course if you prefer the traditional ceremony, the same as everyone else has, and it's what you really want then so be it. It would postpone the wedding for at least a year as everything seems to be booked up a year in advance.'

'Why Bill, how did you know that? Have you been secretly finding out about these things, even before you asked me?'

'Yes my sweet, I confess I have.' The real truth being, he had overheard his next door neighbour's daughter complaining that everything was booked up one year to eighteen months ahead, and she didn't really want to wait that long and was hoping someone would cancel so she could marry sooner. 'I'm really very old-fashioned at heart and I didn't like living under your roof as a lover. I would much prefer to be your husband. I thought we could sell our two houses and buy a little bungalow somewhere. It would be our home and not your mother's or mine.'

Jenny thought she was going to burst with happiness.

'Yes Bill, yes. I'll go along with everything you have planned.' She flung her arms around his neck, kissing him, not caring who was watching them on the train.

★ ★ ★

Tamara was singing softly to herself as she picked up her post. She still hadn't had any second thoughts about her split with Gary. If she was really honest with herself things had got a bit stale and a lot of the excitement and magic had gone out of their relationship, they were just going through the motions for appearance's sake.

A card from Scotland. I do hope she's having a good time, she was really excited about going on her first holiday. Oh my God, Jenny, what have you done?' She shivered as she read the words at the bottom of the card. 'I'm so happy, Love Bill & Jenny Reed.' She sank into her chair wondering why she was feeling so worried and frightened for her friend. How could she marry him, he's so awful. Then she felt a little ashamed of herself for thinking so badly of Bill. He obviously makes her very happy and always seems caring and attentive towards her. Perhaps I've misjudged him. Just because I can't stand the man it doesn't mean to say he won't make her happy. After all I'm a fine one to judge men after my recent disaster; thinking I had found Mr. Right, and look how that turned out. I've made up my mind, for Jenny's sake I'll be really happy and pleased for her and I'll even try and be a bit nicer to Bill when they get back.

The police decided they would pay another visit to Bill Reed and ask a few more questions. They were knocking loudly on his door when Judy Rickman came out of her front door.

'No good knocking there. They ain't in.'

'Do you know when they will be in?'

'No. They're on their honeymoon. She's gone an' married the bleeder. They've been gone weeks.'

The two detectives looked at one another in amazement.

'How do you know, Mrs. Rickman?'

'Her friend, the stuck-up cow, told me.'

'Do you know how we can get in touch with her friend?'

'No, not really. I think she has a flat somewhere in Ocean Village.'

'Does the 'stuck-up cow' have a name?'

asked DC Woods. Harry Harding gave his colleague a warning look.

'Tamara or some fancy name like that. Thinks she's a cut above the rest of us with her fancy name and fancy car.'

'What do you reckon Harry? Do you think it's genuine or he's done a runner with his bird?'

'Well I think they'll have to come back sometime or other. They wouldn't just leave this house, it's worth a bob or two. My bet is they'll be back and when they do we'll be waiting for Mr. William Reed.'

★　★　★

Tamara thought it would be a good time to give her flat a spring clean and remove any traces of Gary, should there be anything left of his. Besides, it would keep her busy and her mind off just how lonely she was actually feeling. In a funny sort of way she missed Jenny and Bill. I wonder how long it will be before they come back. I've had enough of the cleaning, I think I'll watch something on TV. She sat down wearily and turned on the set, just in time to catch the end of a news item. What was that, a girl missing in the Lake District? Oh my God no! It can't be anything to do with Bill. Pull yourself together Tam. Girls go missing every day all over the country, she's probably spent the night with a boyfriend and is too frightened to go home, or has run off with him. I think all the things that have happened to me over the last few months are taking their toll. I'm suspecting everyone and everything. Since Gary left the phone calls and death threats have stopped. It can't have been him surely. He only had to tell me it was over, without resorting to such drastic measures. Now I'm being ridiculous. I think I'd better get off to bed before I have any more insane ideas.

* * *

'I think we'd better be making tracks for home soon my sweet.'

'Oh Bill, do we have to? It's so lovely here I could stay forever.'

'Yes, so could I, but I thought you might want to go home to see your friend and show off your rings. After all it's quite an achievement beating glamour puss to the altar. Who'd have thought it eh?'

'Don't be unkind Bill, she's been through a terrible time of late.'

'I didn't mean to be dear. It was just an observation, with all her money and good looks she hasn't found true happiness. Not like us.' He squeezed her hand and she was brimming over with love for him.

'As soon as we get back we'll put the two houses on the market and perhaps buy a nice little place in the New Forest or Bournemouth. Which would you prefer my dear?'

'Oh Bournemouth definitely. I love the Forest but it's on our door step and that's all mother and I ever did, take a bus ride to one of the forest villages.'

'Well, if it's Bournemouth you prefer perhaps we'll go for a beach apartment, there are some really nice ones.'

Tamara thought she would try really hard to be happy for her friend and have a nice evening meal ready for their return. She must put aside her own feelings of revulsion for Bill and pretend for Jenny's sake she was delighted with the news of their marriage. The following afternoon she left work early to do some shopping for the meal and restock Jenny's fridge with a few essentials. As she put the key in the lock she heard the usual commotion coming from the Rickmans' house a few doors away. My God, that family, don't they ever stop making a noise? As she entered the hall the smell of Jenny's dog was overpowering. I'm sure that's not natural for a dog to smell so awful. How can anything smell that bad and still remain living? He hasn't been here for weeks and I can still smell him all over the house. The smell seems to get right into your clothes.

At nine-thirty a taxi pulled up outside the house. A radiant looking Jenny, Bill and Pepper the dog got out. Tamara had the door open in seconds, flinging her arms around Jenny and kissing her.

'Congratulations! I'm so happy for you. A bit miffed at missing the wedding but never mind. It was so romantic running away to Gretna Green to marry, straight out of a fairy story.'

'Tamara I can't tell you how happy I am. I've so much to tell about our future plans.'

'Time for all that later. I've cooked you both a nice meal, your favourite Jenny, steak and mushrooms.'

After the meal Jenny related all that had happened while they were away, all the places they'd visited both in Scotland and the Lake District, all the funny incidents that occurred. She talked non-stop for at least ten minutes.

'Stop, please Jen. Too much information, my head is spinning. I can't take everything in. What about you Bill, would you like to say anything? Before she starts again. Quick, say something while you have the chance.'

'Well Tamara, Jenny and I have decided to sell up here and buy an apartment in the Bournemouth area.'

The smile froze on Tamara's face. She suddenly felt cold and desolate. He's taking her away, out of my reach. No more dropping in to keep an eye on her, making sure she's safe with him. OK Bournemouth isn't a million miles away, only about twenty-five in fact, but should she need help I won't be able to get to her quickly. Oh God I feel so frightened for her.

Bill was quick to notice the change of expression on Tamara's face and took great pleasure in it. That wasn't to your liking lady. I didn't think it would be; well, you'll just have to lump it. She's my responsibility now not yours.

'Are you alright Tamara? You look upset. Please be happy for me, it's what we both want. Life will be so different there, like being on holiday permanently. Walks along the promenade with Pepper, good fresh sea air. I'm so excited I can hardly wait and of course you must come and visit us as much as you like. Every weekend if you want. Mustn't she Bill?'

'Of course my sweet.' Bill turned to Tamara with a menacing warning look. 'You'll be very welcome at any time.' He turned back to

Jenny, smiling as if he meant every word he had just said.

'Well that's all right then,' beamed Jenny.

The following morning the police paid Jenny and Bill another visit. A look of anger passed over Bill's face as he opened the front door to find DCs Woods and Harding on the step.

'Yes. What do you want?'

'Can we come in please sir? We have a few more questions to ask you.'

'If you must.'

Jenny could not understand the abrupt manner in which he spoke to the two police officers. It was most unlike her Bill, always polite and kind to everyone. Whatever has come over him?

'Can you tell us what you were doing on Friday 19th March, Mr. Reed?'

'I've already answered that question once. How many more times do I have to repeat myself?'

DC Woods continued, quite unperturbed by his outburst.

'We are just rechecking everyone's alibi and asking them if they remember seeing any strangers hanging around that day or anything unusual or out of place in the neighbourhood. For instance, cars parked that don't belong to the residents and are not usually seen around the area.'

'I was here all day with my wife Jenny, and in answer to your other question, I know of nothing else that would help you with your enquiries. If that's all, my wife and I have a very busy day ahead of us and are anxious to get started as soon as possible.'

'That will be all for the moment sir, and congratulations to you both on your marriage.'

Bill watched the policemen from the window as they walked down the road.

'Look at that! They've just walked past all the neighbours' houses and got in their car, and are driving off. I thought they were supposed to be rechecking everyone's alibi. It seems like it was just mine. How dare they.'

'You were a bit sharp with them Bill, so unlike you, and I don't honestly know why you are getting so upset. They are only doing their job.'

'I'm sorry my dear, but the police do tend to waste time asking a lot of innocent people unnecessary questions, instead of getting out there and catching the real criminals. It does annoy me, but I suppose they have to justify their high salaries somehow. Now enough about them. Our first port of call this morning will be the estate agents to get things rolling.'

'What do you reckon to Reed, Harry? Do you think he's for real? A bit jumpy and defensive I thought and what was that awful pong?'

'It's their dog.'

'We've been in some dumps in our time but I have never smelt anything like that before. There must be something wrong with it. That's not a natural dog smell.'

'I think their must be something wrong with their noses if they can't smell it. The house was otherwise clean and tidy and kept in good decorative order. Don, that's it! I've got it. He's our man.'

'What do you mean he's our man, a bit weird perhaps but a rapist . . . ? I can't get my head around that one.'

'I've just remembered something Kendra said about the rapist smelling of dog odours. Back to the station quick as you can and we'll check it out.'

'Surely Kendra would have known about the smell in their house living only three doors away.'

'Can you honestly see the Reeds asking the Rickmans around to dinner or for a quiet evening and a few drinks?'

'No, a quiet evening is the last thing you

would get with the Rickmans and that Judy has some gob on her. Does she ever give it a rest?'

'I would think Kendra hasn't been anywhere near their house so she wouldn't know about the pong that hits you as soon as the front door is opened.'

'Point taken Harry.'

Harry and Don were back at the police station within ten minutes of leaving the Reeds' house.

'Where have you two been? Swanning around in the police car enjoying the sunshine I expect.'

'Watch your mouth Chaveleigh. Anyway, what's it to you where we've been?'

The PC coloured slightly.

'Sarge has been doing his nut. While you were out there's been another rape on the other side of town.'

'What! What time did it happen?'

'About half hour ago.'

'There goes our chief suspect. We were still with him half an hour ago. I felt so sure we had our man. Right, let's have all the details Mike.'

'Sarge says you're to get over to Drayton Park as soon as you can, he's over there now.

'Apparently a young girl had bunked off school and was walking through a lonely bit of the park when she was pounced on from behind.'

'We're on our way.'

'What about some lunch first, Harry? I'm starving.'

'We haven't got time for that, you know what Sergeant Fanstone is like when he gets a bee in his bonnet.'

'But knowing him we'll be there all afternoon. He has no consideration for our bodily needs whatsoever.'

'You'll live.'

★   ★   ★

'We've had a really successful morning. The estate agents seem sure of a quick sale on both properties. Oh I can't believe it Bill. Soon we'll be the owners of a very upmarket apartment in Bournemouth.' Jenny flung her arms around him kissing his face all over in her excitement.

'Steady on Jenny, we're not quite there yet. We still have a lot to do. Firstly we'll have some lunch before the estate agents arrive with their tape measures. I think it best if you deal with this house and I with mine. Hopefully they may be able to include them in the Property Paper which comes out at the end of the week.'

'I do hope so Bill.'

'Perhaps we'll take a trip to Bournemouth tomorrow and have a look at the new apartments, even leave a deposit.'

'You don't think we're tempting fate by putting down a deposit? What if the houses don't sell?'

'Of course they will my chicken. Have some faith. Have I ever let you down?'

'No you haven't. You've always been kind and as good as your word.'

'Well then, stop fussing like a mother hen. All will be well from now on.'

5

By five o'clock DCs Woods and Harding were back at the station mulling over the events of the day, Don Woods still complaining bitterly about missing lunch.

'Look, for Christ's sake go to the pie shop in the precinct and get us both a pie or pasty, and some cream cakes or doughnuts, whatever they have left at this time of day. Hurry up, they'll be closing in half an hour. It looks like it's going to be a long evening.'

Don Woods groaned inwardly. There goes my chance to ask the pretty new secretary out. Still I suppose she'll keep, she isn't going anywhere, unless she runs out screaming by the end of the week.

'Right Don, mealtime over, now let's get down to business. Let's see what we have. Her name is Tracey Sellwood and she is aged fourteen. She should have been in school but bunked off to meet a boyfriend. Before she got to their meeting place she was pounced on from behind. She described her attacker as medium height and build. He was wearing dark clothes and a mask. He had a gruff voice, she wasn't sure whether he had a local accent or not.'

'She didn't mention any dog smell.'

'Perhaps she didn't notice it. She smokes and sometimes smokers don't always have a good sense of smell.'

'Kendra Rickman chain smokes and she smelt it. You don't think we're looking for two different people do you Harry?'

'Don't even think about going down that road. No, I think it's the same fella. The town only has two parks, Moreton Park on the eastern side of town and Drayton Park at the northern end. He knew that everything would be concentrated in the Drayton Park area after the Rickman attack, leaving him to strike in Moreton Park at the other end of town.'

When Bill Reed turned on their television in the evening and heard that a young girl had been attacked that morning in Drayton Park he couldn't have been more pleased.

'Did you hear that Jenny? Another poor unfortunate girl has been attacked in Drayton Park.'

'When?'

'This morning while those two police officers were here harassing me. Then you wonder why I get so uptight with them questioning me, an innocent man. Had they been out patrolling that area perhaps the attack might have been prevented. Well at least I won't be bothered by them this time, I have the perfect alibi.' He gave a coarse laugh. A laugh that Jenny had not heard before and didn't much like the sound of. She shivered slightly as he came into the kitchen.

'Are you cold my sweet?'

'Just a bit. I left the back door open for Pepper as he's been shut in all day. It feels a bit nippy with it open now the sun has moved around to the front of the house. I think I'll close it, he'll have to bark when he wants to come back in.'

'I've a good mind to ring up the police and complain about my treatment.'

'Please don't Bill, you'll only antagonize them and they'll be around here again asking questions about something else.'

'Like what? We have nothing to hide.'

'Let's not talk about such awful things and spoil our lovely day.'

'Very well my sweet. What would you like to talk about?'

'I'll give you three guesses.'

'Bournemouth?'

'You've got it in one. What time train shall we catch tomorrow?'

★ ★ ★

Tamara could not shake off the sense of foreboding she was feeling about her friend's move away from the area. *Why am I feeling like this? I should be happy for her. He obviously adores her even if he doesn't like me very much, and she's over the moon at the prospect of starting a new life in Bournemouth with him, but there is something not quite right and I can't put my finger on it.*

Tamara had just read in the evening paper about the rape of a young girl in Drayton Park, which did nothing to lift her spirits, just added to the sense of doom and gloom she had been experiencing since hearing of the move. *I don't know what Woodfield is coming to. It use to be such a quiet little town, nothing much went on there, now it's not safe to be on the streets, even in broad daylight. I'm so glad I live in town where there's always lots of people around.* The phone rang, interrupting her thoughts; just for an instant the old fear returned. *No, it can't be. I haven't had any of those calls in ages.* She picked up the phone, her hand shaking slightly, her voice sounding croaky.

'Hello.'

'Tam, it's me, Barbara. Are you alright? You sound a bit funny.'

'Yes, of course I am. Have you just rung for

a chat or did you want something?'

'Both really. This might cheer you up. An old school friend of Ken's is flying home from Hong Kong tomorrow and will be spending about a month or so over here. His mother has just died and he has to attend to her estate. His father died years ago.'

'What has this to do with me?'

'I'm just coming to that. He arrives tomorrow, Tuesday, and Ken has suggested we take him for a meal on Friday evening. We were both wondering if you would like to come along and make it a foursome?'

'Oh, I don't know Barbara.'

'Tam . . . you have nothing better to do. Since Gary's gone you've turned into a real middle-aged woman. Whatever happened to the young and full of fun Tamara we've all come to know and love?'

'Oh shut up Barbara. You'll have me in tears in a minute.'

'Well shall I tell Ken to book the table for four or not?'

'Oh go on then, I'll probably live to regret it.'

'No you won't. Don't be so silly, he's gorgeous.'

Tamara felt strangely excited as she got ready for her evening out. I don't know what's the matter with me: it's only a meal with friends, not a date. I have spent the last few days pondering what to wear, trying on God knows what like some silly schoolgirl on her first date. Even anticipating buying something new for the occasion when I have a wardrobe jam-packed with clothes. I must pull myself together. Perhaps I'm turning into a frustrated old maid grasping at straws. Wondering if this might be my last chance of any happiness. A voice on the intercom brought her back to reality.

'Taxi for Miss Watson.'

'Thank you, I'll be down shortly.' Oh hell, the taxi's fifteen minutes early. Just when you don't want it early, any other time it arrives late.

She sat in the lounge of the hotel sipping her drink. She had only been there about five minutes when the Smiths and their guest arrived.

'Tamara, I'd like you to meet Marcus Wheeler-Osman. Marcus, this is my dearest friend Tamara Watson. We all call her Tam at work.'

'Which do you prefer Miss Watson, Tamara or Tam?'

Tamara could hardly speak. He was so handsome. Barbara was right when she said he was gorgeous. He really is! No sign of any grey in his black hair, yet he must be the same age as Ken if they were school friends. Poor chubby Ken hasn't fared as well as Marcus, he's nearly bald and what hair he does have is totally grey, but he's such a sweetie I can understand why Barbara fell for him all those years ago.

'Oh I don't really mind. I get called all sorts, not always good.' Everyone laughed and this seemed to break the ice. The rest of the evening went well and Tamara could not believe how quickly it had passed. It seemed like only minutes ago they had all sat down to dine and now it was all over.

'I do hope I'll see you again sometime Tam.'

'That would be nice.'

'How about we all do something this weekend? Perhaps a drive to the coast and lunch somewhere.'

'I'm so sorry Marcus, Ken and I have a full weekend.'

'Have we? It's news to me.'

Barbara gave him a meaningful look.

'Now Ken, you're not getting away with the decorating that easily, pretending we have nothing on. We have friends coming down from the north next month and the guest bedroom is in real need of a lick of paint, but please don't let us spoil your weekend. You two must go and enjoy yourselves. You don't mind do you Tam? We feel really bad abandoning Marcus but we really do have to get the house ready for our friends.'

'Please don't worry about me. I'll be alright.' Marcus turned to Tamara almost pleadingly.

'I have nothing on this weekend so I'll be happy to accompany you to the coast Marcus.' Marcus could not conceal his pleasure at spending the weekend in Tamara's company.

Tamara awoke early Saturday morning to brilliant sunshine, the sky was blue and not a rain cloud in sight. The weather forecast was for a hot sunny day and Tamara was not disappointed, birds were singing and already the temperature was rising. Marcus had decided on Bournemouth as their first destination, and if they tired of this they could drive further along the coast and possibly reach Devon.

'It doesn't take long these days with the new roads to reach the West Country. We could stay overnight and take a slow drive back on Sunday.'

Tamara was in complete agreement with his plan, in fact she had been in complete agreement with everything he'd said all evening. She was totally mesmerized by this handsome stranger whom she had not known existed twenty-four hours earlier. As she sat waiting for nine o'clock, the arranged time he would call for her, she relived every moment of the evening before. Every look, every glance he had given her were etched on her memory. She looked at the clock. Eight-thirty, still another half hour to wait. She wondered if the clock had stopped. Surely it was more than ten minutes ago when I last looked at the time. I must be in love. It's love at first sight, I never really believed in that romantic stuff before but I suppose it must be true. I've just never experienced it. With Gary it was completely different, he just grew on me and we drifted into a relationship. Tamara Wheeler-Osman . . . that sounds so posh. Mother and Pa would have been so impressed if they were still alive. They were always so snobby, sending me to that private school. I can just hear mother now, telling all her friends. My Tamara is getting married you know, into the Wheeler-Osman family. I expect you have heard of them, millionaires you know. Her daydreaming was interrupted by his voice on the flat intercom.

'Morning Tam, it's Marcus. I hope you're ready?' Ready, I've been ready for hours she thought. I must try and stay calm and not make a fool of myself and spoil things. I don't want him to think I'm desperate.

'Don't bother coming up. I'll be right down.'

They reached Bournemouth in less than an hour. Marcus had hired a smart sports car and was driving a little too fast for her liking. She had the distinct feeling he was out to impress her.

'Do be careful Marcus, there are loads of speed cameras around here. You're not abroad now you know.'

'Sorry Tam I wasn't thinking. What do you think, shall we stay here for lunch and see if there are any tickets left for the evening show at the BIC, or would you rather go on somewhere else?'

'No, let's stay. That's a great idea. We may be lucky and get some tickets for the show I wonder who the star is tonight. As long as it's not some dreadful rock concert I'm happy seeing anybody.'

Marcus laughed. 'I see you share my taste in music. Anything but rock.' He was holding her hand as they strolled along the promenade. She felt happy and content as if she had known him all her life. Suddenly the warm happy feeling was gone and it was replaced by fear. She looked around and could see no reason for this fear that had suddenly enveloped her. Marcus also sensed that something was wrong.

'Are you alright Tam? You look white as a sheet.'

'Yes. I just suddenly feel a bit weak and dizzy.'

'Too much sun my girl. Let's get you into a nice cool restaurant and have some lunch before you collapse from heat exhaustion.' He had barely finished talking when she looked up and saw Jenny and Bill walking towards them. Jenny was beaming with pleasure at the sight of her friend but Bill did not look pleased, he was annoyed at the intrusion.

'Fancy seeing you here Tamara. Do introduce us to your friend. I don't think we've met before. I'm Jenny Reed and this is my husband Bill.'

The introductions over, Marcus suggested they all have lunch together.

'What a lovely idea. I don't know many of Tamara's friends so it will be nice to get to know you Marcus. Don't you think so Bill?' Jenny couldn't help noticing the sour look on Bill's face. It didn't escape Tamara's attention either. This was not what he had planned at all. He wanted to explore the area, alone if possible. He would get rid of Jenny by sending her shopping for curtains for the new apartment. Now that stuck-up bitch has put pay to all that. We'll probably be stuck with them for the rest of the day.

'Will you be staying in Bournemouth over the weekend or are you just here for the day?' Bill asked rather sarcastically. Hoping against hope that they would be moving on as soon as lunch was over.

'Well we were just debating whether to see a show or move on to somewhere else further down the coast. I'll leave it up to Tam, whatever she wants to do suits me fine.'

'A show! What a wonderful idea, we could all go together. What do you think Bill?'

'No darling, we really do need to get back. We have a lot to do tomorrow, seeing solicitors and finalising things on the apartment. A show is a lovely idea — perhaps some other time. After all, we have the 'rest of our lives' to do these things and much more.' Tamara suddenly felt cold again and shivered slightly as he said the words rest of our lives. She inexplicably sensed danger. She had a sense of foreboding like something dreadful was about to happen. She couldn't explain it. There was no reason for her to think such things, and she dared not mention it to Marcus for fear he might think her unstable.

'I think I'd like to move on, perhaps we could stay somewhere in Devon overnight?'

Lunch over, the two couples went their separate ways. Immediately they were on the road again Tamara began to feel much better.

'Thank goodness they've gone. Now we can carry on with our own plans.'

'Bill . . . That is really unkind. I thought Marcus was a lovely man. He's so handsome, I'm really pleased for Tamara. Anyway, what plans? We haven't made any plans.'

'You're right they're well suited to one another. He's full of his own importance just like she is. They deserve one another.' Before Jenny could make any further protest he continued:

'The plans I had made for us, my sweet, did not include those two. I was going to surprise you with a quiet lunch in a really nice restaurant no expense spared. Nothing is too good for my darling wife. Then after lunch I was going to let you loose in the shops to choose anything you wanted, both for yourself and our new home.'

'Were you actually going to traipse around the shops all afternoon with me? I don't believe it.'

'No dear, I was going to sit quietly in the park and wait till you had finished. You know how much I hate the shops, all those people pushing and shoving. I just don't understand how people can actually enjoy that sort of thing.'

Jenny laughed and gave Bill a hug. That explains the long face when Tamara and

Marcus turned up. He really is so kind and sweet, I never thought that one day I would ever be lucky enough to find someone to love me. Mother always said I didn't have what it takes to get a man. Well Mother it just shows how wrong you were. He's wonderful, just wonderful and he's all mine. Till death us do part.

'I suppose it's too late to do any shopping now. What a shame.'

'No it isn't darling, you could shop for an hour and a half before we have to think about starting back. I'll just sit in the park and enjoy the peace and tranquillity.'

As soon as Jenny disappeared into one of the big department stores Bill headed for the park. It's so hot today there'll be plenty of girls with next to nothing on sunbathing in the park, perhaps even some topless ones. I'll just slip my sunglasses on so they won't see me watching them. It was a really clever idea to move to this area, lots of local and imported talent around. The foreign students and tourists would be my best bet. The way some of them dress they're just begging for it.

Back home again in Woodfield Jenny was pottering about the kitchen thinking of the events of the day.

'Are you hungry Jenny? Although we had lunch I'm absolutely starving.'

'Would you like me to cook something?'

'No, you must be tired from all that shopping. How about a fish and chip supper, my treat?'

'That would be nice but it's dark out. Are you sure you want to go back out again? Don't forget there's a rapist still at large out there. It's not really safe after dark any more.'

'My dear Jenny, I'm perfectly safe. I'm not some stupid girl flaunting everything she's got just asking for trouble.'

'I suppose you're right, but be careful — there's still the neighbourhood drunken yobs hanging about the street corners.'

'I'll be back within the hour.'

'An hour! It doesn't take that long to get fish and chips.'

'I thought I might call in at the supermarket. Do we need anything?'

'No, I don't think so. What do you need that can't wait till tomorrow?'

'Never you mind.'

'Well you'd better go there first or the fish and chips will get cold.'

'Yes dear.'

Once outside the house he began to search for his next victim. He was aroused by watching the young girls in the park that afternoon and had to have a young girl at all costs. There seems to be a lot of young people around this evening, must be a party on somewhere. I'll have to be quick, I haven't got long. I need to get to my house and change into dark clothing. Find a girl out alone then get back to the house, change and buy Jenny some flowers from the local shop, and let her think they came from the supermarket.

As he entered the park there was a commotion going on. Two of the local youths were fighting and one was brandishing a knife. Christ, they're going to kill one another; that's all I need, police swarming everywhere. He darted behind a bush just in time, as a big man in his fifties came along the path with his German Shepherd dog.

'Oi, what's going on? Pack it in lads before one of you gets hurt.'

'What's it to you granddad?'

'Plenty. I'm fed up with police crawling around this park all the time, harassing innocent people about the rapes. If you two want to murder each other go somewhere else and do it, not on my patch. Now give me that knife before I set my dog on the pair of you.'

'I'm shaking in my shoes. If you want the knife go and get it.'

The youth tossed the knife into the bushes, landing at Bill's feet. He held his breath thinking any moment he was about to be discovered. The youths ran off shouting and swearing abuse at the man who continued his walk quite unperturbed by what had just taken place.

The park was silent once more. Bill bent down and picked up the knife with his gloved hand. That boy wasn't wearing any gloves so his prints will be all over the knife. I could really have some fun this time. I haven't used a weapon before. He didn't have to wait long for his next victim. A young girl of about seventeen was hurrying along the footpath, looking about her nervously. Bill waited till she had passed him and then pounced on her from behind. She tried to struggle free but he was too strong for her, she couldn't even scream. His hand was over her mouth and the knife at her throat.

'One word out of you and I'll slit your throat.'

'Please don't hurt me. I'll do anything you say.'

'That's more like it.'

He dragged her towards the bushes and threw her to the ground. The girl, in fear of her life, thought it best to try and reason with him.

'The grass is so wet. Please could we go somewhere else? We'll both get soaked.'

She hoped to persuade him to move away from the park, then perhaps she might be able to break free and escape him.

'Shut up. That's the least of your worries. You'll be lying on God's carpet.'

In the distance were the sound of voices and a dog barking. The girl screamed which enraged Bill, and he slashed her throat with the knife. Blood began to pour from the wound; he dropped the knife and ran as fast as he could in the opposite direction to the voices. Two men, a woman and two dogs were soon on the scene. The woman took her coat off and put it around the poor shivering girl. The men and dogs gave chase but Bill was too quick, he was outside the park and had disappeared down one of the many alleyways.

'I think we've lost him Dave. We'd better get back to Jackie and the girl. I don't like leaving them alone — he could double back and have another go.'

'Yeah, I think you're right, John — best leave it to the police.'

'We lost him, Jackie.'

'I've called an ambulance and the police on my mobile. It's lucky I had it with me. I don't always carry it when I'm dog walking. I don't know what made me pick it up tonight. It must have been some sort of premonition.'

In the distance the sound of the ambulance and police sirens could be heard getting closer by the minute. 'Thank God. That didn't take them long.'

6

Chief Inspector Charlie Mann from the Metropolitan police had been put in charge of the operation codenamed Maple. The Woodfield police and Charlie's men, as they had come to be known, were gathered together for a briefing.

'Right everyone, listen up. What we have so far is one unsolved murder and three rapes of local girls which may or may not be connected. Two rapes in Drayton Park and one in Moreton Park. Two were carried out under cover of darkness and one was a lunchtime attack. The lunchtime attack may have been an opportunist attack. He had not planned the attack and just happened to come across the girl alone and vulnerable, so he took a chance, hence the location. Moreton Park is the other side of town and some considerable distance from Drayton Park where the other two rapes and the murder took place. My bet is we're looking for a local man probably residing within the immediate vicinity of Drayton Park. If this is the case it shouldn't take long to track him down and we'll all be back to London before the end of the month sorting out our own patch.'

This last remark incensed DC's Harding and Woods.

'Who the hell does he think he is, coming down here throwing his weight around, like he's some super cop?'

'Did you have something to add, DC Woods? I believe you and DC Harding interviewed several of the local men who live adjacent to Drayton Park, any suspects?'

'Well sir, there was one suspect, Bill Reed. A bit of a weirdo but he had the perfect alibi when the Moreton Park rape took place.'

'What is this watertight alibi?'

'We were interviewing him at the time of the rape, which led me to believe we might be looking for two rapists.'

'Thank you for your theory DC Woods. Facts lad, we deal in facts. It's highly improbable in this tiny backwater of a place that there are two rapists and a murderer at large.'

A few of the Londoners sniggered which enraged Don Woods even more. One of the woman police officers asked how the latest victim was.

'Luckily the wounds to her throat were superficial thanks to the intervention of the three dog walkers, it could have been a whole lot worse. We could have been looking at a second murder. Hopefully the knife he used which was left at the scene will yield some fingerprints or DNA. In the absence of an e-fit or any sort of description we'll be calling in a criminal psychologist to draw up a psychological profile of the rapist. Tomorrow night we'll be staging a reconstruction which will be shown on the Crime Programme in a few weeks time. PC Parker will play the part of Melanie Taylor as she bears an uncanny resemblance to her.'

*　　*　　*

Tamara and Marcus returned from their weekend in the West Country and both felt that something really special had happened between them.

'Tam, I've something to ask you. I know we've only just met but I can't stand the thought of being parted from you. In three weeks time I have to return to Hong Kong and I want you to come with me as my wife.'

'Marcus I . . . I don't know what to say.'

'Please say yes. I know you feel the same about me.'

'I can't just up sticks and move across the other side of the world. What about all my friends?'

'What about them? Would they pass up a chance of a lifetime for you?'

'I suppose you're right, but what about Jenny? We've been friends since we were at school and she depends on me so much.'

'She has her husband Bill and from what I can see they are devoted to one another.'

'But I don't like him and I don't trust him.'

'Darling, you don't have to, he's married to your friend and she's quite happy with him. Stop putting obstacles in the way. Will you marry me or not?'

'I do love you Marcus, and want to marry you more than anything in the world, but I can't be rushed. You'll have to give me more time. I've been married before you know, and after that disaster I thought I would never be able to trust anyone again. After that followed two more disastrous relationships.'

'Stop please, stop Tam, I didn't ask for a history of your past relationships. I've been married as well you know. I was blissfully happy, and when my wife Maria died I thought it was the end of the world and I would never meet anyone again that would mean anything to me, that is until I met you. The instant I saw you I knew there was still some happiness out there for me. If you want more time to think about things I understand — perhaps I did try to rush you into things,

94

but that's how I operate, I see something I want and go after it before it eludes me. I wouldn't have turned out to be such a good businessman if I let things just slip through my fingers.'

'I'm the exact opposite, very cautious and careful. I have an idea! How about if you move in here with me for the remainder of your stay? If we still feel the same about each other at the end of your stay then we'll set a date for our wedding, for sometime next year. Now how does that sound, cautious and careful?'

'Next year!'

'It's only six months away darling. I'm sure you can wait that long.'

'Alright Mrs. Sensible. I'll check out of the hotel in the morning.' The following morning at work Barbara couldn't wait to hear about Tamara's weekend and was astounded to hear how quickly things had moved on.

'He doesn't waste much time does our Marcus. Moving in after only knowing you a couple of days. Well I never.'

'You don't think I'm being silly and on the rebound after Gary do you?'

'No, of course not. You go for it, and I want a definite invite to the wedding — even if it's in Hong Kong I'll be there. Oh, by the way, while you were in the West Country there was another rape in Drayton Park.'

'Oh my God, no.'

'Tam, you've gone quite pale. What is it?'

'I don't know Barbara but I'm scared, suddenly really scared.'

'It's understandable after what you went through with the phone calls and death threats you received. Perhaps you ought to have another word with the police and just remind them of your situation. You'll be safe now with Marcus moving in.'

'I don't know if there's much point going to the police. They'll only ask if I've received any more, and when I tell them I haven't they'll lose interest.'

'I suppose you're right. I suppose we'd better get down to some work before old Patterson comes in and starts moaning.'

★ ★ ★

After the Crime Programme the police were inundated with calls from the public. Chief Inspector Charlie Mann was holding another briefing.

'We had a good response from the general public after last night's programme and there are a lot of lines of enquiry to follow up. We have a clear set of fingerprints on the knife and a report from a member of the public saying that he broke up a fight between two lads aged about seventeen or eighteen. One was brandishing a knife which he threw into the bushes when the man intervened in the fight. Whether or not the lad came back for the knife later on and used it on Melanie Taylor, or whether someone else picked it up, we don't know. My bet is the rapist is this young lad, and he's got a bit nasty this time and thought he would use a knife on his victim. Yes, DS Starkey.'

'It took some guts for the man to break up a fight between two lads, especially with one brandishing a knife.'

'Geoff Grant is over six foot tall and weighs about twenty stone. Apparently he's known to the local police, he's harmless enough unless anyone upsets him. The locals call him the gentle giant. He's a bit of a loner, which brings me to the profile from the criminal sychologist. The man is probably middle-aged, unmarried, and a loner. He has no friends and possibly no family, no one he has to answer to about his comings and goings. Possibly unemployed or if he is working it's only in a part time capacity. The profile seems to fit Geoff Grant but my money is on the young lad. Melanie Taylor is a local girl and would surely have recognized Geoff Grant by his size, even if he was wearing dark clothing and a balaclava. We'll see what the DNA report comes up with. By the way, after last night's programme the media boys have been referring to him as the God's Carpet Rapist.'

'He sounds like a bit of a religious nut to me Chief, which would exclude the lads that were fighting. The young people today don't seem to know the meaning of religion.'

'We'll see, DC Harding, we'll see. He was possibly messing about on the internet and came across one of the religious websites which describes grass as God's carpet, and thought he would use the words 'God's Carpet' to throw everyone off the scent. Making us all think we're looking for an older person not a teenager. Of course there's always the possibility that it is one of those foreign religious cults. There seems to be a few immigrants wondering around Woodfield this summer. Whether they are here legally or not remains to be seen. Then there is the usual influx of language students. I'm putting you and DC Woods in charge of interviewing the foreign contingent in the area.'

Charlie Mann was interrupted by a PC entering the room with the results of the fingerprint report. After reading the report briefly the Chief Inspector looked up smiling at the sea of expectant faces.

'The fingerprints on the knife were

identified as belonging to a local lad known to the police for drug offences, Liam Rickman.'

'But sir, he can't be the rapist. One of the victims, Kendra Rickman, is his sister.'

DC Woods took great pleasure in watching the smile fade from Charlie's face as realization of what had just been said dawned on him.

'Right, we need to get Liam Rickman in for questioning and find out who was the other lad he was fighting with.'

At first Liam Rickman was uncooperative with the police until he realized he could be facing something a lot more serious than a fight with another teenager.

'Right, we'll start again, Rickman. Who were you fighting with and why?'

'I want my brief.'

'Don't be so bloody stupid. You haven't got one and you'll still have to answer the questions anyway, so do us all a favour and let us eliminate you from our enquiries and we can all get home early. On the other hand if you insist on legal representation it will take a bit of time to arrange and you'll be in here a whole lot longer. Now which is it to be?'

'Alright then, what do ya want to know?'

DC Harry Harding breathed a sigh of relief.

'Who were you fighting with two weeks ago on August Bank Holiday Monday in Drayton Park — the night Melanie Taylor was raped and stabbed?'

'I didn't do it. You can't pin that one on me, or Darren — he didn't do it either.' Liam's voice was raised: he was showing panic and fear and began to sweat profusely.

'Darren who?'

'Darren Asher, my sister Danya's ex-boyfriend.'

'Why were you fighting with him and brandishing a knife?'

'Because he wasn't showing respect.'

'In what way?' Harry Harding raised his eyebrows and looked at his colleague Don Woods.

'He said my sister was a slapper and I was a junkie.'

'And you considered him to be lying then?'

Don Woods unsuccessfully tried to stifle a laugh. Liam glared at the two officers. Harry Harding continued his line of questioning.

'Where did you get the knife from?'

'I don't know, I found it a long time ago.'

'Where?'

'On a building site in town.'

'Tell me what happened that night, from the start of the evening.'

'My sister Danya was crying because her boyfriend Darren had just dumped her. Mum was shouting at her to shut up. Kendra was moaning because she couldn't hear the telly and turned it up real loud, so I decided I'd had enough and might as well go to the pub and see my mates.'

'So it was a normal family evening then?' Darren eyed the two officers suspiciously. 'Then what happened?'

'I took a short cut through the park to get to the Viking pub. Then I came face to face with Darren. We started arguing and he pushed me so I threatened him with my knife. Then along come the gentle giant and told us to pack it in. He wanted the knife so I threw it in the bushes and we both ran off.'

'So you came back later and retrieved the knife? Then you saw Melanie Taylor walking along the path and attacked her.'

'No! No! I didn't. I'm no rapist, you can't fit me up for this one.'

'Alright, calm down. You can go now, but you'll be on police bail as we may need to speak to you again later — so don't even think about doing a runner.'

'What do you think Harry? Do you think he's telling the truth or do you think he did do it? after all, his fingerprints were all over the knife.'

'No, he's too thick, all he can think about is where his next fix is coming from. Frankly he's not capable. Did you see his hands shaking? And he was sweating like a pig. His prints are bound to be on the knife because he owned the bloody thing.'

★ ★ ★

Bill Reed was basking in his notoriety. God's Carpet Rapist, he repeated over and over again. At last I'm someone, not just a nobody anymore, and all the females in the area are scared stiff to go out alone at night . . . but there's always a foolhardy one and I'll have her at the first opportunity. All these years women have sneered and looked down on me, except for my lovely Jenny, she respects and loves me. Revenge is sweet! I must think of a way to get rid of Jenny, I'm running out of excuses to be away from her.

'And what are you smiling at darling? You were miles away; come on, a penny for them.'

'I was just thinking it's your birthday tomorrow and I want to do something really special for you, my precious. Can you give me any clues as to what you would like and if it's in my power you shall have it, I promise.'

'Bill, you are so sweet, I have everything I need so don't go spending your money on me. I'm happy just being your wife, Mrs. Bill

Reed, but perhaps there is one thing you might do for me.'

'Tell me what it is and the answer is yes.'

'Well, I would be really happy if you and Tamara tried to get on with each other.'

'It's not me, it's her, the stuck-up cow, she looks down on me all the time.'

'I'm sure she doesn't, you're just imagining it.'

The next day Tamara called after work with a birthday card and present for Jenny.

'I hope you like the present Jenny, I couldn't think what to buy you then it suddenly dawned on me. This would go with your new image.'

She handed Jenny another envelope in addition to the birthday card.

'What's this? Two cards?'

'Open it and you'll see. I hope you'll be pleased with what's inside.' Bill stood in the background scowling at Tamara and thinking, what's she up to now?

'Oh Tamara, thank you, thank you. I don't know what to say. Bill, look — Tamara has booked me a course of driving lessons.'

A smile spread over Bill's face, he looked really pleased for her. Tamara was amazed at his reaction, she was expecting some sarcastic comment. She could only conclude he would gain some personal benefit when Jenny passed her test, she would be driving him around all over the place.

'Tamara that really is most generous of you. I wish I'd thought of it but you have given me an idea for my present. It can only be one thing — a car.'

'A car! Can we afford it Bill? And your present, Tamara, is so expensive as well, are you sure you can afford to spend so much money on me?'

'It's spent so that's that. Just be careful and enjoy yourself.'

'It's no good having lessons if there's no car at the end of it my sweet. Thank you once again Tamara, I would never have thought of such a wonderful present.'

He was beaming from ear to ear with pleasure, Tamara couldn't understand it. Perhaps I've misjudged him all along, he seemed really pleased for Jenny. He had a look on his face like the cat that got the cream. Still, as long as everyone's happy it's made my day as well. They stood at the front door waving good-bye to Tamara.

'Bill, thank you.'

'For what? You haven't got my present yet but we'll start looking tomorrow without fail.'

'No not that silly.'

'What then.'

'For being nice to Tamara.'

'Oh that. Well she wasn't thinking about herself for once and she had obviously put a lot of thought into your present, and that's all that matters to me — you being happy and content.'

'I am, I am, Bill. I feel so happy I could burst.'

The following week Jenny had her first driving lesson. She was gone just over an hour. It's not very long, mused Bill, but enough time I suppose to get to the park and back. Tamara the useless bitch has actually done something useful for once in her life. Thank you so much Tamara for handing it to me on a plate. He laughed out loud, an evil spine-chilling laugh. An hour a week to myself, I must try to persuade Jenny to have evening lessons instead of afternoon ones. Now the evenings are drawing in it's much safer for me after dark.

'Well, how did your lesson go today darling?'

'I'm beginning to get quite brave. I must confess at first I was terrified, traffic seemed to be coming at me from all directions. I felt like screaming with fright and giving up altogether, but my instructor is so reassuring and kind. He said everyone feels like that after their first lesson and I'll soon conquer my fear and enjoy driving. Today was only my second lesson and I felt better already.'

'I was thinking you ought to change from afternoon lessons to evening to give you some experience of night driving.'

Jenny looked horrified. 'Bill, not yet, not for a long time yet. I have a long way to go before I'll feel confident to drive at night.'

The next day Bill had a call from the estate agent telling him he had someone interested in viewing his house at two o'clock that afternoon.

'Would you be available to show the prospective buyer over the house, Mr. Reed, or would you like one of our negotiators to show her around? I know you said you would prefer to be there when people are looking over your home as your possessions are still in the house.'

'No, that's alright, it's no trouble for me to be there at two o'clock. What's the lady's name?'

'A Miss Birch, a professional lady who would like to move down from the London area. I have great hopes for this one Mr. Reed, she seems able to buy the property outright, no chain involved.'

Bill was at his house by one-thirty in plenty of time for the two o'clock viewing. Miss Birch, a professional lady from London. He mimicked the estate agents voice. Sounds to me like another Tamara Watson. At five minutes to two the front doorbell rang. Bill answered it to a very smart lady wearing a white suit and looking uncannily like Tamara.

'Mr. Reed? I'm Jane Birch.'

She had a sugary sweet voice which both excited and annoyed Bill. She extended a white-gloved hand to him. He shook her hand firmly and felt an excitement rising within him.

'Charmed to meet you, Miss Birch. Welcome to my humble abode.'

She wandered from room to room with Bill following close behind, at times she thought he was a bit too close for comfort. She turned around quickly and bumped into him. As he felt the closeness of her body brush against his he knew that she was his next victim. He pushed her against the wall and started tearing at her smart clothes, she was struggling and screaming. She lashed out at his face and scratched him. He banged her head against the wall, again and again, until she slumped to the floor unconscious. When he had finally finished with her body he dragged her to the bathroom and flung her in the bath. I'm going to have to cut her up and get rid of her piece by piece and dump her in the river at high tide. Two hours later he returned home to be greeted by an eager Jenny.

'Well, how did it go? Do you think we have a buyer?'

'She didn't turn up. I waited an hour and a half then decided to go blackberrying.'

'Is that how you got that scratch on your face?'

'Yes, there were some really delicious ones at the back. I reached over trying to avoid the stinging nettles and scratched my face on one of the other bushes. I'm going to ring the estate agent and give him a piece of my mind, and tell him not to send me any more timewasters.'

'Now Bill, don't get too nasty, it's not his fault she didn't turn up. Anyway there may be a good reason for her not turning up. Perhaps she was taken ill or something, no doubt she'll ring the estate agent later and apologize.'

John Hayes was puzzled by Miss Birch not turning up for her two o'clock viewing appointment and confided in a colleague about an inexplicable feeling of unease.

'I really can't understand it Ray, she seemed so keen. I felt it was in the bag. I just can't understand why she's cried off. I think something's happened to her. I've a bad feeling about the whole business.'

'Like what? You're such a drama queen John. Get on the blasted phone and find out why she didn't turn up. She probably missed her train or something.'

'Yes, you're probably right. I'll give her a call right now. Hello Miss Birch, this is John Hayes from Reynolds and Napier Estate Agents. I was wondering if you would like to make another appointment to view the property of Mr. Reed in Marsden Road, or if you are still interested in purchasing a property in this area. If you could give me a call back as soon as you get this message I would be most grateful.'

'I would be most grateful,' mimicked Ray Jones. 'Really John, why do you have to be so polite all the time? You sound like an old woman at times. I think Miss Birch needs a younger man's approach. When she rings back I think I'd better escort her to the next property.'

John wasn't listening, he was deep in thought and still worrying about Miss Birch.

The following day Jenny was busy with the housework and Bill made the excuse of taking back their library books. He had already decided that cutting up the body was a far too messy job and it would be much easier to bury her at the bottom of his garden where there was a mass of trees and shrubs. He dug a hole in the middle of the bushes where it was most dense and hidden from the eyes of the neighbours. I'll have to come back after dark to bury her. I'll slip Jenny some of my sleeping pills in her cocoa and sneak out when she is asleep.

Having successfully completed his mission he was congratulating himself on how easy it had all been.

It was a month later when Reynolds & Napier received a call from a Gillian Clinton.

'Here, you'd better take this one John. It's a Gillian Clinton enquiring about her friend Jane Birch.'

'Hello, John Hayes speaking. How can I be of assistance. Yes, I can confirm that Miss Birch made an appointment to view a property in the area, but she never kept the appointment, the vendor waited for nearly two hours. Since then I have written to her and left a message on her answerphone but she has never got back to me. Have you informed the police of her disappearance?'

'No, not yet. At first I thought that she had decided to take a holiday in the New Forest and view lots of properties while she was in the area. I assumed she would contact me at some point, but I've heard nothing and I am beginning to get really worried.'

'Try to stay calm, perhaps she has met with an accident and is in hospital. You contact the London police and I'll mention it to our local police, I'm sure between us we'll find out where your friend is.'

★   ★   ★

'Look at this, Harry, a report has just come in from Reynolds & Napier Estate Agents about a missing lady from London who never turned up to view one of their properties.'

'Which area Don?'

'Marsden Road.'

'Isn't that where Bill Reed lives?'

'Used to live. He now lives with his wife in her house in Juniper Road.'

'I think it's time we paid another visit to our friend Mr. Reed.'

7

Jenny opened the door to find the same two police officers that had called before. Immediately she saw them, her heart sank. Oh hell, what now! She had visions of Bill sounding off again about police harassment.

'Can we come in please Mrs. Reed? We'd like a few words with your husband please.'

'Bill, it's the police to see you.'

'What is it now?' Bill's face was like thunder.

'Could you tell us where you were early afternoon on Thursday the 3rd of September?' DC Woods eyed him suspiciously.

'How should I know? That was a month ago.'

'Bill darling, wasn't that the day the woman was supposed to view the house and didn't turn up?' Bill could hardly conceal his anger at Jenny supplying the police with this piece of information.

'Which house would that be, sir?'

'It's my house where I lived before marrying Jenny. It's on the market and the estate agent had me waiting in the house for nearly two hours for some woman that never turned up, or probably never even existed.'

'Come now, Mr. Reed. Estate agents don't normally waste people's time. What would be the point?'

Harry Harding continued.

'So you say the lady in question never turned up at all.'

'I've already said, haven't I?'

'Thank you Mr. Reed. That will be all for the moment but we may need to speak to you again.'

Bill slammed the front door shut.

'I didn't realize he owned two houses, Don.'

'According to one of the neighbours he hasn't been married all that long, less than a year.'

'That would probably account for his wife, she's all over him like a rash and very protective. What do you make of her?'

'I think she's a bit over the top. What does she see in him for Christ's sake?'

'Well, she's no oil painting and if he ever crossed her I think she'd turn out to be a right bunny boiler.'

Both men laughed as they walked back to their car. Back at the station DC Don Woods was complaining about having to reinterview all the suspects in the rape cases to see if there was any link with the Jane Birch missing person case. He had to establish who had alibis and who couldn't account for themselves on the afternoon in question.

'Am I ever going to get any social life Harry?'

'What about the typist you had your eyes on a while ago?'

'It seems like she's spoken for. The other evening I saw her boyfriend waiting for her. He's about six foot tall and looks as thick as two short planks.'

'Well there you are then. You being only five foot six you don't stand a chance. She obviously likes taller men, perhaps I ought to get to know her.'

'I'm five foot eight at least, if not more,' replied a very indignant Don Woods.

'Anyway you're married. What would Mrs. Harding have to say about that?'

'Come on, I'm only taking the mick, back to work. Where's our next port of call?'

* * *

Tamara was temporarily lulled into a false sense of security regarding Bill. As soon as she heard from Jenny about the missing woman from London who never arrived at Bill's house, alarm bells began to ring. It's him I just know it. He's responsible for everything, all the rapes and now it may even be murder. The poor woman is obviously dead; according to the papers, she's been

114

missing for nine weeks, not a sighting, nothing. She can't have just disappeared off the face of the earth. What can I do and is Jenny in any danger from him? I suppose I could ring the police anonymously and give his name. I wish Marcus was here to advise me. Tamara's thoughts were interrupted by the phone ringing; she was not expecting to hear the male voice on the other end of the line.

'Hi Tam, it's me, Gary.'

'What do you want Gary? It's rather late and I'm busy.'

'Tam, I've missed you so much. Can we start again please?' His voice was pitiful and pleading and she wondered what she ever saw in him in the first place.

'No, sorry Gary, I'm not interested. I've a new man in my life now. Anyway, what's happened to Barbie doll? Ditched you for a younger model no doubt.'

'Tam, don't be like that. I made a silly mistake and now I'm paying for it. Can't we meet up for a drink sometime, for old time's sake?'

'No Gary, I'm sorry. I'm really happy with Marcus, the happiest I've been in ages, and he's asked me to marry him.'

'Who is this guy and where did you meet him?'

'None of your business.'

'Go to hell then.' He slammed the phone down.

★   ★   ★

Bill thought he had better curb his activities for a while with all the police around, but he was restless and wanted to do something. Suddenly it hit him, Tamara has been getting off lightly, it's time she received more phone calls and threatening letters again; with Mr. Millionaire out of the way it will be even more interesting. The next day was Saturday and Jenny was having her driving lesson. Tamara didn't usually work Saturday mornings so there was a good chance she would be home. He dialled the number; he was breathing heavily, excitement rising in him. She answered almost immediately like she had been waiting for the call.

'Hello Tamara, it's a long time since you've heard my voice, but I've been so busy. I expect you've been reading about me in the newspapers and I didn't want to leave you out of my plans, but rest assured you could be next on my list.' He gave a spine-chilling laugh and then was gone. She felt weak and sick, and poured herself a drink hoping the alcohol would calm her nerves. Why is all this happening to me again? Oh God, am I going to be raped or even murdered? I'm going to phone the police, perhaps this time they will listen to me and not fob me off like I'm some demented woman.

Within half an hour DCs Woods and Harding were pressing the intercom bell to her flat.

'What time did you receive the call Miss Watson?'

'About ten o'clock.'

'And you say you were receiving similar calls about six months ago and then they suddenly stopped. Have you any idea why they stopped?

'No.'

'Did anything change in your life around that time?'

'Like what?'

'Well, perhaps a work colleague left the company or a neighbour moved away, anything that was different from your usual routine.'

'I split up with my boyfriend after five years.'

'Did you finish with him?'

'No, he finished with me for the office bike.' Don Woods smiled and Harry Harding shot him a warning glance and continued with his questioning.

'Have you heard from him since the break-up?'

'Yes last night he phoned me and asked me to take him back. I said no, I have another man in my life now and I was not interested.'

'What was his reaction?'

'He said go to hell and slammed the phone down.'

Both officers looked at one another.

'No, you can't possibly think it was Gary.'

'Did you recognize the voice?'

'No, he uses one of those voice distorters. It's impossible to recognize the voice.'

'I think we had better pay your ex a visit. Can we have his name and address please?'

After the police had left Tamara phoned Jenny and asked if she could come for a chat. When she arrived her heart sank. Bill was sat in the armchair with a smug look on his face.

'What is it, Tamara dear? Sit down and tell us everything, you're obviously very upset.'

Tamara wished Bill would disappear. No such luck, he was firmly ensconced and obviously had no intention of moving. After Tamara had related the whole story to them both, Jenny was as shocked as Tamara to think Gary was about to be arrested.

'No, it can't be him. He wouldn't do that to you.'

'That's what I thought, Jenny, but in one

way it does make sense if you think about it. He wanted to be rid of me so he could carry on with his floozy at the office. Now that's all gone sour he wanted to come crawling back to me and when I rejected him he restarted the hate campaign.'

'And do you think he's responsible for the rapes?'

'No I don't, I think that's down to someone else.' She glanced at Bill as she made the last statement and wasn't sure if it was her imagination, but for a fleeting moment she thought he looked slightly uneasy. 'The thing is, Jenny, he may get stitched up by the police who are anxious for a conviction over the rapes. Everyone locally is up in arms that there has been no arrest yet.'

'I don't think the police could do that without any evidence.'

'Jenny, you know as well as I do that people have been arrested and charged for things they haven't done. You see it all the time on television. People are being released from prison after serving years for things they haven't done. Well at least I can go home and sleep easy tonight knowing he is in custody. Thanks for listening love, I'd better go now.' Once more she glanced at Bill who sat with an expressionless face.

'You were quiet Bill. In fact you didn't say anything the whole time Tamara was here.'

'I daren't my sweet for fear of saying the wrong thing and upsetting her, you know how she's been with me in the past.'

'Yes but that's all over now since her kindness in paying for a set of driving lessons for my birthday. I thought you saw her in a new light and she seemed to be much nicer to you, since you promised to buy me a car. By the way my instructor is putting me in for my test.'

'That's wonderful news, but isn't it a bit soon.'

'No, I'll probably have to wait ages for the test there's a long waiting list.'

★   ★   ★

Gary Stevens could not believe the woman he loved could be so cruel as to get him arrested. She must have taken it harder than I thought when I ditched her and now it's payback time for me. What about Jodie — is she going to tell the police the truth, that I was with her when all these rapes were taking place, or is she going to stick the boot in as punishment for me finishing with her? I've made some mistakes in my life but she must have been one of the biggest. I ruined a good relationship through her. I know I only have myself to blame. She was far too young and immature, but please Jodie, come through for me and speak the truth, he uttered a silent prayer. Almost immediately his prayers were answered and the cell door opened.

'Right, you can go Mr. Stevens. Miss Bowden has confirmed you were with her on the nights in question, but there is still the matter of harassment of Miss Tamara Watson, so we will need to speak to you again regarding this charge.'

'What, just like that I can go, no apology?'

'Don't push your luck.'

Jodie Bowden was tempted to say to the police she had never been out with Gary Stevens, but she knew other people knew different. She had been the talk of the office for months, how she had split up Gary and Tam. She was pleased to have been the centre of attention and was quite proud of herself at how she had managed to pull such a handsome man. As soon as he had finished with her Jodie tried to tell everyone she dumped him as he was much too old for her. Nobody believed her and just assumed Gary had come to his senses.

The first thing Gary did when he got home, ignoring the police warning of not to get in contact with Tamara, was to ring her.

'Hi Tam, it's Gary.'

'Oh it's you, so they let you out then.'

'Please Tam, just tell me one thing, why did you do it to me? You know you meant the world to me once, you still do. I still love you Tam.'

'Oh, spare me the sob story. You're out aren't you? Just leave me alone and don't contact me ever again. Just answer me one thing Gary. Where did you get that voice distorter from? Did you pick it up abroad on one of your trips?'

'No Tam, I haven't got one, you have to believe me. I didn't do it any of it I swear.'

She slammed the phone down. God, how I hate men at times, except my darling Marcus. She settled down to re-read his letter that had come in the morning post, begging her to marry him. I love him so much, I don't know what is making me hesitate in accepting his proposal. I really want to marry him and be with him but I can't stand the thought of living abroad. I think my trouble is I'm too English.

Jodie was furious that Gary hadn't thanked her for confirming he was with her on the night of the rapes. She sulked for a bit and then decided to go out with her friends for the evening. One lived at Woodfield and was throwing a party and Jodie had been invited.

She caught a bus to Woodfield and arrived at 7.30pm. It was dark when she alighted from the bus and shivered in the cold late November air she wished she had worn more clothes, but it was a party and you had to wear the right gear or look a fool. She was walking along the road towards her friend Janine's house when a man with a small dog approached her.

'Good evening young lady.'

Jodie glared at him and didn't answer; she hurried away, her high-heeled shoes making a clicking sound on the pavement, and this sound excited Bill Reed. He turned and started to follow her, she began to run and he quickened his pace, but he was too late — she had reached her destination. She went into a house where a party was obviously taking place. The front door was open and the girl ran in, the music was deafening and every light in the house was on. Young people were everywhere in the garden, sat on the doorstep and in the bedrooms. No one bothered closing any curtains and Bill watched from the shadows the activity of the young people in the upstairs rooms. He was very aroused and knew he had to come back later and kill another victim. There's rich pickings here tonight alright and no doubt the party will go on until the early hours of the morning. I'll have to drug Jenny again and get away.

Jodie was determined to enjoy herself and began drinking as soon as she arrived. By the early hours of the morning the party began to break up. A few people asked Janine if they could crash out for the night but she refused, saying her parents would be back in the morning and she had to get the place cleaned up before their return. She looked at Jodie slumped in a corner and thought, what a state she's in, I'd better call a taxi for her. Another couple, Lucy and Rob, tried to call a taxi to take them home: but none were available for several hours and Janine wanted them out of the house.

'Jodie must have got the last taxi. Now what are we going to do Rob? My parents will go mad if I'm out all night, I'm late enough already.'

'Don't worry, I've got an idea. Jodie is pretty much out of it, when her taxi arrives we'll grab it.'

'But what will she do for one?'

'Well, I don't think Janine will turn her out on the street; she'll just have to stay with her, it's not our problem.'

'But Rob, I feel mean doing that to her.'

'Don't worry about it, she would probably do the same to us if she were sober enough.'

'What makes you think Janine will let her

stay when she wouldn't let us?'

'That's because there's two of us and you know what her parents are like, deeply religious and really old-fashioned. She'll probably make up some story about Jodie coming over for the evening to keep her company and saying she missed her last bus home.'

'Do you really think so Rob?'

'Yes, I'm sure of it. We'd better get out to the front gate before the taxi driver comes and rings the bell.'

No sooner had he spoken than a taxi pulled up at the front gate and the young couple stepped forward.

'Taxi for Jodie Bowden.'

'Yes, that's me.'

'I thought there was only one person to pick up.'

'I thought I might as well give my boyfriend a lift as there aren't any other taxis available for hours.'

'Yeah, there's a big function going on in town plus a couple of other events.'

Jodie staggered to the front gate in time to see her taxi disappearing down the road with Lucy and Rob waving out of the back window. She swore a few obscenities then decided to see if she could hitch a lift home. The alcohol she had consumed through the evening made her relaxed, and she even thought she might walk the seven miles home if she couldn't get a lift. She decided to take a short cut across some wasteland to get to the main road to Southampton. The uneven gravel path caused her to stumble a few times in her high-heeled strapped shoes. She was so busy cursing Lucy and Rob that she didn't hear anyone approaching her. Suddenly she was pounced on from behind, she felt too weak and drunk to offer any resistance. She tried to call out but the words wouldn't come, then suddenly all her pain was gone and Bill was left holding her lifeless body in the moonlight.

It was the following morning before her horribly mutilated body was found by children from the nearby houses. Within ten minutes of the children running home screaming with fear, the police arrived and cordoned off the area. They immediately started a fingertip search for the weapon and any other evidence.

Jenny awoke feeling she'd had a really good night's sleep. As she got out of bed she wobbled slightly and fell against the bedside table. She swung around quickly worrying that she had woken Bill but he was dead to the world. She went downstairs to start breakfast, and as she wandered around the kitchen the calendar on the fridge door caught her attention. 9th November. A year ago today since mother died. A lot has happened in one year mother, a man in your house — my husband sleeping in your bed. I expect you'll be turning in your grave, but there's nothing you can do about it — he's here to stay. She chuckled to herself and thought, how silly, trying to have a conversation with the dead. The phone rang, disturbing her thoughts.

'Hello Jenny, it's me, Tamara. I just rang to make sure you're alright and not feeling too down with it being the anniversary of your mother's death.'

'How kind of you Tamara. No, I'm fine, absolutely fine, really I am. I must go, Bill has just come downstairs for his breakfast. I'll give you a call later.'

'Who was that you were talking to?

'Tamara.'

'Oh.' Bill grunted his disapproval. 'What did she want so early in the morning?'

'Bill it's not early, it's ten-thirty; we both overslept although you look like you haven't slept a wink all night. I had such a lovely sleep although when I woke up I felt a bit wobbly, almost drunk. You haven't been slipping anything into my cocoa have you Bill?' She couldn't help noticing how startled Bill looked at her last remark.

'Like what? What do you mean Jennifer?'

He always called her Jennifer when he was annoyed with her.

'Now, don't go all grumpy on me darling. I meant a little nip of something like brandy or whisky.'

'No of course not, my sweet, I wouldn't dream of doing anything like that.'

'I know you wouldn't. I'm just teasing you my love. Sometimes you take life too seriously. I used to be just like that when mother was alive but since her death I've learned to relax more and be myself. By the way today is a year since her death, the 9th, that's why Tamara was ringing to make sure I wasn't feeling too down, she's such a devoted friend.'

A bit too devoted, thought Bill. I'm going to have to do something about that woman at the first opportunity.

The doorbell rang and two policemen were standing on the step.

'I'm sorry to disturb you both, but we need to ask you a few questions. May we come in?'

'Yes of course officer, and I must apologize for not being dressed so late in the morning.'

'Were you out late last night?'

'No, we were both here all evening. We watched the late-night film and then went to bed.'

'What time would that be?'

Bill interrupted. 'Why are you asking us all these questions?'

'Last night a young girl was murdered on the waste ground not far from here and everyone in the neighbourhood is being asked if they heard or saw anything suspicious between midnight and 4 am this morning.'

'No officer, as soon as the film was finished we both went to bed and were soon sound asleep.'

'Thank you. We'll see ourselves out.'

★　★　★

'Shall we put the television on and see the news bulletins Jenny?'

'Lets not Bill. It's horrible, another young girl murdered practically on our doorstep and the police seem to be getting nowhere. We'll hear all about it on the teatime news. Let's just enjoy today and not think of all the horrible events happening around us. If I wasn't married to you and living on my own I would be terrified. I feel totally safe with you darling.'

Bill smiled but inside he was seething at having to wait till teatime to hear about his latest murder victim. He wanted to just sit and wallow in the glory of it all, watching it unfold before him on the television screen.

God's carpet rapist is now a murderer. I wonder if the police know that yet. Perhaps I should give them a little help by sending a cut-out note. I must be really careful of DNA and fingerprints so I won't be able to use our newspapers, my fingerprints are all over them. I'll have to go out and buy some new ones and keep my gloves on the whole of the time.

'Jenny . . . I'm just going to take Pepper to the park for his walk.'

'I'll come with you.'

'No, don't trouble yourself, I won't be long. I expect you have a few chores to do, we'll go out together later on.'

The park was deserted and as Bill wandered along pondering his next move, he couldn't believe his eyes. A few yards ahead of him in the bushes was a large pile of the free local paper. It's the first time the local youths around here have done something useful, dumping all these papers and not delivering them has helped me no end. Still wearing gloves he picked up several copies of the paper and put them in a carrier bag that was lying near by.

'Quick as you can, Pepper, back to my house.'

The little dog could barely keep up the fast pace. Once inside he soon set about cutting letters from the newspaper and pasting them on a sheet of paper. I think I'll send Tamara one as well. The note to the police read: **GoDs CarPeT RapisT is NoW GodS CARpEt MurDeReR.** On Tamara's sheet he pasted the words: **GoDs CarPeT MuRdereR is CoMing FoR You SoOn.**

His task complete, he went out to the back garden to call Pepper who had been running in and out of the house.

'Pepper, come on in, good boy.' There was no response from the dog. Tutting to himself he began to walk down the path to the end of the garden. He froze in horror; there was Pepper at the very spot he had buried Jane Birch, digging furiously, soil flying in all directions. He grabbed the little dog and practically flung him up the garden path, cursing him and muttering to himself as he tried to fill in the hole Pepper had dug.

'Everything all right Mr. Reed?' Mrs. Johnson's voice came from the other side of the fence.

'Yes thank you Mrs. Johnson, Pepper is trying to destroy the garden and I'm trying to sell the house. I have to try and keep it all together you know. It's not easy keeping two houses going.'

'I don't know what the attraction is at the bottom of your garden. My friend Gwen and her husband Jimmy came to tea last week and their dog was straight over the fence digging in exactly the same spot.'

Bill was white and shaking with rage.

'Mrs. Johnson, I'll thank you to keep your friend's dog under control and confine it to your garden, not let it roam loose in mine destroying my flowers and plants.'

'It wasn't in your garden for long. Jimmy soon jumped the fence, filled in the hole and brought the dog back. No harm done, so don't take that tone of voice with me, Bill Reed.'

She went inside slamming the door loudly, leaving Bill considerably shaken by this revelation. He grabbed Pepper roughly by the collar and put his lead on. He posted the two notes in the nearest post box, not considering how close the box was to their two homes.

'Bill, you were a long time, where have you been? Reynolds & Napier rang while you were out. They have a family interested in your house and they want to view it next Wednesday afternoon. This time I'm coming with you and if this family don't keep the appointment at least we'll have each other for company. Perhaps I could do a bit of cleaning and tidying up whilst we wait. What's the matter with Pepper? He seems very frightened, he's cowering in the corner. Did he get attacked by another dog?'

Bill wished she would stop talking and allow him to think. Would other dogs in the neighbourhood get into the garden and start digging? He must do something quickly, but what?

'Bill, are you listening to me?'

'I'm sorry my sweet, what did you say?'

'Did Pepper get attacked by a dog in the park? He's cowering in the corner and looks really upset about something. Come here my little darling.' Jenny picked Pepper up and began cuddling and stroking him. 'You are obviously both upset about something. Are you going to tell me what it is or do I have to keep guessing?'

'After I walked Pepper in the park I decided to pop around to my house and make sure everything was alright. Apparently Mrs. Johnson's friend's dog had been in my garden digging holes and trampling on the flower beds. When I asked her to keep her friend's dog under control and out of my garden she took exception to it and started shouting and slammed her back door. Poor little Pepper was frightened stiff while all this was going on. He's never seen me cross before, I think I might have frightened him.'

'Come here you pair of softies, you're both

as bad as one another.' She hugged Bill while still cuddling Pepper. 'Don't let that dreadful woman get to you. he can say what she likes, it's only words — and after all, she was in the wrong, not you.

8

Tamara had the local television news on as she was getting ready for work. She heard the post drop through the letter box and rushed to see if there was a letter from Marcus. She scooped up all the mail not noticing the sinister letter addressed to her that was mixed up with the usual amount of junk mail, all she could see was the letter with a foreign stamp. She eagerly ripped open the letter and began to read.

My darling Tam,

It's only been a few weeks since we were together but it seems an eternity. The job that I have loved for so long now seems meaningless without you by my side. My days are empty and I am just wandering around aimlessly. I seem to be doing everything on autopilot and half the time I don't remember if I have done what I was supposed to do. I can't wait for your answer any longer, if you won't marry me because you don't want to live in Hong Kong then I'll sell up, leave my job and settle in Woodfield.

Please Tam, say yes and put me out of my misery. Your devoted lover till the end of time,
Marcus.

Tamara was brimming over with happiness and love for Marcus. Suddenly the happy moment was broken by the newsreader on the television.

'The young girl murdered at Woodfield in the early hours of Saturday morning has been formally identified and named as seventeen-year-old Jodie Bowden. The police are asking for any witnesses who may have seen Jodie on Friday night or in the early hours of Saturday morning to contact them.'

Tamara sat frozen with horror for several minutes. She couldn't move. Gary, you didn't do it did you? Please God, don't let it have been Gary. I must pull myself together and get off to work and leave it to the police to sort out. She was sorting through the junk mail when she came across the death threat letter. She ripped at the envelope, heart pounding, and hands trembling. She read the words aloud over and over again: **'GoDs CarPeT MuRdereR is CoMing FoR You SoOn.'** The police will have to take notice of me this time.

Chief Inspector Charlie Mann was fuming

as he addressed the assembled murder investigation team.

'Look at this! Arrived with the morning's post.' He was waving the letter sent to the station. 'He's laughing at us, playing with us. Telling us he's moved on from rape to murder, as if we needed telling.'

The door opened and DCs Woods and Harding entered the room.

'So nice of you two to join us. You'd better have a jolly good excuse for being late or you'll find yourselves back pounding the beat.'

'Sir, there's a woman in reception with a letter from the murderer saying he's coming for her soon.'

'What woman? Who is she, another crank? I'm surrounded by cranks and idiots.'

'No sir, she's neither a crank nor an idiot.' There was a touch of sarcasm in DC Woods' tone and it didn't go unnoticed by Charlie Mann, who looked sharply at the young DC.

'Well lad, continue. What did she have to say for herself?'

'Her name is Tamara Watson, a very smart business lady. She has been receiving threatening phone calls and death threat messages through the post for the past eleven months. She reported it to the police at the time but nothing came of it. After a period of intense phoning and death threats in the post, it all went quiet, so the police took no further action, assuming it must have been a nasty prank. Then last month the phone calls and threats started again, after she turned down a reconciliation with her ex-boyfriend Gary Stevens. He was brought in for questioning but his ex-girlfriend Jodie Bowden gave him an alibi.'

A gasp of surprise went around the room and a buzz of conversation started until Charlie Mann's voice boomed out calling for silence.

'Right, don't let Miss Watson leave the building and you two bring in Gary Stevens for further questioning.' He gestured to two police officers sat in the front row. 'Woods and Harding come with me. At last we're getting somewhere. We have these three people connected with one another. Tamara Watson, a woman scorned, and Gary Stevens Jack the lad carrying on with both of them. He realised he'd made a mistake with Jodie Bowden and tried to get back with Tamara Watson. When she turned him down he blamed Jodie, who had a reputation as a bit of a slapper, and took revenge by killing her, thinking her death would leave him free to get back with Tamara.'

'But sir, what about the other rapes and murders? It doesn't make sense.'

'Sense and emotion are not what murderers possess. They are very disturbed people. All of the victims were young girls who dressed in much the same way as Jodie and as he probably came across these girls by chance he took the opportunity when it presented itself to assault or murder them.'

'But Jodie gave him the alibi he needed.'

'She probably thought she could blackmail him to go back with her or to obtain money. Which gives him another motive for murdering her. You're quiet, DC Harding. What do you think?'

'I don't know sir, something doesn't seem right. I don't think he's the type to rape and murder women.'

'There's no particular type Harding, I'd have thought you would have learnt that by now, all the years you've been in the force. Still, living in this backwater I suppose you haven't had much experience of crime on this scale.'

DC Harding looked furious but said nothing.

'Then there's Tamara Watson, a woman scorned. Gary Stevens left her for a young girl at least twenty years younger than her. She could also have blamed all her troubles on Jodie Bowden. Perhaps she blamed her for them splitting up.'

The three police officers entered the interview room where Tamara was waiting patiently. They asked her numerous questions about her life with Gary and what sort of person he was. Was he ever violent towards her? Did she think he was capable of murder if pushed too far?

Her head was spinning with all the questions till she could stand it no more and screamed.

'Stop! Please stop! I can't answer any more questions. I'm sure Gary isn't a murderer and if anyone should know it's me. I was with him for five years.'

'Do you still love him Miss Watson?'

'No, of course not. I'm with somebody else now.'

'Do you have any feelings for him at all, a sense of loyalty or even friendship, anything?'

'No, nothing. I have no feelings for him whatsoever, but I do know he would never do anything of a violent nature.'

'You didn't like Jodie Bowden, in fact you referred to her on several occasions as the office bike.'

'No, I didn't like her. I thought she was a cheap little tart. I hope you're not suggesting I had anything to do with her murder.'

'Do you know of anyone who would have had a reason to murder her?'

'No, I don't know anything about her, but I'm sure there is a long list of men friends you could call on who knew her intimately.'

'Thank you Miss Watson, you can go now. We will have the local beat officer call in on you from time to time to make sure you're alright. In the meantime let us know immediately if you receive any further threats through the post or by telephone.'

She made her way home pondering over the morning's events, but the one thing she felt most sure about was that Gary had not murdered Jodie.

'What do you think Don? Do you think she's still carrying a torch for Stevens and is trying to cover for him as best she can?'

'No, I wouldn't think so, Harry. Let's see what Gary Stevens has to say for himself.'

★ ★ ★

Tamara was still worrying what to do next when the phone rang. Her first thought was not to answer it, then she pulled herself together and lifted the receiver.

'Tam, it's me, Marcus. Did you get my letter? Will you please put me out of my misery and marry me?'

'Slow down Marcus, of course I'll marry you, but not yet.'

'Why not?'

'It's difficult, things are going on at the moment and I just can't up sticks and move to Hong Kong.'

'What things?'

'I've been receiving threats again and a young girl has been murdered in Woodfield not far from Jenny's house.'

'Surely, Tam, that is all the more reason to get the hell out of there and come over here with me where you'll be safe.'

'I can't. I just can't. It's hard to explain but I won't leave until the murderer has been caught.'

'It's madness Tam. I'm coming over. I'll catch the first available plane out of here and be with you soon.'

'No Marcus, please don't.' He wasn't listening, he had put the phone down and was already making plans to join her.

★   ★   ★

Bill Reed was reading the morning paper and wallowing in the media coverage the murders had attracted. He was laughing to himself at the stupidity of the police in not even suspecting him. The phone rang in the hall and Jenny called out,

'I'll get it, Bill, don't get up.'

142

He listened for a moment but could not make head nor tail of the conversation Jenny was having with the person on the other end of the line. She had no sooner replaced the receiver when the phone rang again. After about thirty minutes Jenny came into the lounge where Bill was still reading the papers. She thought he looked smug and had a faint smile on his face.

'What have you found to smile about in the paper darling? When I had a quick flit through earlier on it was all doom and gloom about the murder.'

Bill was annoyed he had been caught out but soon recovered his composure.

'I'd stopped reading the paper ages ago — it was too sad for me. I was just staring at the print but not really reading anything. My mind had turned to happier things like the first day I met you in the park. It's my way of coping with all the horror going on around us. I feel almost guilty about how happy we are when the family of that poor girl must be going through hell.'

'Bill you sweetie, you are so kind and caring underneath, although you do your level best to hide it.' She kissed him on the top of his head. Bill was relieved she had accepted his explanation and thought, I can tell her anything and she'll believe it.

'Anyway darling, who were all the phone calls from? We seem very popular today.'

'The first one was from Reynolds & Napier saying they have another prospective buyer for the house. He wants to view tomorrow afternoon at three o'clock. I said it would be alright and I'd ring back if it wasn't. We're not doing anything tomorrow are we?'

'No, that's all right.'

'This time I'm coming with you.'

'Did they say who was interested?'

'Yes, a family called Mason. They have a couple of young children.'

As long as they don't have a dog, thought Bill. If they do I must do all I can to stop the sale going through.

'Who was the other call from?'

'Tamara, she said Marcus is coming over and wants to marry her.'

'Pity he doesn't take her back to Hong Kong with him and keep her there.'

'Bill . . . That's so unkind.'

'I didn't mean it in an unkind way. I was just thinking she's a woman living alone, and with a murderer on the loose she would be far better off away from here, and that Marcus certainly seems to care about her.'

'Yes, I suppose you're right, she would be a lot safer with him. Also she told me the young girl that was murdered was Gary Stevens' ex.

Jodie, the one he left Tamara for. I thought the name sounded familiar but couldn't think where I'd heard it before. The police have arrested him and are holding him for questioning.'

'Well, I'd never have thought it of Stevens. I know he fancied himself as a bit of a ladies' man, but murder! Still, you never can tell with people.'

Bill was secretly delighted Gary had been arrested and couldn't help marvelling at how many times the police had got it wrong.

The next day Bill and Jenny sat waiting for the Mason family to arrive. Jenny was fiddling with the net curtains and saying they could do with a good wash, when a large four-wheel-drive vehicle pulled up outside.

'Bill they're here, complete with two children and a big dog.'

Jenny rushed to the front door to welcome them.

'Hi, I'm Barry Mason and this is my wife Gemma and our children Jack and Chloe.'

'Do come in. This is my husband Bill.'

Bill Reed nodded a greeting in a gruff voice. Inside he was seething. It had to be a family with a blasted dog. I'll have to do my best to put them off.

'I hope you don't mind us bringing our dog in the house? He tends to bark if left alone in the car and I wouldn't want to upset your neighbours.'

'They're a miserable lot alright, very easily upset so I'm sure you're right,' replied Bill sarcastically. Jenny gave Bill a warning look to be quiet.

'Oh, so the neighbours are a bit miserable are they? Perhaps their attitude ought to reflect in the price of the property. Would you consider a lower price offer?'

'No, certainly not Mr. Mason. The price is set and we cannot afford to be flexible as we wouldn't be able to afford the property we are buying.'

'Right then, there's nothing more to be said.'

The dog gave a low growl, looking directly at Bill.

'Now, let's not be too hasty Mr. Mason' perhaps we can come to some agreement. Bill, a small reduction in the asking price should not affect our buying power too much.'

'Mum, can we go and play in the garden? Go on please . . .'

'Be quiet Jack, we are talking to Mr. and Mrs. Reed.'

'Go on, we could take Ben out with us. He doesn't like Mr. Reed. Please . . .'

'Oh, for goodness' sake. Would you mind, Mrs. Reed, if the dog and children went out into the garden, then perhaps we can talk business.'

'I don't think that's a good idea. I've already had one neighbour's dog digging up my plants and running amok in the garden and I don't particularly want a repeat episode thank you very much.'

'Mr. Reed, I can assure you our dog is very well trained and any damage done we would make good.'

'I've had enough of this nonsense. Come on, Gemma, we're out of here, and you can keep your precious house. I wouldn't live here if you paid me a million pounds.'

Barry Mason ushered his family out the front door banging it loudly behind him.

'Oh Bill, see what you've done now. I thought they were really interested, especially Mrs. Mason, she seemed a really sweet person.'

'Well I didn't like him with his bald head and earring. What sort of a man wears an earring? Did you see his arms covered in tattoos, and that boy needed a good slap, completely out of control.'

'That's how the young people are today Bill. I think they were harmless enough, and now we've lost the sale. Please darling, try to be a bit more tolerant of the next people that come to view, or we'll never get rid of the place at this rate.'

'I'm not putting up with rudeness from anyone.'

Jenny sighed in exasperation.

★ ★ ★

Tamara opened the door to a very tired and dishevelled looking Marcus. She smiled to herself as she had never seen the handsome, well-dressed, not-a-hair-out-of-place Marcus looking quite so rough, but he looked even more handsome to her than the last time she saw him. She threw her arms around him, kissing him till he could hardly draw breath.

'I'm so pleased you're here darling. You look absolutely exhausted.'

'Are you alright Tam? I've been really worried about you. I didn't sleep a wink coming over on the plane. It was a hell of a flight.'

Tamara sat him down and proceeded to tell him all that had been happening since he had left. She didn't stop talking for about twenty minutes and when she finally stopped to draw breath she discovered he had fallen asleep, and wondered at which point in her story he had actually gone to sleep.

The next morning he showered, dressed and sat down to a large breakfast. This was the Marcus she loved and she wondered why she had been such a fool in not marrying him the first time he had asked her. Any other woman would have snapped him up without a second thought. As she watched him tucking into his breakfast she made a decision to marry him without any more hesitation. If she had to go and live in Hong Kong then so be it, she'd tell him as soon as he's finished eating.

The look of joy and utter disbelief on his face when she told him convinced her she had made the right decision and that this would probably be her last chance of happiness with anyone. Next week she would be forty-six. Birthdays were not anything to look forward to anymore, but this one would be the best in a long time.

'Darling, do you really mean it? I can't believe you have said yes after so long.'

'It's not that long Marcus. I haven't even known you a year yet. This time last year I didn't even know you existed. And yes I will come and live in Hong Kong with you, if that's where you need to work then I must be by your side as Mrs. Wheeler-Osman.'

'Darling, we needn't go to Hong Kong for at least six months, I have it all worked out. I can do most of my work from home, with all the technology in this day and age I don't really need to be there. We'll need to find a home where I can set up an office to work from, big enough to take a couple of computers, fax machine, plus at least two phone lines. I know you love this flat darling but it really is too small for us now. Your single girl days are over. What do you say Tam? We could start the house hunting tomorrow and you'd have me to come home to every day. You'd never be afraid again.'

'Marcus stop please, you are making my head spin. It's yes, yes, yes, to everything you've said.'

* * *

Gary Stevens was eventually released on police bail pending further enquiries. Chief Inspector Charlie Mann was angry they could not get him to confess to the murder of Jodie Bowden.

'What do you think, sir? Did he do it or not?'

'Of course he did it, Harding. He's a tough nut to crack, but we'll have him, you mark my words.'

'But sir, there was no forensic evidence linking him to the murder scene.'

'He was clever but sooner or later he'll slip up and then we'll have him.'

Gary Stevens arrived home a physical wreck. Once inside his flat he shut the front door and collapsed sobbing uncontrollably. What had he done that was so terrible to deserve this? Was he being punished by the Almighty for ditching Tam for Jodie? Was this his cross he had to bear? Loads of men play away from home and get away with it, so why me God, why me? Never having been a religious man he could not quite understand why he was thinking of God and retribution. After a bit more wallowing in self-pity he pulled himself together and began to think about how he could prove his innocence. Who could have murdered Jodie? Who would want to? She was so easy that she wouldn't have said no to anyone. It must have been a pure coincidence, that she was in the wrong place at the wrong time, or the murderer mistook her for someone else.

★　★　★

'This house hunting is getting really exhausting Marcus, we seem to be getting nowhere fast, all the new properties are far too small. I just don't know what we can do.'

'I think we're looking in the wrong place darling, we need to look at the older-style property. You know, the ones with the two big bay windows in the front and massive long back gardens. I'll get in touch with the estate agents tomorrow and see what he can find for us. I'm sure we'll get something soon, so don't be so despondent.'

'That's it, why didn't I think of it before? Bill Reed's old house. It hasn't got two front bay windows but it has two downstairs rooms, plus a reasonable size kitchen. I'm sure it is just what we are looking for. Shall I ring Jenny to see if it's been sold?'

'It sounds ideal. Let's get onto it right away.'

Tamara returned from the phone looking pleased with herself.

'Jenny said to come around this evening to discuss it with Bill. He was out walking Pepper so I couldn't talk to him right now.'

Jenny and Bill looked very pleased to see them both, especially Marcus. Jenny threw her arms around him, kissing him on the cheek, and Bill shook hands with him, something Tamara had not seen before. Bill did not welcome visitors, especially her. He usually sat in his chair looking sullen and she could almost feel him willing her to leave. This was a total change of heart. Perhaps some of Jenny's nice ways are rubbing off on him, at last he seems almost human. She felt a slight pang of guilt for thinking nasty things about him. The main thing is he makes Jenny very happy, a bit possessive at times, but still, what does that matter so long as they're happy.

'Before we begin talking about Bill's house, I must first give you my good news. I passed my driving test yesterday. It was my first attempt.'

'Jenny, I'm so pleased. You didn't even tell me you were taking it.'

'I know, I didn't want to disappoint you if I failed. Now we can go anywhere we want without relying on public transport all the time. Thank you so much for such a lovely birthday present Tamara. I would never have thought of learning to drive if it wasn't for you.' The two women hugged one another. Bill coughed and wanted to get straight down to business.

'That's enough of that you two, or you'll both be getting emotional any minute.'

'What do you mean any minute, we already are!' Jenny dabbed a tear from her eye.

'I believe you are interested in purchasing my house Marcus.'

'Yes, very interested. We're going to be married as soon as possible and for a while I'm going to work from this country so I need a big enough place to set up an office. Tam seems to think your house would fit the picture.'

'How do you feel about us buying your property Bill?'

'My dear Tamara, I'm delighted. You don't know how relieved I am that my home will be going to someone deserving who will treat it with respect. You don't know what I've had to put up with these past few months. What with people not turning up and then those that did turning out to be the dregs of the earth, with dreadful children running wild and an unruly dog completely out of control. I don't know what the world is coming to these days I'm sure.'

'Now Bill, don't exaggerate, they weren't that bad.'

'Do you like dogs, Marcus?'

'Yes I do, but it's not very practical to have one when we'll be spending most of our time between here and Hong Kong. It wouldn't be fair on the dog.'

'A very wise decision.'

Bill was highly delighted at his reply. That means there won't be any dogs sniffing around the garden. I didn't think lady muck was the dog loving sort but I had to be sure before we complete the sale.

'I'll take you to see the house tomorrow morning. I always think it's much better to see it in daylight, don't you think, Marcus?'

'Yes Bill, but I'm sure it's going to be fine and we'll love it.'

'Now all the business talk is settled, let's talk weddings Tamara. Will you have a big do or a quiet one?'

'I'm not too sure Jenny. I only said yes a few days ago.'

'Tam can have whatever she wants Jenny, and of course you and Bill must come, it wouldn't be the same without you two.'

Tamara was deep in thought on the journey home.

'Penny for them Tam, you were miles away. Are you happy darling?'

'Yes of course I am. At last things are really coming together for me and I'm so pleased for Jenny, Bill seems to have turned over a new leaf. He was like a different person tonight, happy, sociable, being polite. I can't understand it. Perhaps I've been quick to judge him and he sensed it, from now on I must try and be nicer to him.'

The next day they visited Bill's house and Tamara was surprised to see how neat and orderly everything was. She looked out of the window at the neat and tidy garden.

'Bill, you must spend a lot of time here keeping everything up together. I don't know how you manage it.'

'Oh I enjoy it, Tamara, I've always thought there should be a place for everything and everything must be in its place.'

'Well Bill, we'd both be very happy to buy your home. Jenny and I will take a stroll in the garden whilst you and Marcus talk shop.'

'Why? What do you want to go out there for?' Bill replied quite sharply.

'Bill, whatever's the matter with you? If Tamara wants to walk in the garden she can, after all it will soon be her home.'

'Sorry Tamara. I only meant it's very cold out, in spite of the bright sunshine there is quite a chilly wind.'

'I'll live, I'm tougher than you think, you just concentrate on the house negotiations with Marcus.'

The two women went out into the garden leaving Bill scowling out of the kitchen window watching their every move. Marcus couldn't help noticing how Bill's mood had changed, he no longer seemed interested in selling the house and was more intent on watching the women. Extraordinary behaviour, thought Marcus, his mood can change in an instant, he's a bit of a Jekyll and Hyde character. Jenny and Tamara turned and started walking back up the garden path and Marcus couldn't help noticing the look of relief on Bill's face.

'You were saying, Marcus. I'm sure we can get everything tied up pretty quickly so you won't be behind with your work for long.'

The two men shook hands on the deal and Jenny suggested they all have a drink to celebrate.

9

Chief Inspector Charlie Mann sat at his desk pondering his next move. He could feel his temperature rising as well as the anger within. He reached for his blood pressure pills and without thinking he quickly swallowed two tablets, washed down with water straight from the jug on his desk. He didn't bother with the finer things in life like using the glass provided. After several mouthfuls of water it dawned on him that he should have only taken one blood pressure pill and not two. He then thought, what the hell, the bloody things don't work anyway. He was furious that they had to let Gary Stevens go without having enough evidence to charge him with Jodie Bowden's murder. Suddenly his thoughts were interrupted by the door being flung open by DC Don Woods.

'Haven't you ever heard of knocking Woods? I suppose manners are something new to the country bumpkins in this backwater.'

Don Woods ignored his abrasive remarks and continued.

'Sorry sir, but we have a taxi driver at the

desk saying he dropped Jane Birch at the corner of Marsden Road about the time she went missing.'

'Right, take him to interview room two and let's get a proper statement from him.'

'Your full name?'

'John Edward Nicholas, but I'm known to everybody as Johnny the cab.'

'Well Mr. Nicholas why haven't you come forward before now?'

'We moved to Spain a few months ago, and decided not to sell our house but to try and let it, but we didn't have much luck. The people that were going to rent it pulled out at the last moment, which turned out to our advantage in the end. It was my Missus' idea to go and live in Spain. I didn't want to go but she did and what she says goes. Miss Birch was one of my last fares of the day.'

'What date would that be?'

'Thursday 3rdof September. We were off the next day bright and early so I didn't want to work a full afternoon.'

'Did you not hear the news in Spain that this woman had suddenly disappeared off the face of the earth and the whole country was searching for her?'

'No Guv, you see we didn't have a television in the apartment, and we were so busy with settling in that we didn't even buy an English newspaper. I didn't know anything until we decided to come home, and everyone was talking about the murder of the young girl. We only rented the apartment in Spain so it was easy to come back if we didn't like it there. There was an old newspaper on the doormat dated the day after we'd left for Spain. Although we'd cancelled and paid the paper bill they must have got the date wrong and delivered an extra day, and there lo and behold was a picture of Miss Birch on the front page.'

'Right, tell us from the beginning what she said to you and where you picked her up.'

'I picked her up at Southampton Central Station and drove her to Marsden Road, Woodfield.'

'Whereabouts in Marsden Road did you drop her off?'

'The top end nearest the park. She said she was a bit too early for her appointment and would walk around the area and look at the other houses before she kept her appointment at two o'clock.'

'Did you see her enter the park?'

'No, she was stood on the edge of the curb, as I drove off she was looking all around.'

'Did she book a return journey to the train station?'

'No, she said she wasn't sure what time she

159

would finish viewing the house. I remember she said she might wander around the area and find somewhere to eat. There is a local taxi firm operating so there was no need for her to call a Southampton cab, she could use one of the locals when she was ready to leave.'

'Did she say anything during the journey?'

'Only that she lived in London and hated all the hustle and bustle, she was looking for a more leisurely way of life.'

'Thank you Mr. Nicholas, you've been most helpful. If you think of anything further to help us with our enquiries into the disappearance of Jane Birch, please let me know. Here is my direct phone number, you can call me at any time during the day or my mobile number in the evenings.'

'What do you think of that sir?'

'Get straight onto Gary Stevens' employers and check whether he was at work on Thursday 3rd September. If he was absent then we'll haul him back in for more questioning.'

'Do you think she's dead sir?'

'Yes, of course she's dead, Woods. He could hardly be keeping her prisoner in that tiny flat he lives in. I think she wandered into the park and bumped into him. They struck up a conversation and he either murdered her there or took her somewhere else in his car and did it.'

'I don't think he could have murdered her in the park, there are far too many people around at lunchtime.'

'The local schools don't come out until three o'clock and her appointment was at two, Harding, so he had plenty of time before the park was crawling with teenagers, at least an hour.'

'What about the dog walking brigade? They seem to be in the park morning, noon and night, and it was three dog walkers that saved Melanie Taylor from being murdered. He almost succeeded — had it not been for them coming along at that moment, she was about to become the next victim. I just don't think that Stevens is our man, he just doesn't seem the type to call himself the God's Carpet Murderer. That sounds like some sort of nut to me.'

'That's just what he wants us to think, to take the suspicion off him.'

DC Harding said no more but remained unconvinced.

★　★　★

Tamara and Marcus had planned to marry early in May, and Marcus was really pleased that a work colleague and very close friend Lee Chang and his family were willing to

161

make the trip from Hong Kong for the wedding.

'You will absolutely love them darling. I have worked with Lee for the past fifteen years, a very clever and dedicated man. His wife is small, beautiful and very Chinese, Lee is more westernized and prefers his beautiful daughters not to use their Chinese names. Lilly and Lulu are twins, aged seventeen, and Rosie is two years younger. Lee met my mother once and took an immediate liking to her. When their third daughter was born he called her Rosie after my mother Rose Elizabeth, and promised if he had any more daughters he would call the next one Elizabeth. I said enough is enough Lee, you have your hands full with the three you already have. He just laughed and gave me one of his smiles. He is such a happy and contented man, he never complains about anything and is so reliable.'

Tamara sat enthralled listening to Marcus and thinking there was still a lot more she didn't know about him but she had the rest of her life to find out. She sighed contentedly.

'I'm not boring you am I Tam? Going on about my friends all the time.'

'No of course not, I'm fascinated, it sounds like a completely different world living in Hong Kong.'

'I know it's not the bridegroom's place to choose the bridesmaids but I thought it would be a nice idea to have Lee's three daughters as bridesmaids.'

Tamara looked slightly disappointed.

'I'm sorry Tam of course you must have who you want, not who I suggest. Who did you have in mind?'

'Only Jenny, we have been friends since our schooldays.'

'Jenny would have to be Matron of Honour, and with respect, she's not the prettiest of women, lovely person that she is. I'm sorry love, that sounded so unkind and I didn't mean it to. What I was trying to say came out all wrong. I just wanted my beautiful wife surrounded by beautiful people on our special day.'

'I know what you meant Marcus, and I think you're right. Bridesmaids should be young and pretty and after all I didn't even get an invite to their wedding, they ran off to Gretna Green to get married.'

'Good, that's settled then. I'll ring Lee in the morning, he'll be so pleased and honoured.'

★   ★   ★

On checking with Gary Stevens' employers, it was found that he had been absent on the

3rd of September; he had phoned in sick saying he had a temperature and was hoping to return to work the next day. He was brought back to the police station for further questioning in a distraught state, protesting his innocence.

'Can anyone confirm your story?' asked a smug Chief Inspector.

'No, of course not. I was in bed all day and saw no one.'

'Did anyone ring you during that day?'

'No. Everyone would have assumed I was at work so there would be no point in ringing me.'

'Do you usually get a lot of phone calls?'

'No more or less than anyone else I suppose.'

'About how many, five or ten per evening?'

'Don't be so ridiculous, nobody gets ten calls an evening unless they're running a business.'

'What sort of business are you referring to? Ladies of the night perhaps. Do you use that service yourself?'

'Of course not.'

'What never?'

'No, never. I've never had need to, I've always had a girlfriend. That's just for saddos.'

'Oh yes. Of course, you usually have two on the go at once, don't you Mr. Stevens.'

'This is police harassment. I demand to see a solicitor.'

'Have you a solicitor?'

'No.'

'DC Woods, see if you can get hold of the duty solicitor. We'll continue the interview when a solicitor is present.'

After several more hours of questioning in the presence of his solicitor, Gary Stevens was released from police custody once more. Charlie Mann felt more confident that it was only a matter of time before they would be able to charge him with all the crimes, and he could return to London feeling he had gained another feather in his cap, but DCs Woods and Harding did not share his enthusiasm. They felt they were a long way from catching the real killer and a lot of hard work still lay ahead.

* * *

'What are all these rose bushes doing on the kitchen table Bill? We haven't got any room in the garden for any more roses, it's jam-packed tight with shrubs as it is.'

'They're for Tamara's garden. I know she's no gardener and roses are so easy to manage, no trouble at all. I thought I'd plant them at the bottom end as a nice surprise for her. I'll get them in before we hand the keys over next week.'

'It's such a relief that at last your house is sold and to have sold it to our dearest friends is just a wonderful bonus. Now we can concentrate on the apartment in Bournemouth. Are you sure we don't need to sell this house as well before we can complete the purchase?'

'No it's not necessary, we can just about manage it without the sale of your house. If for any reason we're not happy living in Bournemouth we can always come back here.'

Marcus and Tamara were now the owners of Bill Reed's house, and with the wedding only three weeks away, Marcus hit on the idea of letting the Chang family stay in it until they returned from their honeymoon. They had decided to come over a few weeks before the wedding and see some of England. It would be their first family holiday in Europe. Marcus met them at the airport and had a people carrier standing by to take them all to Woodfield. Tamara had stayed at the house to have an evening meal ready for their arrival.

She opened the front door to a sea of happy Chinese faces and was struck by the beauty of the young girls.

'Please come in, you are all very welcome. Did you have a good trip?'

'Oh yes very pleasant. You have a very nice home Tamara.'

'Thank you Mei, please treat it as your own for as long as you're here.'

The meal went down well and everyone was happy except for Rosie. Tamara noticed how quiet and sullen she looked, as if she really didn't want to be here.

On the way home Tamara asked Marcus about her.

'Is Rosie usually so quiet? She hardly said a word all evening.'

'No she isn't, she's usually the noisiest of the three girls and never stops chattering. Perhaps she was just tired after the long flight.'

'Yes, I expect you're right darling. She's not the only one feeling tired, it's been a long day. Let's get to bed.'

Rosie confided in her mother that she didn't want to stay in the house as she was frightened.

'Don't be so silly Rosie, there is nothing to be frightened of.'

'The house is bad, very bad, something really terrible happened here. I can feel it.'

'I think you are wrong Rosie, and you mustn't say anything like that to Marcus or Tamara, they will think we are so ungrateful after the kindness they have shown us.

Besides, nothing bad has happened here. Marcus told your father he bought the house from Tamara's friends. A man called Bill Reed lived here with his mother all his life until she went into a nursing home and eventually died. Then he met Tamara's friend Jenny and married her, and they are living in Jenny's house so they didn't need this one as well and sold it to Marcus. So you see nothing bad has happened here, I think you're probably over tired and letting your imagination run away with you.'

'No Mother, I know I'm right. It has nothing to do with the old lady dying, that is not it. Something else really bad has happened here.'

By this time Mei was feeling really exhausted from the long journey and her youngest daughter's imaginings.

'That's enough Rosie. I don't want to hear another word from you tonight, I'm too tired.'

She put the light out and closed the door on a very frightened Rosie. She went to the big bedroom at the front of the house and got into bed beside Lee who was already in a deep sleep. She lay there for a while thinking about Rosie and her irrational fear of the house. Perhaps she should have slept in the same bedroom as the twins, but Tamara had already made up the little bedroom for her at the back of the house overlooking the garden. Mei soon fell asleep, too exhausted to think any more. She was suddenly woken by an hysterical Rosie screaming. Mei was out of bed like a shot closely followed by the rest of the household.

'Rosie, Rosie please stop. It was only a bad dream.'

'It was not a bad dream Mother, it was real. I saw her.'

'Who? Who did you see Rosie? It's just your family here, no one else.'

'The lady in a white suit.'

'What lady? What white suit?' Lee asked irritably, having been woken from a sound sleep. Between sobs Rosie managed to tell them what she had seen.

'It was not a bad dream. I didn't even go to sleep, I was too frightened. I heard a tapping noise on the window and when I looked I saw a lady's face. She was trying to tell me something, she kept pointing to the bottom of the garden. Then she disappeared, I thought she had fallen, but when I looked out of the window she was stood at the bottom of the garden pointing at the rose bushes. I'm not imagining her, I did see her. You remember what the old aage told you back home. He said I have the gift of second sight and I must not be ignored but encouraged with this great gift that has been bestowed on me.'

'Yes darling, I know and I do believe you, you have inherited your great gift from my family, it seems to pass down from generation to generation.'

'I'm going back to bed. I can't take any more of this talk. Look at the time, it's three o'clock. I might just manage a few more hours' sleep before it's time to get up again. Come on twins, back to your room. Will you both be alright?'

'Yes Father.' They answered in unison.

'Mei, I suggest you make up a bed in our room for now and we'll talk about this tomorrow.'

The next morning the sun shone, the birds were singing and all the trees were thick with blossom. The events of the night before seemed far away and nothing to do with this beautiful English morning in May.

'Breakfast is ready,' Mei called to the rest of the family. The phone rang in the hall and Mei, being the only one up, answered it. 'Hello who is this please?'

'It's me, Tam. I was wandering if the girls could come with me today for a fitting of their bridesmaids' dresses. If you haven't anything else planned.'

'No, that will be alright — we've not had

time to make any plans yet.'

'I'll come and pick them up at eleven o'clock and take them into town to my dressmaker. See you then. Bye.'

'That was Tamara; she's coming to collect you all to take you for your bridesmaids' dresses to be fitted. I don't want one word to be said about what happened last night. Do you understand Rosie?'

'Yes Mother.'

'Good.'

Tamara arrived at eleven to collect the girls.

'Good morning girls. Did you sleep well?'

'Yes Tamara.' The twins both answered, but Tam noticed that Rosie said nothing and was still very quiet. She looked tired and pale as though she had not slept a wink.

'Is anything the matter Rosie? You can tell me if something is bothering you, I promise you it won't go any further, it will be our secret.'

'Mother made me promise not to say anything and I can't break my word to her.' Rosie decided against discussing what had happened and thought it would probably not happen again.

That night there was a repetition of the night before with the lady in a white suit tapping on the window and pointing to the bottom of the garden. Rosie had succeeded in disturbing the whole household's sleep once more and Lee was beginning to lose patience with his youngest daughter.

'Rosie, this has got to stop. It's just bad dreams you're having, no one else has seen this lady in the white suit. Now I don't want to hear another word about it. Tomorrow we'll move your bed into the front bedroom with your sisters.'

Tamara and Marcus had arranged to take the family out the next day and show them some of the local sights. Tamara was quite shocked when she saw how ill Rosie looked; she felt she had to get to the bottom of what was troubling her and decided to broach the subject with Mei.

'Don't worry Tamara, she's just having bad dreams and gets very upset.'

'But why is she, Mei?'

Mei looked embarrassed and hesitated before answering Tamara.

'I think she's not used to living in an English house. She misses our beautiful hilltop home in Hong Kong. I think perhaps she feels hemmed in with all the houses around her; we did consider moving out to a hotel.'

'Oh no, that would be so expensive, Mei.'

In spite of all Tamara's protestations the

family moved out of the house in Marsden Road and into a waterside hotel in Southampton. The colour immediately returned to Rosie's face and she soon regained her cheeky personality. Tamara couldn't help noticing with relief the total change in this lovely young girl. The wedding was fast approaching and Tamara soon forgot about the events of the past few days.

Tamara couldn't have asked for better weather for her wedding; she awoke to blue skies and brilliant sunshine, not a cloud in sight. Everything went without a hitch until the reception when Tamara was introducing the Chang family to some of her friends.

'This is my dearest friend Jenny and her husband Bill.' As she introduced the Chang family to the Reeds she saw the colour drain from Rosie's face and her hands tremble.

'Rosie dear, are you alright? You look quite ill, whatever is the matter?'

'I think all the excitement has caught up with her Tamara, I'll take her outside to get some air. I'm sure she'll be alright in a minute.'

Once outside Mei demanded to know what was troubling Rosie now.

'Rosie, what is the matter with you? Don't tell me you've seen the lady in the white suit again. You've cost your father a lot of money by us moving to this hotel to keep you happy and now you're still not satisfied.'

'Mother, I can't help it.' Rosie began sobbing.

'You must stop all this nonsense at once. I don't know what Marcus and Tamara thought of such behaviour.'

'It's him mother, Mr. Reed. He frightened me.'

'What do you mean, frightened you? He only shook your hand, child.'

Between sobs Rosie tried to explain. 'I think he has something to do with the lady in the white suit. Tamara said he owned the house before they bought it. He is evil Mother.'

'Rosie, what a dreadful thing to say about Marcus and Tamara's friends.'

'Mother please, you know I have the gift of seeing and I wouldn't make things up.'

'I know Rosie, but even if you are right, what can we do about it? We can't go accusing the man of God knows what. We have no proof that anything has happened. Anyway we shall be going home in a few days, so I think it best if we say no more about it.'

'But Mother I would have failed the lady in the white suit, she came to me for help.'

'That's enough now Rosie. I don't want to

hear another word on the subject.'

Rosie's behaviour had not gone unnoticed by Bill Reed. That child seems to know something, but she couldn't possibly. If she had found out anything the whole world would know by now. I think I'm safe for the moment, the sooner they are all back in Hong Kong the better, or their precious daughter might need to be silenced permanently.

Tamara felt slightly uneasy about the child's reaction to Bill and wondered what could have upset her so much. Perhaps that was why she didn't want to stay in his house — I never did get to the bottom of what that was all about. Maybe she just disliked him on sight as I did when I first met him. He's not the most appealing of human beings. Her thoughts were interrupted by Marcus.

'Are you still not ready Tam? How long does it take to pack, for heaven's sake? We are only going for two weeks, not a year. I thought you finished packing last night. I expect I'll have to pay for excess baggage at the airport.'

'Don't exaggerate Marcus, I've finished now. Come on, we'll say good-bye to all our guests and by then the car should be here to take us to the airport.'

10

The honeymoon over, Tamara and Marcus settled down to married life in their new home. It was Thursday afternoon — they had only been home a few days — and Tamara sat alone, reliving the wedding and honeymoon and thinking this must be the happiest time of her life. Never before had she felt so cherished and loved. The clock on the mantel shelf struck two o'clock and she suddenly felt an icy chill as if a door or window had been left open. She shivered and looked around, she felt someone was watching her. She jumped to he feet and pulled herself together, thinking, how ridiculous to feel so cold on such a hot day. I think I'll go into the garden where it's warmer and pick some roses to brighten the place up. The house seems to be a bit gloomy today in spite of the brilliant sunshine outside. As she was cutting the roses the next door neighbour Mrs. Johnson called out.

'Hello, I'm Edith Johnson.'

'Hello Mrs. Johnson, I'm Tamara Wheeler-Osman, nice to meet you.'

'Call me Edith please, although Bill Reed

insisted we address one another as Mr. and Mrs. He was quite a stickler in that way. Have your Chinese friends gone home now?'

'Yes, they returned to Hong Kong a few days after our wedding.'

'They didn't stay long in your house, thank goodness. I was woken two nights running with the young one screaming and yelling in the middle of the night.'

'Oh dear, I'm so sorry Edith if you were disturbed, her parents said she was suffering from nightmares. I didn't realise you could hear anything next door.'

'She screamed loud enough for the whole street to hear, if not the whole neighbourhood. Yelling something about a lady in a white suit in the garden and her father shouting at her to pull herself together.'

'All I can do is apologize Edith.'

'Not your fault dear.'

'Perhaps you would like to come around one afternoon for a cup of tea and look at the wedding photos when we get them.'

'Very kind of you, I'd like that very much.'

Tamara didn't realise she had been clutching the roses tightly and had pricked her fingers badly. Blood was dripping everywhere. She rushed to the kitchen and turned on the cold tap to stem the flow. She turned from the sink after a few minutes to look at the blood she had dripped on the kitchen floor and couldn't believe what she was seeing; pools of blood everywhere, far more than a few pricked fingers could have caused. She stared in disbelief, fear gripping her. Suddenly the blood was gone, and the floor was clean and bright once more, with just a few spots of blood from her fingers which she soon wiped away.

She was unsure whether to tell Marcus what Mrs. Johnson had said. She gave it some thought and then decided there would be no harm in telling him, but she would leave out the pools of blood she had seen over the kitchen floor for fear of him thinking she was quite mad.

'Did you know anything about Rosie having nightmares when you were living in Hong Kong, Marcus?'

'No, it's the first I've heard of it, but Lee did mention one day that she had the gift of second sight. I don't really believe in all that mumbo jumbo so I never pursued that line of conversation, I didn't want to appear rude or disrespectful to his beliefs.'

'The bit I don't understand is the lady in the white suit. No one that has lived in this house had a white suit as far as I know. Bill's mother lived here all her life and she would never have worn a white suit. Judging by the photos at Jenny's, Bill's mum dressed in dark clothing and looked rather dowdy, a bit like Jenny's mum really. I suppose that was how women of their generation dressed.'

'Come on Tam, you don't believe all that second sight stuff. The girl has an overactive imagination.'

That night Tamara couldn't get to sleep, she felt icy cold and very uneasy. She snuggled close to Marcus who was snoring soundly and she eventually drifted into a deep sleep. It seemed she hadn't been asleep long when she was woken by a tapping on the window. She sat bolt upright in bed and looked towards the window frozen with fear. There was a lady in a white suit looking in, she was beckoning to Tamara to follow her. Tamara screamed and shook Marcus but he wouldn't wake up, he seemed dead to the world. Eventually he awoke and couldn't understand why Tamara was so hysterical.

'Now Tam, it was only a dream, nothing to be scared of. I expect it was all that talk about Rosie and the lady in the white suit, you just fell asleep and dreamed about her.'

'No Marcus, I really did see her.'

Marcus thought it best to humour her at this time of night.

'Which window did she look in, the front or the back?'

179

'The back window, the same view as Rosie would have had in the little back bedroom I made up for her.'

'Well she's gone now, so I suggest we try and get some sleep with what's left of the night.'

'But she wanted me to go out into the garden. Perhaps I should go.'

'Tam, don't you dare, you'll be giving Mrs. Johnson a heart attack wondering around the garden in your nightdress. That's how rumours start about ghosts.'

Tamara could not rest and the next day decided to pay Bill and Jenny a visit and ask about the history of the house.

'Did you experience any odd happenings when you lived in the house Bill?'

'Certainly not Tamara, being a good Christian I don't believe in ghosts.'

'It could have been a ghost from long ago, perhaps even a hundred years or so. The house dates back to early Victorian times.'

'Not you as well Jenny, I thought you would have been more sensible than to believe in all that rubbish about ghost and things that go bump in the night.'

Both women ignored him and carried on the conversation as if he wasn't there.

'No, I don't think she could have been a ghost from Victorian times she was dressed too modern in a white suit. No, she definitely belongs to this day and age.'

Tamara couldn't help noticing that Bill visibly paled when she mentioned the white suit. He knows something alright and is not letting on. The white suit rings a bell with me as well but I can't think for the life of me why it does. Hopefully it will come back to me later on.

Bill was beginning to feel the need to kill again. He was irritable and restless and could quite cheerfully have killed Tamara there and then given the opportunity. The door bell rang and Bill went to answer it. On the step stood a young girl in her twenties wearing heavy make-up.

'Yes, what do you want?' Bill asked sharply.

'I've come for the cosmetic catalogue and to see if your wife wants to order anything this month?'

Jenny rushed to the door on hearing the young girl's voice.

'I'm so sorry dear, I haven't had time to look at it yet, I've been too busy. I did want to order a few things. Would it be possible for you to come back tomorrow afternoon?

'Alright then, I will.'

'Thank you so much dear, bye.'

'Painted little harlot.'

'Bill, don't be so unkind. The poor girl is a

single parent and struggles to bring up her little girl by herself, she has no family and works really hard. I think she only wears all that heavy make-up to advertise what she's selling. Oh, I've just remembered we were going to Bournemouth tomorrow to the apartment, the girl will call back for the catalogue and I won't be here.'

'Leave it on the step.'

'I wanted to ask her advice on one of the cosmetics.'

'Huh, her give you advice, it should be the other way around.'

'Now I've passed my driving test Tamara, I was going to drive down to the apartment tomorrow to sort out a few things.'

'You carry on, I have plenty of work here to get on with so leave a note and I'll see the girl gets the catalogue. Perhaps you could take Tamara with you for company.'

'Please say you'll come Tamara, it would be fun and I'd really value your advice on some of the furnishings.'

'Yes that would be really nice Jenny, we could have a girls' day out. Are you sure you don't mind me going in your place Bill?'

'No not at all you carry on and enjoy yourselves. In fact I might have a surprise for you when you get back, Jenny.'

Already a plan was forming in his mind for

his next victim. He rang the local DIY store and ordered some paving slabs and quick-drying cement, while Jenny was out walking Pepper. Then he knocked on the Rickmans' door and asked if Roy could give him a hand laying the slabs and if he could borrow or hire a cement mixer.

'Yeah I can do that providing it's cash in hand and you keep it to yourself. If anyone asks I'm doing a favour for a neighbour free of charge.'

'Yes of course, I never discuss my private life with the neighbours.'

'Good, glad to hear it.'

'May I ask how your daughter Kendra is bearing up after her terrible ordeal last year?'

'No you may not.' Roy Rickman slammed the door in his face.

His next thought was to ring Tamara and ask her to keep Jenny out as long as possible so the surprise he had planned for her would be finished.

'Yes of course I will Bill. Can I ask what the surprise is?'

'I'm going to get some concrete paving slabs laid by the back door making a nice patio for Jenny to sit and enjoy the fruits of my labour in the garden.'

'I didn't know you were DIY-inclined Bill.'

'No I'm not, I'm getting help from an

unemployed labourer three doors down. He'll be working hard and late into the evening to get everything done in time so I would be grateful if you could take Jenny for an evening meal somewhere. All expenses paid by me of course. I must go, Jenny has just come in the back door.'

Jenny and Tamara set off after lunch the next day. They had been gone about an hour: Bill was waiting for the delivery men outside the Rickmans' house, having just finished digging a deep hole where the patio was to be laid, when he saw Joanne Thorn walking up the road. He felt a sense of excitement at what he was about to do, telling himself to stay calm for fear of frightening the girl away. At the same moment a lorry pulled up with the paving slabs. Bill left Roy Rickman to deal with the delivery. He hurried away with Joanne Thorn following close behind.

'Your wife said to call back for the cosmetic catalogue.'

'Ah yes, so she did. She has an order for you with a query on one of your products. Now let me see, where did she leave it? You'd better step inside a moment out of the heat, I think she left it in the kitchen, come on through.'

The unsuspecting girl followed him through to the back of the house. He turned and grabbed her neck, his hands around her throat choking her. She broke free from him and screamed, he grabbed a vase from the hall table and smashed it over her head and the girl passed out. She lay on the floor, tiny and pathetic-looking. He took the largest knife from the block on the kitchen unit and plunged it into her heart. After making sure she was dead he fetched a black bin liner and put her body in it. He then dragged her body out of the back door and pushed it into the hole. He quickly filled it in with earth and finished with a layer of rubble on top as Roy Rickman had instructed him to do. The neighbours on one side were a young couple who were out at work all day and on the other side lived Mrs. Jones, an elderly blind lady, so Bill felt quite confident he hadn't been seen dragging the body out and pushing it into the hole. Roy Rickman called out from three gardens down.

'Have you got everything ready? The cement mixer will be here in half an hour.'

'Yes, I've just been burying some rubbish and have finished putting the bricks and rubble on top ready for the cement to be poured.'

'Right, make sure you have the money up front before I start, I have to pay for the mixer when it arrives.'

Bill was wondering what to do with the

excess soil that was left after the body had been buried. Then it suddenly dawned on him what to do with it, he would build a rockery, Jenny was always going on about having an alpine rockery in the garden. He walked back into the house congratulating himself on a job well done when he noticed the cosmetic catalogue lying on the kitchen table. He swore to himself at his own stupidity. Hell and damnation! What am I going to do with this, I should have buried it with the body.

Too late. Roy Rickman was banging on the front door for the money.

'Right, a hundred and fifty quid.'

'A hundred and fifty pounds? You said it would only be a hundred.'

'I forgot to add the rental of the mixer for a day, plus the rubble and shuttering I supplied.'

'A day's hire! But we only want it for a few hours.'

'Can't help that they're only rented by the day.'

'And as for the rubble you supplied, that came from your broken wall so it didn't cost you anything.'

'Do I send the driver around the back with the mixer or not? You'd better make your mind up quickly, he's other deliveries to make.'

'Very well then, I've seen cowboys like you on the television robbing people of their life's savings.'

Roy Rickman looked menacingly at Bill as if he was going to hit him, then he thought better of it and turned away.

'Right mate, around the back.'

Just before dark the job was completed, Bill was satisfied. The patio area looked good and in the corner of the garden stood a little mound of earth with rubble dotted about the earth. He thought it almost looked like a shrine. In loving memory of the cosmetic girl no longer among us to hawk her wares. He laughed to himself then remembered he hadn't disposed of the catalogue and Jenny would be back at any moment. He remembered seeing a rubbish skip three roads away when he was walking Pepper. It was dark now so no one would see him throw the catalogue in the skip. He had just arrived back at the house when Jenny and Tamara pulled up outside. Bill went to the door to meet them both.

'Did you have a nice time girls?'

'Oh yes darling, Tamara took me to this little pub in the Forest and we had the most wonderful meal — all paid for by you I believe. Thank you so much Bill.' She threw her arms around his neck and kissed him.

'Now come inside both of you and see the surprise I have for you Jenny.'

He switched on the outdoor lights to the garden to reveal the new patio.

'Bill, a patio! It's lovely. You couldn't possibly have done it all by yourself whilst we were out.'

'No I had help from Roy Rickman.'

'Roy Rickman! I thought you hated the man.'

'I do but he has his uses. Over there in the corner is the alpine rockery you always wanted. First thing tomorrow morning we'll go to the garden centre and you can choose all the plants you need to fill it.'

★ ★ ★

Sarah Cawte was frantic with worry over her friend Joanne Thorn and decided to call the police.

'Hello, I'd like to report a missing person, my friend Joanne has been missing since this afternoon.' The voice on the other end of the phone was not at all helpful.

'Can you come down to the station and make a statement?'

'No I can't. I've got two babies here, mine and Joanne's. Can't you send someone around?'

'How long has she been missing?'

'Since this afternoon.'

'Well that's only a few hours and she might turn up yet. Perhaps she has decided to go out on the razzle and left you holding the baby, so to speak.'

'No, Joanne wouldn't do that she thinks too much of her little girl to just go off and leave her. There's a sick bastard out there murdering women and I think he's got Joanne.'

'Now calm down, I'm sure she will be back before morning. If not, then we'll send someone around to speak to you.'

Sarah slammed the phone down crying hysterically and cursing the police for being useless.

*   *   *

The next morning Sarah was up early after a sleepless night. She dressed the two toddlers, put them in a buggy and set off for the police station.

'Sir, it looks like we have another missing person on our hands. A young girl has just reported her friend missing, she hasn't been home all night. She only went out for half an hour to collect a cosmetic catalogue from someone in Juniper Road.'

189

'Right Harding, let's get more details and a photo of the missing girl.'

Sarah Cawte sat sobbing in the interview room. Two toddlers sat silently in a buggy at her side.

'Lets start at the beginning Miss Cawte, or would you prefer me to call you Sarah?'

The girl nodded her head in agreement.

'Well Sarah, you told the police constable that your friend would only be gone for a short while to collect a catalogue.'

'Yes, she only had one to collect from a lady in Juniper Road, she'd collected all the others the day before but a lady asked her to call back as she hadn't had time to look at the book and she wanted to order some things.'

'Do you know the name of the lady Sarah?'

'No I don't, Joanne didn't say.'

'Do you know how old she was? Was she young like yourself or perhaps an older lady?'

'I think she was older, because she said her husband was a bit of a weirdo. She said he was a grumpy old weirdo and she hoped he didn't answer the door as he always looked at her like she was a piece of dirt. She's dead isn't she?' Sarah began sobbing again.

'Now Sarah, we mustn't jump to any conclusions just yet. She's only been missing for less than twenty-four hours. There's still time for her to come walking through the door full of excuses and the minute she does, you let us know.'

Sarah sniffed, wiped her nose and nodded her agreement.

'Would you like someone to see you home?'

'No, I'll be alright. I have some shopping to do.'

'Have you a recent photo of your friend that we can borrow?'

'Yes, I have one that was taken a few weeks ago.'

'Good, a PC will call around this afternoon to collect it. That should give you time to do your shopping and look for the photo. Goodbye Sarah and try not to worry too much.'

'Do you think we have another victim, sir?'

'Of course we bloody have, Woods, he's struck again right under our noses. I want a full search of the area, get onto it right away Woods.'

'Yes sir.'

'Harding, do we know anyone in Juniper Road that fits the description of 'weirdo'?'

'Bill Reed springs to mind.'

'Anyone else?'

'No. The only other oddball is Roy Rickman, father of Kendra, one of the rape victims, but I would describe him more as a loud-mouthed layabout.'

'Right, get around to Juniper Road and see

what our Mr. Reed was up to yesterday afternoon.'

Bill and Jenny were just about to have tea on their new patio when the police rang the doorbell.

'Isn't it marvellous the amount of people who ring the bell right on mealtimes? I think they do it on purpose just to annoy us.'

'Shall I go and see who it is Bill?'

'No I'll go, you stay there.'

'May we come in Mr. Reed? We'd like to ask you a few questions.'

'Not you two again. How many more times are you going to pester me?'

'Who is it Bill?'

'The police dear.'

'Where were you yesterday afternoon?'

'I was here all afternoon.'

'Can anyone verify that?'

'Yes, Roy Rickman three doors down. He was here all afternoon and best part of the evening laying a patio for me.'

'Did a young lady call to collect a cosmetic catalogue?'

'Yes she did, my wife was out for the day and left an order for her.'

'That's right I did.'

'What time would that be?'

'I'm not sure, early afternoon. I gave her the catalogue soon after my paving slabs arrived from the DIY store. Then Roy Rickman arrived about fifteen minutes later with the cement mixer.'

'Did you see which direction she walked after you gave her the catalogue?'

'No I was far too busy to bother about where she was going. I wanted the patio finished before my wife got home. I just handed over the catalogue and she left.'

'Did Roy Rickman see the girl?'

'I have no idea, you'll have to ask him. He was in and out of his front door waiting for the cement mixer to arrive, he may have seen her. Why all these questions about the cosmetic rep?'

'After leaving here the girl never reached home.'

'Oh my God!' Jenny let out a gasp. 'I hope nothing has happened to that poor little girl.'

'So do we Mrs. Reed, so do we. We'll see ourselves out, get back to your tea.'

'Right, Roy Rickman next.'

Roy Rickman came to the door wearing a red vest-type tee shirt and looking like he hadn't washed or shaved for days.

'We'd like to ask you a few questions about what you were doing yesterday afternoon?'

'Look, if it's about the work I did for Reed, I did it as a favour — no money changed hands, I swear.'

'We're not Social Services Mr. Rickman, and we're not here to talk about your benefit fraud. Did you see a young girl collecting a catalogue from Mr. Reed's yesterday afternoon?'

'Come to think of it I did see a young girl walk up the road.'

'What time would that be?'

'Somewhere around two o'clock. I was looking out for the cement mixer to arrive, a mate was bringing one around for Reed's patio job.'

'Did you see her walk back down the road?'

'No. I went back inside, the Missus was yelling out she had a mug of tea for me.'

'Right, that will be all Mr. Rickman.'

The two police officers walked back to their car pondering over the fact that a young girl had completely disappeared in the space of minutes.

'Do you think she was dragged into a car Harry?'

'It's got to be something like that Don, how else could she disappear without a trace so quickly? Rickman and Reed are alibis for one another. Rickman looks capable of anything and he's big enough and strong enough to overpower and kill a young girl in seconds, but he couldn't possibly dispose of a body in such a short time with so many people about and his wife Judy supplying mugs of tea to all and sundry.'

'What about Reed?'

'I think he was more obsessed with his patio and getting it finished in time before his wife returned. Besides I think he's too finicky to gets his hands dirty murdering a young girl. Did you see how orderly the house and garden were? Not even a flower dared be out of place. Anyway what would he do with the body in such a short space of time?'

'Put it under the patio.'

'What, with all those delivery men calling in quick succession and both the Rickmans hanging around? He'd have to be pretty damn quick.'

'I wonder if one of the lorry drivers could have picked her up.'

'Maybe, but they would have had to pick her up after delivering the paving slabs and cement mixer, not before, as Reed or Rickman wouldn't have seen her. Either way she would have been seen by one of the people on the street at the time.'

'I think she knew the killer, Don, and accepted a lift from him. That would seem the most feasible explanation. It takes just seconds for a car to stop and for her to jump in and the car to drive off.'

'Charlie is going to do his nut with yet

another murder on our patch.'

'We don't know for sure it's a murder yet. It's more likely she has run off with a boyfriend and will turn up again in a few weeks.'

11

Chief Inspector Charlie Mann was unhappy as all hope of promotion and an early retirement seemed to be slipping away. His superiors were leaning on him hard to get a result and he was not in the best of health. He had high blood pressure, was overweight, and his smoking, heavy drinking and consumption of junk food in large amounts did nothing to remedy the situation. There were times when he sat alone pondering over his past life and how different things could have been if his wife Maureen hadn't run off with a teacher from the school where she worked. She said his job wasn't the be all and end all of life and he should make time to care for her and take her out sometimes. She couldn't stand any more sitting at home alone, waiting for the phone to ring or someone to come to the door to tell her he'd been killed or seriously injured.

Perhaps if we'd had children together it might have made a difference, and now she has a son with that poncy teacher. I can kiss good-bye to any chance of a reconciliation. Where the hell did I go wrong? I had it all once, good looks, women falling at my feet, working my way up through the ranks. I used to be the blue-eyed boy of the force destined for the top; and now look at me, I could be forced to resign or worse still demoted if I don't get a result PDQ.

He or she has got to be local, all the crime scenes seem to centre around the same area within a two mile radius of one another, which might suggest the murderer can't drive. His thoughts were interrupted by DC Harding.

'Excuse me sir, Gary Stevens is in the outer office making a complaint about paint being daubed on his flat saying 'murderer' and 'rapist'. Also missiles have been thrown through his window.'

'What does he expect us to do about it? Obviously someone else seems to think he's guilty.'

'He's demanding to know how his name has been leaked to the public as it was not mentioned by the press, and he wants police protection.'

'How the hell should I know? Tell him to go away and stop wasting police time.'

'But he's making an official complaint.'

'Well get the necessary paperwork done then get rid of him as fast as you can. There'll be a briefing at two o'clock this afternoon.'

The Operation Maple team sat waiting for Chief Inspector Mann to appear, no one dared be late for his briefings. By two-thirty everyone was beginning to feel restless and some people had decided he was not going to show when suddenly the door burst open and a very red-faced Charlie Mann stood there. Harry Harding noticed there were beads of sweat on his brow, his hands were trembling uncontrollably, and concluded he had been drinking again and they would all be in for a rough time. Although he disliked the man intensely, as did the whole of the Woodfield police, in a way he felt sorry for him. His wife had left him and he was the most disliked man in the force. Perhaps he should leave the police and do something else. I don't know what I would do if I were in his position.

'Are you with us DC Harding, or miles away with the fairies?'

A titter went around the room and Harry Harding felt the anger rise in him and wondered why he had any pity for such an obnoxious man.

'Now I have grabbed Harding's attention we'll carry on. Joanne Thorn's cosmetic catalogue has been found in a skip in Letchworth Gardens, which is within a quarter of a mile of Juniper Road where she was last seen. Mr. and Mrs. Stride at number five were about to put some rubbish in the skip when they caught a man rummaging about inside it. On challenging him he ran off dropping Joanne's catalogue on the way. The couple have only just moved into the area and are not familiar with the locals but managed to give a good description of him. They said he was a really big man very tall and weighing about twenty stone, which sounds remarkably like Geoff Grant — the 'gentle giant' as he has been nicknamed by the locals. DS Starkey, get Geoff Grant in for an identity parade and we'll see if the Strides can pick him out. He was on the scene at the time Melanie Taylor was stabbed. So far we have two murders, one attempted murder, two rapes and two missing persons, all within a two-mile radius of one another. The perpetrator of these crimes has got to be a local man, so why can't we catch him?'

'Do you think it could be more than one person sir?'

'No I do not, DS Starkey. For starters the same people's names keep cropping up time and time again, in some way each has been connected with one of the victims. The first victim, Alice Jones, was murdered eighteen months ago in Drayton Park. No particular leads or suspects in this case. The only thing to tie her in with the other crimes was the location Drayton Park. Next came the rape of Kendra Rickman, which would rule out the two males in the Rickman family, the father Roy and brother Liam. Although there is always the possibility it could have been one of Liam Rickman's druggie friends or any of the lowlife he seems to hang around with. Next came Tracey Sellwood, raped at lunchtime on the other side of the town in Moreton Park. Did she bunk off school to meet one of the teenage layabouts and things got out of hand and he raped her? She swears blind she didn't know her attacker. Melanie Taylor was stabbed and raped in Drayton Park and was saved by three dog walkers. Prior to the stabbing Liam Rickman was fighting with Danya Rickman's boy-friend Darren Asher, who owned the knife which was used on Melanie Taylor. The fight was broken up by the local 'gentle giant' Geoff Grant. Did he then keep the knife and attack Melanie Taylor? And would he use the words 'God's Carpet' when he told her to lie down on the wet grass? I don't think these words are within his vocabulary. Missing person Jane Birch came to view Bill Reed's house for sale, but never kept her two o'clock appointment. Bill Reed was being interviewed by the police at the time Tracey

Sellwood was raped, but his name crops up again when Joanne Thorn the cosmetic agent went missing. She was collecting the catalogue, found in the skip, from Bill Reed's house and was never seen again. His alibi was Roy Rickman and a man delivering paving slabs for his patio. The other murder victim, Jodie Bowden, was found on waste ground near to the park and was the ex-girlfriend of Gary Stevens who is also acquainted with Bill Reed. Then there's Tamara Watson, another ex-girlfriend of Gary Stevens, she's been receiving menacing phone calls and death threat letters for the past year or so. In the absence of any forensic evidence we are precisely no further forward than day one. This is not a good situation. Not good for me and not good for you, when I'm being leaned on by the powers that be for a speedy conclusion to all these crimes. I'm not a happy man! You will check, then check again, every one of the suspects' alibis; someone, somewhere knows who the murderer is. All weekend leave is cancelled.'

A moan went around the room.

'I want this serial killer caught and caught soon. I'll have him if it's the last thing I ever do.'

Chief Inspector Mann broke into a fit of

coughing. He was red in the face and slumped into a chair. One of the PCs rushed over and handed him a glass of water.

'It probably will be his last thing if he don't give up the booze and fags,' muttered Harry Harding.

Geoff Grant was brought in for questioning before an identity parade was set up. He admitted to searching through the rubbish and picking up the cosmetic catalogue. He didn't know why he picked it up except that he had it in his hand when the Strides' porch light came on. He was startled, so he dropped the catalogue and ran away. He was looking through their rubbish for any items that he might be able to sell for a bit of beer money.

Charlie Mann decided to cancel the identity parade as Grant had admitted rummaging through the Strides' skip, and he believed his intentions were purely for finding things of any value. It seemed to be a favourite pastime of the local oddballs to rummage around in other people's rubbish. After the meeting dispersed he sat for a long time pondering his next step and cursing the murderer for eluding arrest for so long. The next morning's post did nothing to lift the depression he was slowly sinking into. There in the post in large cut-out letters was a message from the murderer:

**THere WILL be MoRe BLOOD
Spilt oN GodS CarPet.
CaTch mE if YOU Can.**

He picked up the letter, hands trembling.
He could feel the anger rising inside him, his
throat became dry as he read the letter over
and over again. His anger was replaced by
rage, a burning rage. Suddenly he understood
the meaning of 'seeing red', it was like a
massive sea of redness before him which
seemed to be engulfing him. It was the last
thing he saw before he slumped forward onto
his desk. A PC brought in his morning cup
of coffee and screamed to her colleagues for
assistance.

'Help! I think the Chief's snuffed it!'

Several police officers rushed into the
room. PC Andy Richardson immediately
began resuscitation.

'Someone call an ambulance, he's stopped
breathing.'

After a few moments he began breathing
again.

'Phew, that was a close one. I really
thought we had lost him.'

'Well done Andy, perhaps you'll get a
medal for saving the Chief's life.'

The mood in the room began to lighten as
the first panic was over.

204

'He's not out of the woods yet by any means. Sometimes with heart attacks there's more than one. He could have another one at any moment. Where the hell is that ambulance?'

The ambulance arrived minutes later and Chief Inspector Mann was taken to hospital.

'Do you think he's going to make it Harry?'

'Dunno Don, he looked pretty rough. God knows who we'll get to take over the investigation. Another smart Alec from London I suppose.'

The late editions of the local evening paper carried several pages on the collapse of Chief Inspector Mann who was heading Operation Maple. It then went on to show photos of all the victims, listing all the murders, rapes and missing persons. Giving descriptions of what each victim was wearing, dates, times and places where the attacks occurred.

Tamara arrived home from work and popped her head around the office door where Marcus was working, he was so engrossed in his work he hadn't heard her come in.

'Hello darling, would you like a cup of tea? I'm absolutely parched, before I start the evening meal I must have a cuppa to unwind. It's been one hell of a day and old Patterson has been in a foul mood all day. I don't know who rattled his cage.'

'No thanks Tam, I had one about ten minutes ago and I must finish what I'm doing before I stop again. Take your time with our meal. Don't start right away as I really must finish this report.'

'What time would you like it then?'

'Another hour and a half should see me finished.'

'OK then.'

Tamara took herself off to the kitchen leaving Marcus in peace to finish what he was doing. She made a cup of tea and decided to drink it in the lounge where she could curl up on the sofa in comfort, collecting the evening paper from the letter box on the way. She put the tea down and unfolded the paper. The headlines read, **Chief Inspector Rushed to Hospital.** She carried on reading the account of how he was taken to hospital after collapsing with a heart attack and was in a critical condition. She turned to page two and looked at the photos of the victims. The first three photos were of the rape victims, Kendra Rickman, Tracey Sellwood, and Melanie Taylor who was stabbed. Next came the two photos of the murder victims Alice Jones and Jodie Bowden. She still felt a slight annoyance as she looked at the photo of Jodie Bowden, although the poor girl was dead she could still evoke emotions of anger and resentment. Perhaps it was just a matter of pride that a common slip of a girl could take away her man. She felt slightly ashamed that she should still harbour such resentment towards her after all this time, and anyway she had married Marcus the man of her dreams. She brushed the thoughts aside and carried on reading the rest of the report. Next came the photo of the two missing persons, Jane Birch and Joanne Thorn. She let out a scream when she saw the face of Jane Birch, loud enough to bring Marcus rushing from the office.

'Whatever's happened Tam?'

'It's her.'

'Who?'

'The lady in the white suit, the one I keep seeing in my nightmares pleading with me to help her. Look, it even says in the paper that she was wearing a white suit on the day of her disappearance. Oh Marcus, what does it all mean?'

'Now calm down Tam, and let's talk about this sensibly.'

'Oh, why do you always have to be so bloody sensible?'

Marcus was quite shocked, she had never spoken to him in that tone before. He put it down to some sort of temporary hysteria brought on by the newspaper article, her nerves certainly seemed pretty bad of late.

Tamara instantly regretted the way she had snapped at him and immediately apologized.

'Apology accepted Tam. Now let's be calm and start again. We may have the answer to your nightmares. The mind sometimes plays tricks on us, and somewhere buried in the subconscious are things that we have stored up without even knowing it. At some point you have read about Jane Birch's disappearance and a description of her in a white suit. You said to me yourself the white suit rang a bell but you couldn't think why.'

'Yes, that's right, I did.'

'Well she was also linked to this house in as much as she had an appointment to view it and never turned up. All this somehow got jumbled up in your mind and the consequence is the nightmares you've been having. After all darling you have been through a pretty traumatic time recently with the break-up with Gary after five years, plus all the nasty letters you were receiving. It's no wonder everything got jumbled in your mind.'

'I suppose you could be right.'

'Now how about a smile, and put that blasted newspaper down. I don't want you reading anything more about those poor unfortunate women, and then my sweet I shall take you out for a meal to save you cooking. Is it a deal?

'Yes, a deal.'

Tamara was not entirely convinced what Marcus was saying was correct but she was willing to give him the benefit of the doubt.

★   ★   ★

Several days later the replacement for Charlie Mann arrived. He was tall, slim, with grey thinning hair, a severe looking military type. A man of few words, but when he did speak he caught everyone's attention; several felt nervous in his presence and they were right to be so. Chief Inspector Frederick Boulter did not suffer fools gladly, he had no room for slackers or incompetents in his team. Anyone fitting either description was quickly off the team and transferred elsewhere. If he had his way they would have been out of the force altogether. After their first meeting with the new Chief Inspector, Harry Harding and Don Woods were speculating as to how long he would last heading Operation Maple.

'I've been told by some of the London boys that he doesn't take kindly to failure and heads will start rolling if there's not a quick result.'

'We have run ourselves ragged taking statements and then rechecking them. All our leave has been cancelled, what more does he expect Don?'

'Blood! He wouldn't care if we all ended up in the cardiac ward alongside Mann, as long as he got a result.'

'Has anyone heard how he is?'

'The last bulletin said he was still on the critical list. Some of the lads reckon it was the note from the murderer that triggered the heart attack.'

'You could well be right Don.'

'He's a cheeky bastard, but one day he'll slip up and then we'll have him Harry.'

* * *

Bill Reed was delighted to read in the newspaper that the Chief Inspector heading Operation Maple had been rushed to hospital with a heart attack. He felt smug and satisfied with his work. Sending him my last little message might have tipped him over the edge. Perhaps I should start looking for my next victim to show everyone I'm a man of my word. Jenny is going to Tamara's this evening to have her hair coloured and won't be back till quite late. I've told her I'm staying in to watch my favourite television programme so all I have to do is video it and then I'll be able to discuss the programme with her when she gets back.

I think I'll try my luck at the copse end of the park tonight and see which young lady will be unlucky enough to pass my way. He could not contain his cruel laugh. Jenny heard him from the kitchen and called out.

'What are you laughing at Bill?'

'Nothing my sweet, I was coughing not laughing, just clearing my throat. How about a nice cup of tea? I'm parched.'

'What time are you going to Tamara's?'

'Sevenish. Why? Will you miss me darling?'

'Of course I will sweetheart, but I also value some quiet time on my own watching TV. You know we don't like watching the same programmes and I do so enjoy the history ones. It's a good opportunity to watch a bit of history without feeling that I'm being selfish and you're just sat there bored to tears.'

'You selfish, never. You're the most unselfish man I've ever met.'

That evening Bill waited till it was almost dark then left by the back garden gate and headed towards the park. He settled down behind some trees on the edge of the park and waited. He didn't have to wait long before he heard female voices in the distance getting closer. Damn my luck, there's three of them, far too many for me to handle. He sank back into the darkness behind the clump of trees. Time was getting on and he wondered if he was going to be unlucky tonight. The next moment he heard a female voice screeching and shouting at a youth.

'You can get stuffed Tommy Shields! You're dumped and I never want to see you again so don't try and follow me.'

'I wouldn't dream of it. I've been trying to ditch you for months. Go find yourself some other sucker to whinge at you spoilt brat.'

Bill waited patiently for the tirade of verbal abuse to finish. At last both had decided enough was enough and walked off in opposite directions. As luck would have it the girl walked in Bill's direction and the boy ran off quickly in the opposite direction and was soon out of sight. All was now still and quiet once more except for the girl's footsteps on the gravel path. She was getting closer, suddenly Bill stepped out in front of her brandishing a kitchen knife. Suddenly aware of the danger she was in she began to run as fast as she could but Bill was faster and wrestled the girl onto the grass. She was screaming, kicking, and fighting hard for her life but her attacker was far too strong for her. The last words she ever heard was her murderer muttering 'More blood on God's carpet.'

Bill decided not to bother concealing the victim's body as he wanted it to be found as soon as possible, so he could enjoy reading the headlines in the paper the next day. He had just managed to change out of the blood-stained clothing and back into the clothes he was wearing when Jenny had left the house. In the still night air the sounds seemed to be amplified and he heard her car coming, long before it turned the corner of the road. He only just managed to drop the blood-stained clothing under a floorboard in his potting shed and get back into the house just as Jenny was putting her key in the lock. He quickly sat down and turned the television on.

'Hello darling, you look nice. Tamara has done you proud. Is there no end to that woman's talents? That colour really suits you.'

Jenny was not too sure whether he was being sarcastic or not. She had the strangest feeling that he hadn't been watching television, he had been out somewhere.

'Bill have you been in all evening?'

'Of course I have. Why do you ask?'

'Oh I don't know. The house seems cold like no one has been here for a while.'

'I had to turn the fire off as I was falling asleep and missing my programme. I'll turn it back on for you.'

'Did you enjoy your programme?' And

before he could answer she asked another question. 'Why is the video recording?'

'Because my sweet I kept falling asleep and missing bits so I decided to record the programme and then I could play back the parts I had missed. You know how much I was looking forward to seeing the programme.'

Jenny had the distinct feeling he was lying to her and it unnerved her. Never before had she mistrusted him. What would be the reasons for lying? Where would he go that he didn't want her to know about? Oh no, please God not another woman. Don't let it be another woman, I couldn't bear it. Am I just being silly, he wouldn't do that to me would he? He's a man and most men are not to be trusted. Look at poor Tamara — she is beautiful, clever and has a good job with loads of money, she had everything going for her and yet Gary Stevens cheated on her for a younger woman. The more she thought about it the more upset she got. I've got to go to bed before I say something stupid that I'll regret later.

'Are you alright darling? You're very quiet.'

'Yes I'm just tired, I'm off to bed.'

'I'll be up in a bit. I'm just going to catch up on the bits I missed in my programme. Would you like me to bring you up some supper or a drink?'

'No thank you.'

For the first time since their marriage they were both glad to be free of one another, each one not having to keep up the pretence any longer. Jenny lay awake for ages pondering over the possibilities that Bill, the only love in her life, had betrayed her for another woman. She tossed and turned and couldn't get to sleep, then she suddenly caught sight of the alarm clock. She had been in bed a whole hour and Bill had still not joined her.

Was he watching the whole of the history programme or was he watching something else? Worse still was he avoiding her? Did he have a guilty conscience and couldn't face her and was waiting for her to fall asleep? When he eventually comes up to bed I'll pretend to be asleep so he doesn't suspect anything, but I'll be watching him very carefully from now on.

Bill was flitting through the programme making sure he could remember the salient points and of course the ending. He sat thinking about the evening and making sure he had covered his tracks. Had he forgotten anything? The kitchen knife was still in my jacket pocket when I dropped it under the floorboards. I hope Jenny doesn't notice one is missing from the knife block before I can retrieve it. As soon as she is out shopping tomorrow I'll burn the clothes in my garden incinerator and make sure the knife is thoroughly clean before I replace it in the block. I wonder why she was acting so strangely when she came in. I hope she doesn't suspect anything; she couldn't possibly, no one knows about the murder yet. It must have been something Tamara said to upset her, probably about me — that woman has never liked me. Could be her age? Women of a certain age do start acting peculiarly. Oh well, tomorrow is another day and I have the morning papers to look forward to. I expect Miss whatever her name is will be found by then. Let me think, what was it the boy called her? No I can't remember, he called her many things, none of them very nice, but I can't recall him calling her by name. Still I'll soon know, in fact everyone will know tomorrow, her name will be on everyone's lips.

Bill Reed switched off all the lights and walked upstairs to bed.

12

The next morning Jenny woke early after a restless night. Bill was still asleep so she decided to ring Tamara and ask if she could come over and have a serious talk with her.

'Of course you can Jenny. Has something happened with your hair? Are you not happy with the colour? I'm sure I can do something with it.'

'No Tamara it's nothing like that, the colour is fine, you did an excellent job. I'll explain as soon as I see you. Bye.'

Tamara replaced the receiver with a puzzled look on her face.

'What's the matter Tam? you look worried.'

'I don't know. That was Jenny, she needs to speak to me urgently, but she wouldn't say what about, she sounded pretty upset.'

'Here she is just pulling up outside. You'd think she'd walk on such a lovely morning, as she only lives a few blocks away, and show off her new hair colour. Do you want me to make myself scarce?'

'Yes please darling.'

'Jenny come in. Would you like a cup of tea?'

'Yes please, it might calm me down.'

Tamara noticed how pale she looked and her hand was trembling.

'What is it dear? You know you can tell me anything, just like our old school days together, all those girlie secrets we used to share.'

'It's Bill. I think he's seeing another woman.'

'No . . . Jenny, I can't imagine him doing that. Whatever makes you think that?'

'Well last night when I got home he seemed quite strange. In fact the whole house felt strange.'

'In what way strange?'

'I can't quite find the words to explain. The house seemed to have a bad feeling about it, almost sinister, and Bill looked furtive as if he'd been up to something behind my back. I had the feeling he'd just got back indoors seconds before me. The whole house was cold and he hadn't even put the heating on. We usually need it on at about eight thirty, sometimes eight o'clock on a cold day, and the video was recording.'

'What's so strange about that?'

'Well he made a big thing about staying in to watch his favourite history programme in peace, and when I asked him what he was recording he said he kept falling asleep in the middle of watching the programme, so he started recording the rest of the programme so he could pick up on the parts he'd missed. This morning when I checked the video recorder the whole programme was recorded from the start, not just the middle part as he had said. He deliberately recorded the whole programme to watch later so he could talk about it with me and I wouldn't suspect he'd been out.'

'But another woman Jen, it just doesn't sound like him at all. He always seems devoted to you and can't do enough for you.'

'You've changed your tune, I thought you couldn't stand him.'

'That's not fair Jenny, I've made a real effort with him for your sake and I do feel we've been getting on a lot better lately. Anyway it doesn't matter what we think of one another, it's what he thinks of you that is important and one of the reasons I have made an effort to be nice to him is because he thinks so much of you, and as long as he treats you OK then that's fine by me.'

'I know Tamara, you're right. I'm sorry.'

'Perhaps he's planning one of his surprises for you. Something he had to do when you weren't around.'

A smile began to spread over Jenny's face. 'You know I think you're right Tamara.

Thank you so much, I've been really silly imagining all sorts of things and getting myself worked up over nothing. I think I'll go home and cook him a nice breakfast if he's up. Sometimes he sleeps like a log as though he's thoroughly exhausted and another time he's up with the lark.'

Marcus was in the hall reading the morning paper as Tamara went to see Jenny out.

'Oh my God, not another one.' He turned to the two women, holding up the front page headlines.

'Another poor girl has been murdered in the park last night.'

Now it was Tamara's turn to feel worried and upset. If Bill had in fact been out last night he could have committed the murder and just got back to the house in time before Jenny came in. She glanced at Jenny who was still smiling and saying her good-byes. Obviously she hasn't made that connection between Bill and the murders, which might be a blessing. As long as she acts normally she is safe but if he ever gets an inkling that she suspects him then her life may be in danger.

Marcus continued reading aloud without noticing the impact this latest murder was having on Tamara.

'The poor girl's name won't be released till

the next of kin have been informed. Anyway what was so important that Jenny had to rush around here so early to talk to you?'

'She had some silly idea that Bill was seeing another woman and that he was out last night when she was here.'

'Oh dear! It looks like the honeymoon period is over and cracks are beginning to appear. Do you think it's true? Personally I wouldn't have put him down as the womanising sort. Not wishing to sound unkind about your friends Tam, but he's hardly God's gift to women. I always thought he was very lucky to get a nice woman like Jenny.'

'No, I don't think it's true either. After all who would look twice at him? No, if he was out last night he was up to something else.'

'Such as? You don't honestly think he's a burglar.'

'No silly, something far more serious.'

'What? Come on Tam, tell me what's on your mind.'

'Murder.'

'Murder!!!' Marcus repeated, totally shocked at such a suggestion. 'Tam, I know you don't like the man but that's going a bit far.'

'It all seems to add up to me. I think he was the one all along, making the phone calls and sending me the death threat letters, and to think I thought poor Gary was responsible.'

Marcus flinched at the 'poor Gary' part of the statement. He secretly felt jealous of this man who had shared her life for five years. He often had doubts about her truly loving him, or did she only marry him on the rebound? Was it to teach Gary Stevens a lesson, playing him at his own game? Tamara was still talking, totally unaware of what Marcus was thinking.

'And then there was the missing woman Jane Birch. I'm sure he knows something about her. Perhaps she did call here on that afternoon and he murdered her.'

'And what did he do with the body in broad daylight?'

'I don't know, perhaps she's under the floorboards.'

'Oh no Tam, I'm not pulling all the floorboards up in every room just to satisfy your wild fancies about Bill Reed. Whatever you may think of him I don't believe he's capable of murder. Now I think enough's been said on the subject, let's talk about something else please.'

It looks like I'm on my own over this one. I can't expect any help from Marcus, he thinks I'm being ridiculous, and if I tell Jenny she'll either not speak to me again or she'll be very frightened and I might put her life in danger.

Oh hell, what am I going to do? I really do need help on this one and I've no one to turn to. There is one person who'd like to see Bill Reed behind bars, Gary. He would be only too pleased to clear his name. Someone at work said he's been made the target of a hate campaign by his neighbours, 'murderer' painted on his front door and his flat windows smashed. Yes, he's definitely the one to ask for help. I'll ring him the first chance I get.

Gary Stevens at first decided not to answer his phone when it rang that evening. More abusive phone calls this evening I suppose. Something in the persistence of the ringing made him answer it. Whoever it was wasn't going to give up very easily.

'Yes.' He hissed down the phone.

'Gary, it's me, Tam.'

'What do you want? I suppose you're having a good laugh at my expense.'

'Don't be stupid Gary. You should know me better than that. I'm hurt that you should think that of me.'

'Alright, cut the crap. What do you want?'

'Can we meet up? It's really important that I talk to you.'

'What's up, lover boy dumped you already? That marriage didn't last long.'

'Gary, shut up and listen. It's about the

murders, I think I know who the murderer is. It's Bill Reed.'

'What! Creepy Bill! He wouldn't be capable or man enough to rape and kill young girls.'

'You think, well I know different. Look we really do need to meet up and discuss this. I'll come to your flat after work tomorrow. I have to go now. Bye.'

'Who was that darling?'

'No one.'

'What do you mean no one? It had to be someone unless you make a practise of talking into your mobile when no one is there.'

'What I meant was no one of any importance, only someone trying to sell something or other.'

'What?'

'Does it matter what? I was just going to put the news on to see if there was anything more on the latest murder.'

Marcus felt irritated that she had obviously lied to him. Who could she have been phoning that she didn't want me to know about? The television news reporter interrupted his thoughts.

'The girl found murdered on the edge of Drayton Park last night has been named as Jessica Hale. Anyone who has any information or saw Jessica Hale yesterday evening should contact the police on the number shown at the bottom of the screen. A sixteen-year-old youth is at present in police custody being questioned in connection with Jessica's murder.'

'I think I'll go and have a shower darling, I can't listen to any more about that poor girl. I still can't believe all these dreadful murders are happening on our own doorstep.'

As soon as Tamara had left the room Marcus picked up her mobile and checked the last number she'd called. Gary Stevens! Oh my God, he's not on the scene again. Tam, how could you do this to me? I thought you loved me. He buried his head in his hands not knowing what to do next. How could she? I love her so much and I thought she loved me too. What a fool I've been. What am I going to do? Should I confront her with it when she comes down or should I just wait and see what happens next? He decided to say nothing and monitor her every move to see if he could catch her out. Perhaps she would just be straight with him and confess everything and ask his forgiveness. He would just have to wait and see and if he could find it in his heart to forgive her. He wasn't sure. The only thing he knew for sure was that he couldn't face a showdown right now.

★ ★ ★

Bill Reed was also listening to the latest television bulletin on the dead girl. He was savouring every small detail given about his latest victim. Jenny was busy in the kitchen cooking a meal. 'Jessica Hale,' he murmured her name several times.

'Did you say something Bill?'

'No darling just humming to myself.'

That's funny I could have sworn he said something like a name. It didn't sound much like humming to me.

Bill continued to watch the news item laughing to himself. So the police have arrested that half-witted boyfriend of hers no doubt, as if he would be capable of anything, let alone murder. Wrong again Chief Inspector, you're not much better than the last one at solving crimes.

★ ★ ★

The following day Tamara phoned Marcus from work, saying she had to work late as a lot of work had come in over the weekend, and she would be about an hour late. Marcus listened to Tamara chatting, telling him lie after lie till he could listen no more and abruptly ended the conversation saying he was rather busy himself.

'How about coming for a drink after work

Tam, with some of the girls? It's Linda's birthday from Buying Office. I'm sure Marcus won't mind if you're a bit late home.'

'I'm sorry Barbara but I have another appointment I really must keep.'

'Not a job interview I hope?'

'No, nothing like that. It's a private matter. I'll tell you about it sometime but not just now, it's very confidential.'

'I'm intrigued. See you tomorrow.'

'Yes, bye Barbara, say happy birthday to Linda for me and if there is a collection put the usual in for me and I'll square you up tomorrow. Bye . . . '

Gary Stevens opened the front door to his ex-girlfriend with a sneer on his face.

'So what's all this about, that you have to share with me that you can't share with lover boy?'

'Are you going to let me in or not? What I have to say might help you out of your current predicament and I haven't got a lot of time. I need to get home within an hour.'

'Yeah OK, come in then. Fire away, I'm all ears.'

'I think Bill Reed has been committing all the murders.'

Gary gasped with surprise. 'Bill Reed! Have you gone totally mad Tam?'

'I know it sounds ridiculous but it all fits

and I am so worried about Jenny, I feel she's in real danger. She already suspects something is not quite right, but thinks he's seeing another woman. If she should ever find out the truth and confront him, then I think he would kill her without a second thought. You must help me Gary, please.'

'What do you expect me to do?'

'I don't know.'

'Won't lover boy help you then?'

'He has a name you know, Marcus, and no he doesn't believe Bill is capable of murder.'

'How are we supposed to prove it? The police won't believe a word I say, they'll think I'm just shifting the blame.'

'I don't know yet but I'll think of something. Look, I have to — go will you help me or not?'

'I suppose, but I can't think for the life of me how we can prove he's the one.'

Tamara put the key in her front door and as soon as she entered the hall was shocked to find Marcus standing there waiting for her.

'Hello Marcus. What are you doing in the hall?'

'Just waiting for you darling.'

Tamara thought he sounded strange and remote.

'Did you manage to finish all your work?'

'Yes thank you. I got through stacks of it.'

'Stop lying to me Tam. You weren't at work, I phoned about fifteen minutes ago and the cleaner answered. She said everyone had left at five o'clock and she and the other cleaner were the only ones in the building.'

'She's not supposed to answer the phones, she's there to clean the office and nothing else. She always did fancy herself as a secretary.'

'Stop and stop now, Tam, you're avoiding the issue, I don't give a damn about the cleaners. Where were you? — and no lies please. I know you've been seeing Gary Stevens again. Why Tam? Just please tell me why. I've given you everything you want, I've even said you don't need to work any more, but no, you insisted and now I know why.'

Tamara was totally shocked that she had been found out so soon.

'No, it's not like it seems.'

'No, it never is.'

'Please Marcus let me explain.'

'Go on I'm listening but how you're going to talk your way out of this one is beyond me.'

'I went to see Gary Stevens tonight because I'm scared, really scared.'

'Why ask for his help? Why didn't you ask me? I'm your husband for God,s sake, or was that just an excuse because you're still in love with him?'

'That's not true, he means nothing to me

and I did ask you for help but you wouldn't listen to me.'

'What help? I don't recall you ever asking me for any help.'

'I told you about Bill Reed but you didn't believe me, and I'm so worried for the safety of Jenny, I had to do something. You've got to believe me Marcus. Gary Stevens means nothing to me, I swear. I only turned to him because I knew he would be the one person to help me and it would also prove his innocence. The police are still watching his flat you know, and monitoring his movements.'

'Oh Tam, don't be so damn ridiculous. Why would they waste valuable police resources on a nobody like Gary Stevens?'

'You know that he's been arrested several times and then released without charge through lack of evidence, because he is innocent and no one seems to believe him.'

'Except you, the devoted ex-girlfriend.'

'Marcus, don't be so cruel. My friend's life is at stake and all you can do is make jealous cracks about Gary.'

'Well, you've no need to worry about any of your precious friends that seem to mean so much to you, as the police have caught the murderer.'

'What?'

'There it is in the evening paper. Go on,

read it for yourself.' He threw the evening paper at her and walked away.

She sank into a chair, totally exhausted and shocked by Marcus's outburst, and began to read. *Local man has confessed to five murders and three attempted murders.*

'So you see, darling, you needn't have contacted your ex after all.'

★ ★ ★

Chief Inspector Boulter was congratulating himself on making an arrest so soon after being assigned to the Woodfield murders. He had been here less than a month and someone has been charged. The fact that someone had walked into the police station and confessed to all the rapes and murders, and was not caught by police detection, did not make any difference. He would take all the credit for solving the crimes and it would be beneficial in his next promotion bid.

'Well done men. Your diligence and hard work have paid off at last. If Geoff Grant had not confessed, I think it would only have been a matter of time before we caught him.'

'Poor sod didn't do it, Don.'

'Why did he confess then, Harry? I must admit I would never have had him down as a rapist and serial killer. I know he was in the park the night Melanie Taylor was stabbed and his dabs were all over the cosmetic catalogue belonging to Joanne Thorn, but murder? He seems too soft.'

'You have it in one Don, the man is not right in the head. The locals call him the 'gentle giant', and as for confessing, there are hundreds of nutcases out there, all trying to gain notoriety or bring some excitement into their sad little lives, by confessing to any and every crime going.'

'What do you reckon we ought to do about it Harry? I bet the poor sod's sat in a cell scared stiff.'

'I think we'll have a chat with the people in his local, The Viking, and see what they have to say about him.'

The landlord and landlady of The Viking were not at all pleased to see the police back on their doorstep asking even more questions.

'Oh gawd, John, the law's back again frightening half our customers away. What do they want this time? They've got poor old Geoff for the murders; what more do they want, blood?'

'Evening gentlemen. What can I get you?'

'Nothing thanks, we're still on duty.'

'How can I help you then?'

'We'd like to ask you and your wife a few questions about Geoff Grant.'

232

'What do you want to know?'

'How often does he come in here?'

'Every evening usually.'

'Was he in here the day before yesterday and did you notice anything unusual about him? Did he say anything about the murders or that he was going to confess?'

'No, a few of the locals were having a bit of a laugh with him, saying they knew he was the murderer all along and his secret was safe with them.'

'You mean baiting the village idiot.' Don Woods said rather sarcastically.

Harry Harding signalled to Don Woods to be quiet and carried on questioning John Pearcey.

'And what was Geoff's response?'

'He looked a bit upset and left.'

'Did anyone go after him?'

'One of my regulars called after him but he wouldn't come back, not even for a pint.'

'Which regular would that be?'

'I can't remember; the pub was full that night and I just heard the voice.'

'And you couldn't recognize whose voice it was.'

'Nope. All the locals sound the same to me when they've had a few.'

'You're not from around here are you?'

'No, London. The missus and I took over this place about a year ago.'

'About the time the murders started.'

'Here, I hope you're not suggesting I had anything to do with any of them.'

'I'm not suggesting anything Mr. Pearcey. Goodnight.'

'That's it Don, he didn't do it. Thanks to the local joker, the poor sod thought he ought to confess before he was dragged off in a police wagon.'

'Now what we gonna do Harry? Boulter won't listen to any of this, he is too busy congratulating himself on a result.'

'We can only try Don, we can only try. If we don't succeed a few years down the line I can see our Chief Inspector appearing on one of those wrongful arrest programmes that are so popular on television these days. Trying to justify Geoff Grant's conviction and spouting off about all the circumstantial evidence, not mentioning the lack of any forensic evidence. Meanwhile, the real murderer is free to carry on his killing spree.'

Chief Inspector Boulter was not pleased when he heard that Don Woods and Harry Harding had been to The Viking interviewing people, when the case was closed as far as he was concerned. What did they think they were playing at, undermining his authority? The murderer was locked up and that was an end to the matter.

13

Jenny was not at all happy, she was watching Bill closely for any telltale signs of his infidelity. He seemed to be taking every opportunity to walk the dog alone, or to send her off shopping or on some errand or other, even encouraging her to see more of Tamara. He just wants me out of the way. Well, Bill Reed, I think I'll set a little trap.

'Bill darling, Tamara has asked me over to her house tomorrow evening for one of those lingerie parties, girls only. I thought it might be fun. You don't mind, do you?'

'Of course not, my sweet, you go and have a nice time and buy yourself something nice. What time is it?'

'About seven-thirty.'

'Be sure to take the car.'

'But I can walk, it's only a few streets away.'

'No, I insist. It's dark at seven-thirty and you never know who's about.'

'But they've caught the murderer now.'

'Jenny, I really must insist.'

She could hear the anger rising in his voice and thought, he really wants me out of the way so he can meet his fancy woman. I wonder who the hell she is?

'Alright Bill, I give in. If it makes you happy I'll take the car.'

Her plans were nearly ruined when Tamara arrived, also deeply unhappy and in need of a friendly chat. When Jenny answered the door to her she was surprised how startled she looked at seeing her.

'Hello Jen. I thought we ought to get together for a girls' night in. I haven't seen much of you lately.'

'But you'll be seeing her tomorrow at your party.'

Tamara was just about to say, what party? when she caught sight of Jenny behind Bill's back signalling her to say nothing.

'Don't tell me the lingerie party is cancelled. I was really looking forward to buying a few things.'

'No, I just wanted to make another date for the two of us to have lunch or something.'

Jenny felt relieved that Tamara had cottoned on to her deception so quickly and Bill seemed satisfied with the explanation for Tamara's presence.

'I'll leave you girls to it. I'll take Pepper for a walk and buy my paper at the same time. Do you need anything from the shop Jenny?'

'No thanks, I'm OK for everything.'

'What's all this about a lingerie party?'

'Well, I'm setting a trap. I'll take the car, park it outside your house, then walk back and watch our house. As soon as he comes out I'm going to follow him. I'll soon find out who his bit on the side is and I'll give her a piece of my mind. I might even teach her a lesson she'll not forget in a hurry, messing with another woman's husband.'

Tamara was quite shocked at the venomous way in which her friend was talking; she had never seen this side of her before. She was all fired up with hatred and anger, convinced she was right, and nothing could persuade her otherwise.

'Jenny dear, do calm down. I've never seen you like this before and you're jumping to conclusions without any proof. I'm sure you've got it all wrong and there is a perfectly reasonable explanation for Bill's behaviour.'

'You talked me round before Tamara, but you'll not do it this time. I know there's something wrong, dreadfully wrong, and I won't rest till I find out what is going on. Now what did you want to talk to me about?'

'Oh, it's nothing really, just Marcus and I having a silly quarrel about Gary Stevens. He's under the impression I married him on the rebound and don't truly love him, but I do, I really do, I love him with all my heart. How to convince him is the real problem.

Look, I'll come with you tomorrow night. I'm worried in case you do something stupid.'

'Like what?'

'Well, if there is someone else, which I'm sure there isn't, then you might resort to violence and could get arrested.'

Jenny reluctantly agreed that Tamara could come with her.

★ ★ ★

Charlie Mann had been released from hospital after his heart attack. He had been told to take things easy, and that he would be unable ever to return to his former employment as the job was far too stressful. His job was the only thing he had left in his life; he thought, what's the good of living with no purpose in life and no one to share it with?

'I hear Charlie's been released from hospital, Harry, and he's been hanging around the station. He looks terrible.'

'You think he'd want to get as far away from this place as possible, not hang around outside. What does he hope to achieve by that? He should accept his early retirement gracefully and settle down to a comfortable old age, doing gardening, reading books or something.'

'Can't imagine big Charlie doing anything like that Don.'

That evening Charlie decided he would do something positive; he would patrol the parks and isolated areas where all the previous murders and rapes had taken place. He too felt that the wrong man had been arrested. Poor fool, not quite right in the head, and Boulter had to grab at the first idiot to confess just to make himself look good. Well, Chief Inspector Frederick Boulter, you'll be proved wrong and I'm going to be the one to catch him. You just sit back behind your desk, or rather my desk, feeling smug and self-righteous while I go out and catch him for you. I might not be in the force anymore but nothing will stop me now. He's mine and I've been after him for far too long to just give up. I'll have him if it's the last thing I do.

Jenny knocked at Tamara's door just before seven thirty. At the same time Charlie Mann took up position behind some bushes not far from Tamara's house. The two women walked silently down the street together. They decided it would save time to take a short cut through the park which would get them back to Jenny's house a lot quicker than walking around the road. Jenny was determined to follow Bill at all costs and find out exactly what he had been up to. Tamara felt a little nervous at walking through the park in the dark.

'Do you really think it's safe to walk through the park, Jenny?'

'Of course it is, Tamara, don't be so silly, they've caught the murderer, haven't they? And after all there are two of us, we're hardly like some defenceless young girl. How I feel at the moment, I could cheerfully murder anyone who stops me from carrying out my mission.'

Once again Tamara was shocked at the venom and anger within her friend. Talk about a woman scorned, she doesn't know anything for sure and already she's out for revenge.

'I did hear someone say they thought poor Geoff Grant was innocent and was stitched up by the police, it wouldn't be the first time they got it wrong.'

'Shut up Tamara and let me think. You don't have to come along. I didn't ask you, it was your idea.'

'I know, I'm sorry, Jen, I'll be quiet from now on I promise.'

They were half-way along the path when a twig snapped, startling both women, and they could just make out a figure of a man behind the bushes. He stepped forward and tried to assure them that it was alright and he was harmless, but neither woman was prepared to wait for an explanation and ran down the path screaming.

'Stupid bitches!' he yelled after them.

They didn't stop running until they got back to the road and both stood under a streetlight, trembling with fear.

'I've had enough Jenny. I'm going home and I suggest you do the same or come home with me. Which is it going to be?'

'I think I'll go home Tamara, I'll tell Bill the party was cancelled because the women didn't turn up.'

When Jenny reached home the house was in darkness; just as she thought, Bill had gone out. It was only eight o'clock and he had not expected her home for another two or three hours. She was fuming, all the anger and suspicion had returned, she would have it out with him the minute he came in.

Charlie Mann had resumed his watch behind a big oak tree surround by undergrowth. He made sure he was well hidden from view this time. He hoped the two women would not do anything stupid like calling the police.

Tamara was toying with the idea of calling the police and reporting the prowler in the park when Marcus came in.

'You look a bit flustered and on edge. What have you been up to now? Not more assignations with Gary Stevens I hope.'

'Oh, give it a rest for heaven's sake, Marcus. If you must know I was out with Jenny.'

'Doing what? I can check up on you. I only have to pick up the phone and ring Jenny to find out.'

'Go ahead, do what you like. See if I care.'

'Well, I'm waiting. What were you doing out with Jenny? No lies please.'

After Tamara had finished telling him everything that had happened and how she was about to call the police, he seemed to believe her.

'Well, I'll give you one thing; you're persistent if nothing else, but I don't really think you can call the police on such flimsy evidence of a man in the bushes — probably just relieving himself. Anyway, they've got someone for the murders.'

'I think they've got the wrong man.'

'You would. You always know best, even better than the police. I'm off to bed.'

'But it's early yet.'

'I know, I just want some peace and time to think.'

Tamara was hurt by his words and wondered if things would ever be the same again between them.

★ ★ ★

242

Charlie Mann was beginning to feel uncomfortable and cold, and began to think it wasn't such a clever idea to be out on such a damp, dismal evening. He felt he was the only fool in the world out alone. Apart from the two women, he had seen no one else in the past hour. He was about to give up on the idea when he could just make out a young woman who had walked under the streetlight at the entrance to the park and was walking his way. She looked about seventeen or eighteen and had long blonde hair. He thought he had better stay concealed for fear of frightening her. I don't know what she's thinking of, walking through the park alone in the dark; still, I suppose she thinks it's safe with the murderer safely under lock and key.

The young girl had walked past totally unaware of his presence. As he looked towards the street light once more he saw a man entering the park who was walking quite fast in the same direction as the girl. There was something strangely familiar about the man but he couldn't quite put his finger on what it was. Suddenly the man began to sprint after the girl; he was on the grass and not the path so she had no idea there was anyone behind her. He grabbed her and she began to scream and struggle. Charlie was calling out to him to stop, but he had a pain in his arm and a searing pain in his chest. He couldn't run very fast and he knew what was happening to him; another heart attack. He must go on and try and avert another murder. Please God, let me be in time to save the girl, give me the strength to get to her in time and then you can take me if you want. He reached Bill Reed in time to see him let go of the lifeless body of the girl. He had strangled her — she lay on the ground, her face deathly white in the moonlight. He was too late to save her. Her murderer stood smirking at him in the moonlight. It was Bill Reed. All this time it was him all along; Bill Reed, the henpecked wimp, a serial killer. He tried to raise a hand but he couldn't, he felt weak, his life was ebbing away from him and he fell to the ground close to where the girl lay. The last thing he heard was the chilling laughter of the killer.

Bill Reed stood over the two bodies, laughing to himself and thinking, two birds with one stone — and one an ex-police chief, what more could I have asked for? Then a sudden thought struck him. He could rear-range the bodies and place Charlie Mann's hands around the dead girl's throat, so it would look like he had strangled her, then collapsed. He had just completed the task when he heard a man's voice in the distance, calling.

'Emma, are you there? It's Dad. Emma, Emma . . .'

'Well Emma, your father's coming for you so you won't be there for long. Then you'll soon be all over the papers tomorrow.'

He ran off in the opposite direction to where the voice was coming from. He had just reached the park entrance when he heard the most horrific scream.

'Emma, no, no not my Emma,' followed by sobbing and wailing. He felt pleased with his handiwork and hoped her father hadn't disturbed the position of the bodies.

★　★　★

Jenny was waiting for his return and flew at him the moment we walked through the door.

'Where the hell have you been?' Before he could answer she started hurling accusations at him. He was totally shocked; he had never seen her like this before. He didn't know she had it in her. He had thought of her as a mouse, who was totally devoted to him, in his power and who would do anything for him. It took him a few minutes to recover his composure from the onslaught of verbal abuse.

'Now darling, what's all this about? Why are you upsetting yourself so?'

'Don't you 'darling' me, Bill Reed. I know what you've been up to.'

For a few seconds he thought she really did know what he had been up to, but he soon realized she was completely on the wrong track when she continued screaming at him about another woman.

'I know you've been seeing another woman. Who is she? I suppose she's a lot younger than me. Go on, tell me.' She began beating him on the chest with clenched fists till eventually she collapsed in a heap, all her anger spent.

He cradled her in his arms, rocking her backwards and forwards, talking softly to her like she was a baby. Eventually she stopped sobbing, she felt limp in his arms.

'Now then, sweetheart, what's all this about? You know there could never be any other woman in my life. You are everything to me, and frankly I'm quite hurt that you could even think such a thing. Wherever did you get such a foolish idea from?'

'Well, you were out when I got back. Where did you go? You seem to be going off a lot on your own lately and I thought you were seeing another woman. We always used to do everything together and I thought you didn't

246

love me anymore. What am I supposed to think when you exclude me from everything and you just seem to want to be on your own all the time?'

'I only want to be on my own sometimes. I just need to think things through at the end of the day.'

'What things? Are you ill?' Unwittingly she had given him the explanation he was desperately searching for.'

'I don't really know, my darling, if I'm ill or not. I've been getting the most blinding headaches and I've been worried that I might have something seriously wrong with me. The headaches always seem worse in the evenings, that is why I've needed to go out in the cool evening air — it seemed to help ease the pain.'

'But why didn't you tell me?'

'I didn't want to worry you. I thought they might just go away in time on their own.'

'Why haven't you been to the doctor's? I'm going to make an appointment for you first thing in the morning, and I don't want any arguments. I'll come with you if you like.'

'I don't think that will be necessary, Jennifer, I'm not a child. I'm perfectly capable of seeing the doctor by myself.'

'Just as you like, but will you please forgive me for my terrible outburst and thinking such dreadful things of you?'

'Of course, darling, it's forgotten already and we'll say no more about it.'

The following morning Jenny was up first and rang the surgery for an appointment. Bill seemed to be sleeping in late this morning. I think I'll leave him a bit longer, he seems exhausted, poor love. His appointment isn't till eleven so I think I'll leave him for another half an hour. She was about to give him a call when she heard his footsteps on the stairs.

'How are you feeling this morning darling? I've booked an appointment with Doctor Stainer at eleven o'clock. Are you sure you don't want me to drive you there?'

'No darling, I'll be fine. You know how much I enjoy walking and the headache has gone now. In fact, I feel a bit of a fraud going there at all, taking up the doctor's time; I'm sure there are a lot more people sicker than me that could do with the appointment.'

'Stop and stop now, I won't hear another word. You'll take the appointment and put both our minds at rest.'

'Alright sweetheart, you win.'

He kissed her on the cheek and thought, God, what a woman.

★ ★ ★

Tamara heard first on the breakfast news that another girl had been murdered and police were asking for anyone in the park yesterday evening between the hours of seven and ten o'clock to contact them. She immediately rang Jenny.

'Can you talk, Jen?'

'Yes, Bill is at the doctor's; but it's alright, he's explained everything to me about why he's been acting so strangely lately. He's been having these terrible headaches and imagined he was seriously ill, and was going out in the fresh air to clear his head. I feel terrible, Tamara, for doubting him. You were right all along, and to think I flew at him when he got in last night accusing him of all sorts.'

Tamara nearly dropped the receiver when she heard the words 'when he got in', so he had been out yet again when a murder had taken place. It's him, I just know it. She felt hysterical, she must keep calm for Jenny's sake.

'Anyway Tamara, what were you going to say to me before I started prattling on?'

'Jenny, another girl has been murdered in the park sometime between seven and ten. We were there at seven and there was that man loitering in the bushes. Do you think we should tell the police?'

There was silence at the other end of the line.

'I don't really know. I suppose so. I expect they'll be doing their usual door to door enquires like they've done with all the other murders.'

★ ★ ★

Chief Inspector Boulter could hardly contain his rage, another girl murdered on his patch. He was going to have to admit he was wrong about Geoff Grant and, worse still, one of his own was implicated in the murder. He paced up and down several times, preparing himself for the morning briefing. The station was a hive of activity and a crowd of reporters were gathered in the media suite awaiting a statement regarding the sixth murder victim.

He braced himself for the deluge of questions that would be fired at him and the flashlights from cameras going off every second. *God, how I hate this part of police work.* He took a deep breath and entered the room where the press were waiting for him.

'Good morning ladies and gentlemen. Sadly there has been another young girl murdered.'

A young reporter eager to get in first with his questions stood up.

'How do you feel about arresting the wrong man while the real murderer was free to kill again?'

Chief Inspector Boulter held up his hand for silence, disregarding the question that had just been fired at him.

'Please allow me to finish my statement and I will answer any questions that I can afterwards. Yesterday evening between the hours of seven and ten, seventeen-year-old Emma Dewey was murdered in Drayton Park. The first person on the scene was the girl's father who was worried about her walking home through the park after dark and had decided to meet her. Unfortunately he came upon a most dreadful scene, that of his daughter lying strangled on the path about twenty yards from the entrance. We would ask all members of the public that were in the park that evening to come forward and contact their nearest police station. That is all the information I can give you at this moment. A further statement will be issued later.'

'Is there any truth in the rumour that two bodies were found in the park?'

Another reporter was on his feet asking questions. Frederick Boulter knew he was not going to get away from the press conference for a long while yet.

'Yes, I can confirm two bodies were found

at the scene of the crime. May I ask how you came upon that piece of information?'

'Good reporting. One of the neighbours saw two bodies being taken away. Was the other body male or female?'

'The other body was that of a male.'

'Did he kill the girl then commit suicide?'

'I cannot comment further on the other victim until a post-mortem has been carried out. I have nothing further to add at this stage. Thank you all for coming.'

He walked away with a barrage of questions ringing in his ears. As the reporters rushed from the room down the stairs and out into the street their footsteps were like a crash of thunder in his ears. He sank in his chair wondering what he would do next. He poured himself a drink and immediately thought, he had better not go down the same road as Charlie Mann.

The post mortem confirmed that Charlie Mann had suffered a massive heart attack and both victims had died at approximately the same time. Did Charlie Mann strangle her and then die before he could carry out a sexual act? Or was there someone else at the scene who had placed his hands around the girl's throat to make it look like he was responsible for the murder? What was Charlie Mann doing at the murder scene? Was it a coincidence that he just happened to be in Drayton Park at that time? He'd been drinking, and drink is always a prelude to some crime or other. Had he been the serial rapist and murderer all along? It would explain the lack of forensic evidence, he would have known how important that was and would make sure he left none. All these thoughts were keeping him awake at night, he kept going over and over in his mind all the evidence gathered, but he still could not believe Charlie Mann, an ex-police officer was, a serial killer.

'Sir, we've just had a member of the public report that she and another woman were in Drayton Park at seven on the evening of the murders, but were frightened out of the park by a man hiding in the bushes. They ran back to the entrance and never continued their journey through the park.'

'Did they get a good look at the man?'

'Not really, they were too scared to hang around and ran as fast as they could out of the park, but they did hear his voice. He called out after them, 'silly bitches'.'

'Did he have a local accent?'

'They thought it sounded like a London accent but couldn't be sure.'

'Bring them both in Woods, I'd like to have a word with them.'

'Two people spring to mind with London accents. Charlie Mann and the landlord of The Viking pub.'

'Bring him in as well and we'll see if he has an alibi.'

Bill Reed was not at all pleased that his wife had to go down to the police station and give a statement.

'What on earth were the pair of you doing in the park? You should have kept to the roads at that time of night. I suppose it was all Tamara's idea.'

'No, no it wasn't, Bill, please don't blame Tamara; it was all my fault and anyway the man we saw could have been the murderer.'

'What man? Did you recognize him?'

'No, he called us silly bitches and we ran like mad.'

'Well, you best tell the police all this, it does sound like you came across the murderer and had a lucky escape. I suppose he couldn't attack both of you so he decided against it, especially when he got a look at Tamara.'

'Don't joke Bill it's not funny.'

'I know, I'm sorry, off you go and try and remember as much as you can to help the police catch the killer as soon as possible. There have been far too many murders.'

As soon as Jenny was out the door Bill

Reed could contain his laughter no longer. He sat down in the chair rocking backwards and forwards with laughter till his sides hurt. Then he decided to switch on the television for the latest news bulletin. The newsreader was giving the name of the murdered victim as seventeen-year-old Emma Dewey.

'Come on, name the other body you idiot.'

'The other body found at the scene of crime has yet to be formally identified and an announcement will be made after the next of kin have been informed.'

'What a load of twaddle.' The police are trying to cover their tracks and can't bring themselves to admit that one of their own is involved; it gets even better. My wife and her stuck-up friend are down the police station helping to point the finger at Chief Inspector Charlie Mann. I mean, ex-Chief Inspector. He gave another one of his blood-curdling laughs then settled down to await the return of his wife.

★　★　★

By the time statements had been taken from Jenny, Tamara and the landlord of The Viking, Frederick Boulter felt they were no nearer in finding the murderer than before.

Mrs. Wheeler-Osman had described the

man in the bushes as not very tall and quite fat. The landlord of The Viking was tall and slim so that ruled him out; and besides, there was the big annual darts tournament yesterday evening, The Viking against the Hungry Hound pub, and dozens of people could verify he never left the bar all evening. The only thing linking him to the murder was a London accent, and there seems to be an abundance of Londoners who have moved down to this backwater. I can't see what the attraction is myself. The most obvious choice is Charlie Mann, he fits perfectly the description given by the two women. Charlie Mann might have been a lot of things but I can't believe he is a serial murderer.

A few days later the identity of the other body was disclosed to the press and made front page news in all the papers including the nationals.

14

The strain of the past few months was beginning to show on the face of Frederick Boulter. He looked pale and drawn and seemed to lack his usual confidence. He had not long been in charge of Operation Maple and already he had made a serious mistake in arresting the wrong man while the killer was free to kill again.

'I can't get my head around Charlie Mann being the serial killer Harry. It's just not in his nature, but what the hell was he doing at the murder scene with his hands around the girl's throat?'

'I don't know Don, but one thing is for sure, if he's not the murderer the real killer will strike again and quite soon, he won't be able to help himself. He's either very lucky or damn clever, I'm not sure which. I feel certain he's someone we've already inter-viewed and is local. I think Charlie Mann was probably staking out the park in the hope of catching the killer red-handed and the actual shock of seeing him in action finished the poor sod off.'

'That's it Harry, you've hit the nail right on

the head. He was conducting his own stake-out and may even have tried to stop the killing when he had another heart attack. The killer placed Charlie's hands around the girl's throat. I bet he couldn't believe his luck. Do you think we ought to suggest a stake-out of the park to Boulter?'

'I dunno, Don, at the moment he's wandering around like a bear with a sore head, worried about his promotion going down the Swannee.'

* ★ ★ ★

After spending a sleepless night Tamara sat in the kitchen drinking coffee and wondering what she should do for the best. Should she tell the police that she suspected her friend's husband as the serial killer, or worse still, should she tell Jenny — her best friend — first? She decided against the latter. Jenny would never speak to her again; but was her life in danger? She thought not: as long as Jenny knew nothing, she gave him respectability as a happily married middle-aged man enjoying life with his wife. Would the police believe her or would they think it was the ravings of some madwoman?

'Tam, what are you doing up so early? You spent half the night tossing and turning in bed, I hardly got any sleep.'

'I'm thinking of going to the police and telling them Bill Reed is the serial killer.'

'Tam, have you taken leave of your senses? I absolutely forbid it.'

'You forbid it! Who do you think you are, some Victorian dictatorial husband who has his wife totally under his control? Just get stuffed, Marcus, I'll go to the police if I want to, I don't need your say-so.'

'No you don't, but you do need some proof. They'll just think you're some stupid menopausal woman with a vendetta against her friend's husband.'

Much as she hated to admit it he was absolutely right. How can I get some proof? I must think. Think Tam, think, there has got to be some proof out there somewhere. I need someone to help me with this and there is no one at all I can turn to. Suddenly she felt calm, a feeling of peace came over her and it was almost as if someone was telling her what to do. Into her mind came the image of the lady in a white suit, Jane Birch. She was saying 'the bottom of the garden' over and over again and then she was gone. That's it, she's buried in the garden under the rose bushes. Luckily Marcus had left the house, so she quickly dressed and rushed out into the garden, shovel in hand, and began digging.

The rose bushes had grown quite large and were really hard to shift. She tugged at one with all her might, but to no avail: she could not shift it and only succeeded in pricking her fingers on the thorns; her blood began to drip everywhere. It stained the white petals of the roses and it reminded her of the lady in the white suit stained with blood, calling for help. Tears began to roll down her cheeks until she was sobbing uncontrollably. I can't help her, I don't know what to do, I'm not strong enough. Marcus returned to find her collapsed on the lawn with blood all over her clothes and the grass around her stained red.

'Tam, what have you done? Oh my God!' He picked her up and carried her indoors. 'Tell me, what on earth has happened to you?' His first thought was that she had slashed her wrists as there was so much blood around and it was all his fault. Between gulps and sobs she managed to tell him what she was trying to do.

'I was trying to dig up the rose bushes because I think Jane Birch is buried there and when I tugged at the bush the thorns pricked all my fingers.'

'My poor darling.' He put his arms around her. 'Please don't cry. I am so sorry. What have I made you do in desperation? I've accused you of all sorts and now I realise it was just my jealous imagination. Please forgive me darling.'

'Of course I will. I'm so pleased that at last you believe me.'

After attending to her fingers they both sat down for a long talk.

'What are we going do to next? Should we let the police dig up the rose bed or should we do it ourselves?'

Marcus was thoughtful for a moment; he didn't want to upset her any further by telling her the idea of Jane Birch buried in their back garden was totally ridiculous.

'I'll dig up the rose garden before we inform the police, but first I have to go to Hong Kong on urgent business and I want you to come with me. It will do you good to get away from things for a while.'

'But what about Jane Birch?'

'No buts, the rest will do you good. If Jane Birch is there she certainly won't be going anywhere, and she'll keep till we get back.'

'In the meantime Bill Reed is walking around free to kill again.'

'A week or two won't make any difference and you need to feel stronger before we invite the police and everything it entails into our back garden. There will be press camped out on our doorstep morning noon and night, and quite frankly I don't feel you're well enough to cope with all that.'

She reluctantly had to agree with him. 'I suppose you're right.'

★ ★ ★

Bill Reed realized that if the police were to believe that Charlie Mann had been the serial killer all along, he would not be able to kill again. Then a thought began to form in his mind that if he was to continue his killing spree he must do it elsewhere.

'Jenny, how about us getting away and staying in our apartment in Bournemouth? We've spent a lot of money on it and have hardly used it this year. I think we deserve a really nice rest and to spend some quality time together. After all, none of us ever know how long we have left.'

He saw the look of consternation on her face and knew he had won. Once more she was in his power and would do anything he asked for fear of losing him. He had assured her the doctor said everything was fine and the headaches were nothing to worry about, but now and again he would drop little hints about doctors making mistakes and not always being right. He had planted doubt in her mind that everything may not be alright. She was worried that she might lose the one and only love of her life and felt remorse at having doubted his loyalty to her.

'Of course we must go. You're absolutely right Bill. How long will we go for? I need to know how much to pack.'

'Shall we say a month to start with? You never know, if it starts to feel like home we might sell up here and stay down there permanent. Although we have both grown up in this area it is not the nice place we knew as children. It's not safe to be on the streets any more with all these young girls being killed. I know they've caught the killer now, but the whole place has unpleasant memories. Our lovely childhood memories have been tarnished forever.'

The following day the pair set off for Bournemouth.

* * *

Three weeks had passed since the last murder and everything was quiet. Reluctantly, the police had to admit it was beginning to look more certain as time passed that Charlie Mann was the serial killer. Operation Maple was being scaled down. Extra police called in to help with the search for the killer were returning to their own units. DCs Don Woods and Harry Harding could still not come to terms with him being the killer.

'I still don't get it Harry. Charlie Mann was brought down from London to help us solve the rape cases which later became murders, so how could he be the killer when the rapes started before he got here?'

'I put the same question to Boulter and he said the rapes were probably some local nutter, and when Charlie and his men arrived he got the idea to murder and the blame would be put on the rapist when he was caught.'

'You don't believe that do you Harry?'

'No of course not, but I don't see what else we can do at the moment Don. One thing is for sure: the killer will strike again, and Charlie Mann will be exonerated.'

★ ★ ★

Bill Reed resumed his responsibility of taking Pepper out for a walk last thing at night and was highly delighted to see so many young girls wandering the streets in Bournemouth late at night. The whole place had a wonderful holiday atmosphere, young people out enjoying themselves, he would soon change all that. He alone, Bill Reed would strike fear into the place, after all he was an accomplished serial killer too clever for the police to apprehend. He returned home feeling quite elated and must plan his next victim carefully.

'I must say Bill you seemed to have cheered up a lot since we've been here. Are your headaches less troublesome?'

'Yes dear, it must be the sea air doing me a power of good.'

'I do worry about you going out so late with Pepper.'

'I'm perfectly safe here, it's not Woodfield; and anyway I was safe there, the serial killer never ever killed any men.'

As he said the words thoughts began to form in his head about murdering young men. Of course that would really throw the police they would still be thinking one of their own was the serial killer at Woodfield and down here I could start a whole new killing spree on useless drunk young men.

'What are you thinking Bill?'

'Nothing at all dear.'

'You must have been thinking something, you were miles away.'

'Nothing of any importance my sweet.'

'Perhaps I'll come out with you tomorrow night.'

'No!'

Jenny was quite alarmed at the sharpness of his answer and immediately began to think that he was up to no good again. He recovered quickly with an explanation for his concern over her coming with him.

'No darling, I wouldn't like you to hear all the bad language from the youngsters coming out of the night clubs and pubs. It really is bad you know. You'd think the police would have more control. I thought it was an offence to use such language in the street, but there you are, no one seems to care.'

He was quite relieved to see Jenny had forgotten about the sharp way he'd spoken to her. The way she was so easily fooled never ceased to amaze him.

The next night it was pouring with rain so his plans were spoilt. The rain continued to fall for the next three days and he was beginning to feel restless till eventually he could stand it no more and decided to go out in the rain with Pepper.

'Darling you'll be soaked. Are you sure about going out, it isn't really necessary you know, Pepper can make do with the balcony.'

'No, it'll be alright. I won't be long.'

'Don't forget the umbrella in the hall.'

'No I won't.'

A few moments later Jenny went into the hall and found the umbrella still there. I suppose if I hurry I can catch him up, he hasn't been gone more than five minutes. She grabbed her raincoat and dashed out into the street just in time to see him disappearing around the corner at the end of the road in the direction of the beach. She called to him but her words were lost on the wind and the rain seemed to be coming down even heavier than before. She tried to run to catch him up but the wind was against her and she seemed to be making hardly any progress at all. Bill was completely unaware that Jenny was following him. He had just noticed a group of young people arguing. One of the young men decided to separate from the rest of the group and go his own way. He shouted a few obscenities at the group and stumbled towards the beach. He was very drunk and hardly capable of walking let alone finding his way home. He started to go down the steps to the beach but only managed to get half way before he fell, landing with a heavy thump on the sand. Bill had been watching from a doorway and stepped forward after checking no one was in sight. In an instant he was down the steps and on the beach. The young man had managed to stand up and stagger a few feet before being violently sick. Bill was on to him before he was aware anyone else was on the beach. His hands closed around the young man's throat, he was squeezing hard when he heard Jenny calling. 'Bill, are you there?' He froze on the spot, hands still around the boy's throat. Pepper immediately recognized his mistress's voice and barked loudly to attract her attention. She turned just in time to see Bill loosen his grip on the young man's throat.

'Bill what on earth are you doing? Stop! Stop at once or you'll kill him.'

'Jenny my love, he almost killed me! I was trying to stop him.'

The young man managed to whisper, 'liar' before he passed out.

'Oh my God Bill, is he dead?'

'No of course he isn't, he's stupid drunk.'

'We'd better call an ambulance.'

'I don't think so, he attacked me and if he hadn't been so drunk he could have killed me.'

'It didn't look that way to me, more like the other way round.'

'Jenny what are you saying?'

'I'm saying I'm calling the police and an ambulance. We can't leave him here in this weather, he could die.'

That's precisely as I intended my sweet until you came along and spoiled everything, thought Bill.

Jenny ran to a nearby phone box and called the police and ambulance. She waited with the young man till they arrived, a disgruntled husband beside her complaining bitterly about the youth of today and how he had been attacked first and he was only defending himself.

The shock of being attacked seemed to sober up the young man and in a croaky voice he told the police his name was Peter Dumaresq and his father was one of the local dignitaries. The paramedics said he had severe bruising to his throat but could find no sign of any other injuries; they would take him to hospital for a check up and as soon as he was over the effects of the alcohol he should be able to go home. A policeman would accompany him in the ambulance and take a statement from him at the hospital. Another policeman turned to Bill and said, 'Now sir, is there somewhere we can go to hear your side of the story?'

'Please come back to our apartment officer and I'll make us all a cup of tea, we live quite close by.'

'Thank you madam, that would be very nice.'

Once inside their apartment Bill was beginning to panic and curse his luck for picking one of the local rich kids for his next victim. How was he going to talk his way out of this one? Everyone including the police will believe daddy's spoilt little brat.

'Are you alright sir? Your hands are trembling.'

'I think so officer, it's just the shock setting in. I've never been attacked before and I'm finding the whole episode very upsetting. It will take me a long time to get over this.'

'Right sir, shall we start? Beginning with the moment you left your flat.'

'I was taking our dog Pepper for his last walk of the day. I was heading for the beach so I could let him off the lead when I came across a group of young people the worse for drink. They were swearing and shouting at one another and I could sense trouble brewing so I hurried by as quickly as I could, hoping that they hadn't noticed me. I walked down the steps to the beach and had just let Pepper off the lead when someone came at me from behind. He jumped on my back and started shouting, 'Give me your money old man'. When I said I hadn't got any money he shouted, 'liar, liar!' I managed to break free from him but he came after me. He was so strong and I was very frightened. I turned and put my hands around his throat to try and ward him off and the next thing I heard was my dear wife's voice calling my name. Bless her she saved my life.'

Jenny felt uneasy; this was not quite how she had witnessed the situation. She hadn't seen the youth attack her husband in any way.

'Now Mrs. Reed, we'd like your version of what happened.'

'Well.' Jenny was hesitant, not sure how she should answer for fear of incriminating her husband. All eyes were on her including Bill's.

'Don't be nervous, please continue.'

'My husband decided to take our dog for a walk and he forgot to take the umbrella. I discovered it still in the hall about five minutes after he left. He couldn't have gone far so I ran after him with it. I just caught sight of him turning the corner at the end of the road and heading towards the beach. I called out but my words were lost on the wind and he didn't hear me. By the time I caught up with him he was on the beach grappling with the boy.'

'Did you hear what anyone was saying?'

'I heard the boy say 'liar' as my husband turned and said, 'he's attacking me'.'

'So you didn't hear the boy ask for money.'

'No. Those were the only words I heard.'

The two police officers looked at one another.

'That will be all for tonight. Come down to the station tomorrow morning and make a formal statement.'

★ ★ ★

Back at the station the police officers compared notes and the statement taken from Peter Dumaresq at the hospital was very different from the version given by Bill Reed.

'We can expect hell tomorrow morning from Robert Dumaresq. I can just hear him now. 'My son being attacked, it's a total disgrace, where were the boys in blue while he was practically murdered? Sat in a nice warm police car whiling the night away instead of being out there keeping the peace.' I'm glad I'll be off duty by then Rew.'

'Yes Sarge. What do you make of it all Sarge? Do you think young Dumaresq is telling the truth that the old geezer did attack him first?'

'I dunno. Dumaresq junior is not opposed to popping the odd pill or two and he was really very drunk. Perhaps he was hallucinating and the older man was really in fear of his life, he panicked and just grabbed his throat. No doubt Dumaresq senior will want to press charges, you mark my words.'

True to the sergeant,s words, the next morning Robert Dumaresq was at the police station insisting that charges of attempted murder be brought against the man who attacked his son. Bill Reed was outraged that he should be brought before a court over a young pipsqueak that should be taken out of society anyway. What use was he in society? What use were any of the young people of today? All they were good for was taking drugs, fighting and boozing.

The police wanted to drop all charges due to insufficient evidence, but Robert Dumaresq was having none of it and decided on taking out a private prosecution against Bill Reed.

Jenny was terrified of the consequences. Would her Bill be found guilty and sent to jail?

Robert Dumaresq certainly seemed to wield a lot of power in the town, and he also had plenty of money and could hire the best lawyer to be had. And what did they have? Nothing. All their savings had gone on their dream apartment. And now I wish we'd never bought it. At home there was a serial killer on the loose and we came down here for a few weeks' peace and quiet — and now this has happened. When is it all going to end? She felt uneasy about Bill and how she had found him trying to choke the life out of the young boy. It didn't look like the boy was putting up any resistance at all let alone trying to murder Bill. Something didn't ring true in Bill's version of events.

★ ★ ★

Tamara and Marcus had returned from their trip to Hong Kong and things were back to normal, no more quarrels or jealousies, all their differences forgotten. The two weeks they were supposed to be away had turned into two months.

'I must just pop next door to Edith and tell her we're back and give her the present we've brought her.'

'Don't be too long darling, I'm starving.'

'Hello Edith, how have things been?'

'Very quiet my dear, no more murders so it looks as though the policeman was the murderer after all.'

'That's good news, so we can all sleep easy in our beds again.' As she said these words the old feeling of fear seemed to come back to her once more, as if things were still not right. She told herself not to be so silly and after a few more brief words with Edith excused herself and went back to Marcus.

'Edith said there haven't been any more murders while we've been away.'

'Thank God. Does that mean I'm excused from digging up the rose bed?'

Tamara hesitated for a moment and then answered. 'Yes, I suppose so.'

Tamara had a good night's sleep in spite of her feelings of unease, and when the phone rang she was not expecting to hear the bombshell that Jenny was about to drop.

'Good God! Bill arrested for attempted murder.'

At hearing these words Marcus put down his paper and took an interest.

'Jenny, whatever's happened? Don't cry dear. Where are you? I'll come at once.'

'I'm in Bournemouth. I'll drive to Wood-field this afternoon. I just need to get away from the place, it's all so upsetting. Please help me Tamara, I just don't know what to do.'

'Of course I will, we'll be here all day. Drive carefully. Bye.'

'Well, what did you make of that Marcus? Perhaps I was right all along — Bill is the murderer after all.'

'Now please Tam, don't start. Let's wait and see what Jenny has to say about it all. It must be some ghastly mistake.'

Jenny arrived just after two o'clock, white as a sheet and looking very distressed.

'Sit down Jenny, and tell us all about it. Would you like a cup of tea?'

'Not at the moment thank you.' She looked at her two friends' faces waiting for her to begin, but she couldn't find the words to tell them that her husband had done something terrible.

'I don't know where to start.'

'Just take your time Jenny.' Marcus replied kindly to this poor distressed woman. 'We have plenty of time, we're not going anywhere.'

'Well it started one rainy evening two weeks ago. You were still away and I didn't have anyone to talk to or confide in. Bill took Pepper out for a walk in the pouring rain and forgot to take the umbrella. I discovered he'd left it behind about five minutes later and went after him with it. With the wind blowing and the rain lashing down, he didn't hear me call him, so I ran after him. I saw him on the beach with his hands around a youth's throat strangling him. I called out, 'Bill stop, please stop', and when he saw me he let go of the youth who slumped on the sand coughing and choking.'

'But he was alright wasn't he?'

'Yes Tamara, only just, a few minutes later and I think he would have killed him.'

'What reason did he give for such extraordinary behaviour?'

'He said the youth had attacked him first and wanted money and he was only defending himself; but Marcus, there wasn't any time for him to attack Bill because I was right there a few minutes behind him. The police have dropped the charges because of insufficient evidence.'

'Well there you are then, nothing more to worry about. This lad was probably a known criminal and the police believed Bill's version of things.'

'No Marcus, it's not over by a long way yet. The boy was known to the police because he comes from a very rich family and his father is taking out a private prosecution against Bill.'

'Oh I see. That throws a whole different light on the matter. Have you got a good lawyer?'

'No we haven't much money left after buying the apartment. Perhaps we could sell our house up here to pay for his defence.'

'Well if you need any help at all — either financial or otherwise — you only have to ask. You know I'm not short of a bob or two.'

Tamara sat there outraged; much as she loved her friend and would do anything to help, she certainly didn't want to assist a killer in any way at all. She felt that at last he had got what was coming to him and good on the boy's father for going after him.

'You're very quiet Tam. Haven't you got anything to say for yourself?'

'I'm just so utterly shocked Marcus. I really don't know what to say that will help Jenny.'

In the meantime a plan was forming in her mind to tip off the police in Woodfield that he had been arrested on a charge of attempted murder. Then perhaps they might take a fresh look at the crimes up here. Strangulation was how most of the girls were killed. It's him, I know it. I'm even more convinced than before. How am I going to inform the police without them knowing it was me? Perhaps if I made an anonymous call from a phone box they wouldn't be able to trace me. Yes, that's it, that's what I'll do.

Marcus had been watching Tamara's reaction and thought, I hope she doesn't do anything stupid like calling the police and having our back garden dug up. Oh my God, what an unholy mess. I used to lead a really quiet life once.

★ ★ ★

Tamara and Marcus were at Jenny's side when Bill's case was heard at the Magistrates Court. Marcus was very encouraging and said it would probably be thrown out and not get as far as the Crown Court. After all the police didn't think there was a case to answer, and Bill was of previous good character and had never been arrested in his life for anything, not even a small misdemeanour. Marcus and Jenny were very shocked when the case was sent to the Crown Court and not dismissed. Bill was given a date to appear at Winchester Crown Court for a preliminary hearing. Only Tamara was elated but had to appear calm for the sake of her friend. She sat there thinking, yes, yes at last justice will be done.

15

The next evening Bill's arrest was all over the local paper. The headlines read **Local Woodfield Man Arrested for Attempted Murder.** It was also mentioned on the early evening television news. Tamara was elated; she didn't have to do anything, the law was catching up with him at last. There was to be a preliminary hearing at Winchester Crown Court. Tamara was determined she would be in court throughout all the proceedings. As far as anyone else was concerned she was there to support her friend but the truth was she was there to see the long hated Bill Reed get what he deserved.

★ ★ ★

Don Woods couldn't believe his eyes when he picked up the evening newspaper. He had just slipped out to buy the usual teatime treat of doughnuts and thought he might as well buy a paper at the same time. He burst into Harry Harding's office waving the local paper.

'Harry, take a look at this lot. Bill Reed arrested in Bournemouth on an attempted murder charge. Are you thinking what I'm thinking?'

'I'm already one jump ahead of you Don. Perhaps poor old Charlie's name will be cleared after all.'

'Even if he's found guilty of attempted murder and goes inside, how's that going to help us nail him for the murders? He's hardly going to confess, he knows if he does he'll be banged up for the rest of his natural.'

'I always thought there was something odd about him but I couldn't quite explain what.'

'What do we do next Harry?'

'Check back over all his alibis when each murder took place.'

'Christ, you sound like Boulter.'

'It's the only way Don. It looks like we've a long evening ahead of us. Bye the way, where's the doughnuts?'

'I forgot them, when I saw the headlines in the paper I came straight back to the office.'

'I suggest you go back and get them and some sandwiches as well. We're in for a long night.'

DC Harry Harding took out the file on the very first murder of Alice Jones and realized Bill Reed had not been questioned in connection with this murder; so in point of fact he had no alibi, as none was required. Next came the rape of Kendra Rickman, the local good time girl. It was presumed she was raped by one of her previous boyfriends or someone her brother knew. His alibi was given by his newly acquired wife. While we were questioning him the rape of a schoolgirl took place at Moreton Park on the other side of Woodfield. Could this have been someone else unconnected to the other rapes and murders? Tracey Sellwood said the man was young and tall, neither description fitting Bill Reed. It could have been an unplanned rape, someone saw the opportunity and took it. Melanie Taylor, stabbed in the neck but saved by dog walkers. Again, alibi supplied by wife. Jane Birch still missing, a prospective buyer for his house who he claims never kept the viewing appointment. Jodie Bowden murdered late at night, wife supplied alibi. The victim was known to Mrs. Reed's best friend. Joannne Thorn the cosmetic seller called at Bill Reed's for a catalogue and was never seen again. Alibi provided by Roy Rickman and a delivery man, but was there a time when they were out of sight and he could have disposed of the body? Jessica Hale and Emma Dewey, both murdered in the park. Mrs. Reed his alibi yet again, saying the same thing as with all the other murders — that Bill had been indoors all evening and never left the house after dark. Well Mrs. Reed, I don't believe you.

Don Woods returned with the doughnuts and sandwiches.

'Did you find anything Harry?'

'Only that all his alibis were supplied by his wife with the exception of one given by Roy Rickman and a delivery man.'

'Oh yes, and he's a good upstanding pillar of society, I don't think. Each one backed the other's story up, so no joy there. Do you think Roy Rickman had anything to do with the Joanne Thorn murder?'

'No, he did seem to have genuine alibis for all the murders. He was usually mouthing off at one of his family and all of Juniper Road could vouch for his whereabouts at the time the girls were murdered in the park.'

'What next Harry?'

'I think we'll take a drive down to Bournemouth tomorrow and have a word with Mrs. Reed and see if she is still happy to back up all the alibis. Also we'll have a word with our colleagues in the Dorset force and get their opinion on Bill Reed.'

The next morning their first port of call was Bournemouth police station where they obtained Jennifer Reed's address. Harry asked off the record what the general feeling was as to Bill Reed's guilt or innocence. PC Rew was the officer on duty that night and he was a bit undecided as to who to believe.

'Peter Dumaresq was well known to the police, a rich spoilt kid who only had to ask and daddy supplied. He had crashed numerous cars bought by his father, had been arrested for fighting and being drunk. He'd spent many a night in a police cell till his father came and bailed him out the next morning, but in spite of his record I tended to believe him. He was totally incapable of putting up any sort of fight. As for Bill Reed, there is something sinister and creepy about him. I've seen that strange look before when I was working up north and a serial killer was caught on our patch. He had the same eyes as Bill Reed and the same cold calculating stare. I tell you that man has the makings of a killer if ever I saw one.'

'Thank you so much, you don't know how much help you've been.'

'That's alright, you're welcome; don't forget it's off the record and only my opinion. If it had been up to me and not the powers that be I'd have arrested him long ago. Anyway, why are the Hampshire police so interested in him?'

'He's been questioned in the past about the murders and rapes of young girls in our area. He's always had alibis at the time of the murders, mostly provided by his wife, so when we learned he'd been arrested for attempting to strangle a local youth we became very interested indeed.'

'I thought they caught someone for the Hampshire murders, wasn't it one of our lot?'

'We never believed that was true, we think he was framed. Anyway we'll be attending the court case so we'll see you again soon. Now we'll see what Mrs. Reed has to say for herself Don.'

It didn't take the pair long to locate the apartment on the sea front where the Reeds were staying. Don Woods knocked loudly on the door, startling Jenny whose nerves were shattered from the lack of sleep and worrying about Bill. She opened the door slowly.

At once she recognized the two DCs. 'Oh it's you two. What do you want?'

'We'd like to ask you a few questions regarding the night the boy was attacked on the beach by your husband.'

'What's it got to do with you? I've answered enough questions from the local police. Why are you two getting involved?'

'Mrs. Reed we have reason to believe your husband may have been involved in the Woodfield murders.'

'How dare you! I know what you're up to, you just want to exonerate one of your own. Well you won't succeed, Bill is innocent so don't you dare try and drag him into the

Woodfield murders. What happened to Bill here is completely different from those young girls in Woodfield that were murdered. He was set upon by a youth who has been in trouble with the police loads of times, and because his father is rich and doesn't know what to do with his money he's brought this case against my innocent husband. I'd like you to leave now.'

Any misgivings Jenny had about her husband's innocence before had now gone. She had talked herself into believing he was totally innocent and was being hounded on all sides.

'Well what did you make of that Harry? Didn't I tell you before she looked like a bunny boiler and would defend her man to the end?'

'It proves one thing Don, she would certainly lie to protect him. What the hell she sees in him is beyond me.'

'Well she's no oil painting, I suppose it was a case of any port in a storm. In her mind even Bill Reed was better than no one.'

★　★　★

Following the directions hearings at Winchester Crown Court the High Court Judge had ordered that the trial be heard by a

286

senior Judge at Bournemouth Crown Court. Jenny was pleased about this as it meant they didn't have to travel and she hoped there would be less press coverage in Woodfield.

The day before the trial Tamara and Marcus stayed the night with Jenny and Bill. Tamara was a great help to Jenny who was in a terrible state. She couldn't make up her mind what to wear.

'Should I wear my black suit Tamara, or does it look too solemn? My pale blue suit looks too summery. Oh dear, I just don't know what to wear. I want to create a good impression.' She sat on the bed and began to cry.

'Don't cry Jenny. I'll look in your wardrobe and find something suitable. Ah yes . . . This is the one to wear, the bottle green dress and matching jacket. Not too dowdy and not too bright. Perfect . . . '

The four arrived at the court a half hour before the case was due to be heard. Tamara, looking around, caught the eye of DC Don Woods.

'Isn't that the two policemen from Woodfield? What on earth are they doing here?'

'Yes, they came around yesterday morning, poking their noses in where they don't belong and accusing Bill of being implicated in the

Woodfield murders. Have you ever heard such nonsense?'

Tamara's heart missed a beat. Yes . . . at last someone else is on to him. Marcus gave Tamara a warning look so she said nothing further. Don Woods was quick to notice the interest in their presence shown by Tamara and made a mental note to speak to her later.

'Did you see that Harry? I'm sure that woman looked pleased to see us. I get the feeling she wants to tell me something.'

'What, like she really fancies you? Dream on Don, she's married to the millionaire bloke that's with her.'

'No stupid, about Bill Reed. If it's all the same to you I'd like to have a word with her at some point.'

'Be my guest, but you'll get nothing from her. She's on very good terms with Mrs. Reed — that's why she's here, to give her friend support.'

'What if she's here to see Bill Reed get what's coming to him?'

As everyone took their seats at the start of the trial Tamara looked around and caught Don Woods' attention once more. He smiled and nodded to her. I'm sure he knows I'm bursting to tell him something. Perhaps in the break I can separate from Marcus and have a word with him. Unfortunately in the break the two DCs had a phone call summoning them back to Woodfield immediately. There had been a terrorist scare at Southampton Central railway station. Tamara was thoroughly disappointed when they disappeared and felt the moment was lost once more.

After the recess everyone settled back in their seats to listen to the evidence of Peter Dumaresq. Marcus had managed to secure a top London lawyer for Bill, Benjamin Walters. He was an equal match for the Dumaresq lawyer Joshua Soars. Marcus glanced across at Robert Dumaresq and thought, you won't buy your son out of this one quite so easily.

The barrister asked Peter to tell the court what happened on the night of the attack.

'I met up with my friends at about seven o'clock, we had a few drinks and then thought we would go on to a nightclub. Then an argument started between me and Jake Prowting.'

'What was the argument about?' Joshua Soars was on his feet gently guiding Peter Dumaresq through his evidence.

'He had been flirting with my girlfriend all evening and began taunting me, saying he could have her quite easily if he wanted to.'

'And what was your girlfriend's response to this?'

'She said, don't take any notice of him

Peter, he's not worth it, but I did take notice — I wanted to kill him. He just went on and on, so in the end I just walked away.'

'Where did you go?'

'On to the beach. I thought I would sit there for a while to cool off. As I got to the beach steps I slipped and fell down onto the sand. I stood up, and walked along the beach, then suddenly I was jumped on from behind. At first I thought it was Jake, I managed to turn around and was surprised to see this old boy with a mad stare in his eyes. I was caught off guard and he put his hands around my throat and started squeezing really hard. My strength was ebbing away, then this woman called out, Bill what are you doing? Stop you'll kill him!'

'Would it be fair to say you were incapable of fighting with anyone that night as you were more than a little drunk?'

'Yes sir.'

'Could you have fought with anyone on that night?'

'No sir, that's why I walked away from Jake.'

'No further questions.'

Benjamin Walters was on his feet to cross-examine Peter Dumaresq.

'You have just told the court you wanted to kill Jake Prowting.'

'Yes that's right.'

'Would you say Jake Prowting was a fit young man?'

'Yes I would.'

'Fitter and tougher than you?'

'Yes, no, well I don't know.'

'Isn't it the case Mr. Dumaresq that you knew Jake Prowting could get the better of you and this left you feeling angry and frustrated?'

'No.'

'I put it to you that you were so wound up and angry that you walked off'in a rage and vented your anger on a defenceless elderly man walking his dog on the beach. Isn't that what really happened?'

'No! It's not true, he attacked me first.' A torrent of anger and obscenities came from Peter Dumaresq and the judge had to warn him about his behaviour. He told him to calm down and just answer the questions.

Marcus was pleased with Benjamin Walters' efforts in defending Bill. He whispered to Tamara, 'Good old Ben, he's one of the best.'

'How do you know him?'

'We were at the same public school; we were great friends then and have continued to be so ever since.'

'I see the old boys' network is still working,' Tamara whispered sarcastically.

291

'For God's sake Tam, I'm trying to help your friend. Think how Jenny must feel with her husband sat there in the dock being wrongly accused.'

'Who said he was wrongly accused? I think he did it.'

'Shush . . . be quiet or we'll be turned out of court.'

Tamara's thoughts turned to Jenny, sitting in the witness room waiting to be called to give evidence. She wondered if she should have stayed outside as well but she didn't want to miss anything. I would really like to see Bill Reed go down for this.

A statement was read to the jury from the hospital doctor who attended to Peter Dumaresq on the night of the attack. He said Peter Dumaresq had severe bruising on his neck and haemorrhages in his eyes consistent with being strangled. Although the bruises were quite severe, there was no long term damage sustained and he was released from hospital the next morning.

Several of Peter's friends were called to the witness box and all testified that he was in no fit state to attack anyone, although none of them had seen the attack take place.

As the four drove back to the apartment, Jenny and Bill sat silently staring out of the window.

'Jenny, are you alright?'

Jenny was miles away and then suddenly became aware she was being spoken to.

'Sorry Tamara, did you say something?'

'I was only asking if you were alright.'

'As well as I can be with the possibility my husband may be locked up for something he didn't do.'

'Now don't upset yourself Jenny. It's not over by a long way and Ben Walters is really doing well. He'll come up trumps for us you'll see.'

'I'm sure you're right Marcus but I can't help worrying.'

The next morning was bright and sunny for a November day. Tamara thought that although it was a nice day it was cold both inside and out. What I wouldn't give to be a hundred miles away from all this, or still in Hong Kong enjoying the company of Marcus's friends. As soon as they all settled back in court Tamara perked up when she saw the two police officers across the courtroom. She glanced at Marcus to make sure he wasn't watching her, before smiling across at the two men.

'Look at that Harry, didn't I tell you she wants to speak to us?'

'Yes, I must say there seems to be something on her mind alright.'

Tamara turned her attention back to Bill as she heard Benjamin Walters' voice.

Bill's barrister was on his feet asking for Bill's account of the attack.

'Can you tell the court what happened on the night of 2nd November?'

'The weather was very bad on that night so I thought I would take our dog for a quick walk. As I approached the beach I saw a group of young people arguing. I slipped by hoping they wouldn't see me.'

'Do you normally walk your dog on the beach that late at night?'

'Not usually as late as I did that night. I was waiting for the rain to stop but it didn't so I had to go anyway.'

'You say you slipped by the youngsters arguing, hoping they wouldn't see you. Why was that?'

'I felt intimidated by such a large group of them shouting and swearing and obviously the worse for drink.'

'What happened when you reached the beach?'

'One of the group had left the others and went down on the beach. I cursed my luck but then thought one on his own was obviously harmless, but I soon learnt different. I'd only taken a few steps when he turned around and started asking me for money in a most threatening manner. When I said I hadn't any he attacked me. I don't remember what happened next. I only remember my dear wife calling to me.'

'No further questions.'

Joshua Soars was on his feet in a flash ready to cross-examine Bill. Tamara thought he looked quite formidable and hoped he would be able to shake the confidence of smarmy Bill. He had put up quite a good show of turning things around and making out he was the victim not the aggressor. She had glanced at the jury several times while Bill was giving his evidence and thought a few of them had sympathetic looks on their faces. So far things seem to be going well for Bill and she hoped a few of the stronger jurors would be able to see through his tissue of lies.

'Did you say the group of youths were *obviously the worse for drink*? And you said one of them became separated from the others?'

'Yes.'

'Would you say the one on his own was too drunk to be able to attack someone?'

'No, definitely not.'

'What about too drunk to be able to defend himself.'

'No! He attacked me!'

'Come, come Mr. Reed, we've heard it was

Peter Dumaresq who went to hospital that night with throat injuries, not you.'

Bill became very red in the face. Beads of sweat were on his brow and he began to stammer when answering the prosecution's questions.

'I . . . I . . . only know how frightened I was on that dreadful night. I feared for my life.'

'Mr. Reed I would say that if anyone feared for their life it was Peter Dumaresq not you. The only reason you didn't go on to kill him was because your wife called out to you, *Bill stop, you're killing him.*'

'No . . . no, I don't remember her saying that.'

'Do you like young people Mr. Reed?'

'Not especially.'

'Do you dislike them to the extent that you wanted to kill one of them when the opportunity came your way?'

'No, no, no. It's not true.'

Bill became even more agitated and was relieved to hear the barrister say, no further questions. Next Jenny was called to the witness box. As she came through the door and walked towards the witness box Tamara felt an urge of sympathy and guilt towards her friend. How would she cope if Bill was found guilty? She would go to pieces completely and here she was wishing her friend's husband would be found guilty. She turned her attention back to Jenny who was now giving her version of what happened on the night. When she had finished Joshua Soars began his cross-examination.

'Mrs. Reed why did you run after your husband with an umbrella in such appalling weather conditions?'

'We are very close and I was frightened he would catch a cold if he was soaked to the skin.'

'I put it to you that you were probably worried about what he might do in the state of mind he was in. Perhaps you had quarrelled and he was angry?'

'I object to this line of questioning. It is pure conjecture regarding the state of my client's mind.'

The judge agreed. 'Please stick to the facts Mr. Soars, and not speculate as to the state of mind of this witness or the defendant.'

'Mrs. Reed, had you and your husband quarrelled that evening?'

'No, certainly not, we never quarrel.'

'Never! Not many of the people sitting in this courtroom in all honesty could admit to never having had a quarrel during their married life. How long have you been married Mrs. Reed?'

'I must object again Your Honour, these

questions are irrelevant.'

'Mr. Soars, where are these questions leading?'

'I was just trying to ascertain the state of mind of Bill Reed when he left the flat that night in such appalling weather conditions.'

'Continue Mr. Soars.'

'I'll repeat the question. How long have you been married Mrs. Reed?'

'Two years.'

'So one could say you were still in the honeymoon period and had not really got as far as seeing each other's bad points.'

'I suppose so.'

'When you reached the beach you say you saw your husband struggling with Peter Dumaresq.'

'Yes that's right.'

'And you called out, *stop Bill you're killing him.*'

'I don't remember.'

'But you did see your husband with his hands around Peter Dumaresq's throat.'

Jenny didn't answer and the judge had to request she answer the question. After a long pause she answered.

'Yes that's right.'

'And what did you deduce from the sight of your husband trying to throttle a young man?'

'I thought that he was trying to defend himself. He is such a kind gentle man that he must have been in fear of his life to do something like that.'

'No further questions.'

Tamara glanced across at Bill and saw the same smug look on his face she had seen so many times before and come to loathe. The judge was speaking and Tamara saw her chance to slip away from Marcus.

'We will adjourn till after lunch. Everyone back by two o'clock when we'll hear the prosecution's closing speech.'

'Marcus I must go to the ladies'. Look after Jenny for me please, I won't be long.'

She almost ran to catch up with DCs Woods and Harding.

'Please can I have a word?'

Don Woods turned around smiling.

'Yes of course.'

'I haven't got long, I have to get back to my husband and friend, but I think you ought to know I think Bill Reed is the Woodfield killer.'

'And what do you base that statement on? Have you any evidence to support your claim?'

'Yes, no, not really. Look, I can't talk here, my husband is coming.'

Don Woods handed her a card with his mobile phone number on.

'Well what do you think of that Harry? Didn't I tell you she wanted to talk?'

'Let's hope she has something concrete to base her claims on.'

After lunch the prosecution's barrister Joshua Soars began his closing speech, followed by Mr. Benjamin Walters' defence speech. Tamara had to admit he was really convincing in the arguments he put forward in Bill Reed's defence. Finally the judge gave his summing up before the jury retired to consider their verdict. Tamara wondered how long they would take to deliver their verdict. By four-fifteen they had still not reached a verdict and they were released by the judge to resume their deliberations the following morning.

The next morning the court resumed. After several hours the jury returned to the courtroom and the foreman was standing ready to read out the verdict. The court was deathly silent. Tamara could feel Jenny shaking in the seat next to her; she gripped her hand and whispered, 'Try not to worry Jen, I'm sure it will work out for the best.' Jenny gave her a strange look and she realised she should have phrased her words better.

The jury had reached a not guilty verdict. Tamara could not believe her ears. He had his hands around the boy's throat for God's sake, didn't they hear the evidence? Jenny began to sob, tears of relief ran down her face. Marcus was smiling and on his feet. Only Tamara was not pleased and this didn't go unnoticed by the two police officers.

'I am so grateful to the jury for recognising the truth I'll never say anything against the British justice system again,' sobbed Jenny.

Tamara sat fuming, thinking, I could say a few words about the judicial system.

'I'm going to take you all out for a meal to celebrate.'

'Thank you Marcus, but the meal should be on us, I don't know how we are ever going to repay you for all the kindness you have shown us both.'

'Say no more about it. Now where shall we go for this meal? Somewhere posh I think.'

16

A few days later Tamara contacted DC. Woods asking him to meet her in Southampton as she did not want to be seen in Woodfield talking to him. She told Marcus she was doing some early Christmas shopping in Southampton and didn't want him to come with her as she hoped to buy his Christmas present. As Tamara approached the meeting place Don Woods was already waiting for her.

'Well now Mrs. Wheeler-Osman, what's all this about Bill Reed then? I'm intrigued. What makes you suspect he's the Woodfield killer?'

'I've never liked the man.'

'That's no reason to make a serious accusation against him. Have you any proof to back up your statement?'

Tamara began to tell him everything, from the bad dreams of the lady in a white suit that both she and the Chinese girl had, and how he always seemed to be out when the murders took place. Finally she mentioned the evening in the park when the last girl was murdered. He listened carefully to all she had said; his face was expressionless. So she didn't know if he took her seriously or not. Perhaps he thought her a crank.

'You say you broached the subject with your husband and he didn't believe you.'

'Yes, he said I was imagining things and subconsciously, with all these horrific murders going on in Woodfield and the death threats I had received in the past, I'd put two and two together and came up with the person I disliked the most, Bill Reed. It's not true, I feel so sure he's responsible for all those poor girls' deaths. I've tried to like him for the sake of Jenny, my dearest friend, whom I care about so much, but I can't, I just can't. There's something about him that doesn't ring true. Please help me, please tell me you believe me and I'm not going crazy.'

'Yes, I do believe you Mrs. Wheeler-Osman, but first we need proof. We can't just go and arrest him on your say-so, as yet you have given me no proof of what you are claiming.'

'But in our back garden under the rose bushes lies the truth. I'm sure Jane Birch is buried there. You must come and dig up our back garden.'

'What do you think your husband would say about that?'

'Oh, I don't know, I'll cross that bridge

when I come to it.'

'It's not that easy. I'll need a warrant to search the garden and they are not granted easily, especially on the say-so of a member of the public who thinks there may be a body buried there. And besides, to all intents and purposes the case is closed and the killer has been found.'

'Do you honestly believe that a policeman killed all those girls and raped the others?'

'No, no I don't. Leave it with me Mrs. Wheeler-Osman, I'll speak to my superiors and get back to you. In the meantime I'd be grateful if you kept this conversation to yourself.'

'Absolutely, I'm just so pleased someone at last is prepared to listen to me, I've felt so alone with no one to confide in.'

Tamara reached home feeling elated that at last Bill Reed may get what he deserved. Not realizing that she hadn't bought a single present.

'Well, you haven't done very well Tam.'

'What do you mean Marcus?'

'Where are all these Christmas presents you went into town to buy? You don't seem to have purchased a single one.'

'Oh I know. It was just bedlam in town, people were everywhere, it was a job to park. I'll just have to try again some other time.'

'But it can only get worse with the run-up to Christmas.'

Tamara was getting slightly irritated by his questioning.

'Well, I'll order from mail order catalogues or off the internet. Don't go on about it.'

'Alright, don't get so ratty. I've got a better idea. How about doing your Christmas shopping in Hong Kong? I've had a phone call while you were out, I'm needed over there right away. Now Bill's trial is over you needn't worry about Jenny anymore and I thought it would be a nice pre-Christmas break for you. You said how much you wanted to get away during the trial, well now's your chance.'

'When do you need to go?'

'The day after tomorrow.'

'So soon. Is it that urgent?'

'Yes darling, I'm afraid it is.'

'Look Marcus, I know I said I wanted to get away but there is so much to do here and I haven't even written a single card yet. You go without me and I'll have all the Christmas arrangements completed by the time you get back. How long will you be gone for?'

'Two weeks.'

She saw the hurt look on his face and felt slightly guilty, but she would make it up to him once all this was over. An ideal opportunity to have the garden dug up; if she was wrong he'd be none the wiser, and she would drop the subject and have to admit to herself that she was wrong.

A few days later with Marcus safely out of the way she rang DC Woods.

'Hello Mrs. Wheeler-Osman, I was about to contact you to have another chat.'

'You can come around this afternoon if you like, my husband is away for two weeks.'

Don Woods arrived soon after lunch. As soon as Tamara opened the door she could tell by his face that all was not well.

'I'm sorry Mrs. Wheeler-Osman, I have some bad news for you. My Superintendent won't hear of us digging up your back garden. As I thought, I was told in no uncertain terms that the case is closed. I'm afraid I can do nothing further.'

'But there must be something you can do? You can't give up just like that.' Tears sprang to her eyes, and she bit her lip hard to stop herself from crying. She felt once more she had been regarded as a fool, the police probably thought she was some neurotic woman with a big imagination. Then a thought suddenly struck her, her face immediately brightening.

'You believe me don't you?'

'Yes, but as I've already explained my hands are tied.'

'But what if you came to a friend's house and did some gardening for her while her husband was abroad, like removing the rose bushes from the bottom of her garden?'

He hesitated for a while, mulling over what she had just suggested to him.

'OK, you win. I have this weekend off, how about I start Saturday morning?'

'What about your wife or girlfriend, will she mind?'

'I have no one to answer to. I'm fancy free.'

'Even better, then no one will be any the wiser.'

She awoke early Saturday morning having hardly slept during the night. She drew back the bedroom curtains to a bright frosty morning and was grateful it wasn't raining although the rain would have left the ground softer. DC Woods arrived dead on ten o'clock as promised.

'Please come in DC Woods.'

'Call me Don please. If we are to make it an informal thing, friends working together in the garden, then you must call me Don and I'll call you Tamara.'

'I'd prefer Tam.'

'OK Tam, let's get to it.'

They had just started digging when Tamara

thought she heard the front doorbell.

'I think that was my doorbell. I'd better go and check as I'm not expecting anyone, it's probably someone collecting for something. I won't be long.'

Tamara froze with shock when she opened her front door and on the steps stood Jenny and Bill.

'Hello Tamara. Well, don't look so shocked, we've come to take you shopping then treat you to lunch. We thought you must be really lonely with Marcus away for two weeks, so no excuses — go and get changed and then we'll go.'

'It's really sweet of you Jenny but I have heaps to do. Would you be very upset if we made it another day, next week perhaps?'

'What have you got to do that's so important it can't wait? After all you have two weeks to do it in. The least you can do is ask us in for a few minutes I need to use your bathroom after the journey up from Bournemouth.'

'Yes of course, come in both of you.'

Tamara prayed Don Woods would stay in the garden and not come looking for her, but she was out of luck. Just as Jenny emerged from the bathroom he came in the back door.

'Tam, what's keeping you? I hope you're not leaving me to do all the hard work!'

'So this is why you're so reluctant to take up our offer of lunch. I'm really surprised at you Tamara. How could you? I just can't believe you would do such a thing to Marcus.'

'Please let me explain Jenny, it's not what you think. Don has come to help make a few changes in the garden and it's a birthday surprise for Marcus when he gets back.'

'Don, is it? Since when have the police extended their duties to landscape gardening? Really Tamara this all sounds very suspicious to me. I think it's time we left, Bill.'

'Jenny, wait, please . . .'

Tamara glanced at Bill who had been silent all through Jenny's outburst. He had gone quite pale, his hands were shaking and he had beads of sweat on his brow. He stuttered good-bye as Jenny flounced off to her car and slammed the door without another look at her friend on the doorstep.

'Well that's torn it. What do you think she'll do? She won't contact your husband will she?'

'No, she doesn't have his address in Hong Kong — she'll have to wait until he gets back to spill the beans, and by that time we'll have finished digging and know one way or the other if Jane Birch is buried there.'

'What if she's not? What will your husband say about me being here?'

'Oh, you worry too much. I'll cross that

bridge when I come to it. Now back to the digging.'

Bill was panic-stricken and didn't believe for one moment that Tamara had the policeman around for gardening purposes. He guessed they were onto him and were searching the back garden for Jane Birch's body. He had to act fast and get away as soon as possible.

'Why Bill you look really upset. I didn't think you liked Tamara very much. I thought you'd be pleased she's been caught out.'

'That's not strictly true: I've come to like Tamara since we called a truce. I know we started off on the wrong foot, but recently she's been a lot nicer to me and I saw another side to her which I've begun to like. But after this shock I'm beginning to think my first impression of her was right.'

'I'm just so upset Bill, I don't know what to do for the best. I couldn't look Marcus in the face again knowing her dirty little secret, and he's been so kind to us.'

Jenny pulled the car over and began to cry uncontrollably. Bill put his arm around her and tried to comfort her as best he could. At the same time he was making plans for his escape.

'Jenny darling, I was about to plan a surprise for you to celebrate my release. It

310

was going to be later on in the year but I think I'll bring it forward to now, and it may solve your dilemma over facing Marcus when he gets back.'

'How do you mean? What surprise?'

'Well, I was planning an around-the-world trip. We could stop off at any place that took your fancy for as long as you liked. So we'll get home and book some flights, and throw some clothes in a bag and we'll be away.'

'Oh Bill, you always cheer me up. But where will we go?'

'We'll go, my sweet, to whichever country has flights available. Won't it be exciting, being just free spirits wandering the world?'

'How long for?'

'Till we get fed up and want to come home or the money runs out, whichever comes first.'

'But what about Pepper? I couldn't possibly leave him indefinitely.'

'We'll take him with us. Haven't you heard of pet passports?'

'But why all the rush?'

'So we'll be out of the country before Marcus returns and you won't have to face him.'

Tamara and Don went back to the task of removing the rose bushes.

'If she's not buried here what happens

then? Will we have to dig up the rest of the garden? I don't think I can stand all this hard graft.'

Suddenly a dog from next door took a flying leap over the fence and landed at Don Woods's feet. He stopped digging to make a fuss of the dog.

'Hello fella, what do you want then? Perhaps he wants to help with the digging.'

'Mrs. Johnson must have her doggy friends visiting. I believe there was a quarrel one time and Bill was furious over their dog digging in the rose beds. He got quite nasty with Mrs. Johnson and wouldn't speak to her for ages.'

Both looked at one another, realization dawning on what Tamara had just said.

'Perhaps the dog can save us a lot of time by leading us to the spot where she is buried. Let him have a sniff around and see if he starts digging again. What's his name?'

'Um, Jason, I think.'

'Good boy Jason! Come on then, do some digging.'

The dog wagged his tail as if he understood and immediately started digging under the white rose bush. Mrs. Johnson rushed out apologizing and calling the dog to come back into her garden.

'It's alright Edith, please don't apologize, the dog is fine with us. Please go back to your visitors and don't worry about him.'

'But your beautiful roses, he'll ruin them, Mr. Reed was quite particular about the dog being in the garden.'

'Don't worry about Bill Reed. I live here now, not him, and the roses are being dug up anyway. The dog thinks he is helping us with the digging so it's alright, really it is. You go indoors and see to your visitors and we'll bring the dog back to you when we've finished here.'

'Well, if you're sure.' A worried-looking Mrs. Johnson went back into her house.

'Thank goodness for that! I don't want her upsetting herself when we find the body.'

'You are so sure she's here, aren't you, Tam?'

'Yes I am. Look at Jason, he's going mad digging away frantically.'

'Oh my God, I can see something white. Stay back Tam I think we've found her, keep hold of the dog.'

Don got on his mobile and called for backup. In minutes the police would be swarming all over the back garden. Tamara could imagine the headlines in the local paper: **Body Found in Garden at Marsden Road.** Marcus's words came flooding back to her. *Are you prepared for police swarming all over our house and garden and the press* camped out on our doorstep morning, noon and night? Within minutes the police arrived and a white tent was put up over the spot where the body was found. Tamara was deathly white and trembling, still holding onto the dog's collar. Don Woods put an arm around Tamara.

'Come on Tam, let's take Jason home and perhaps Mrs. Johnson will make you a nice cup of tea. Have you anyone who can put you up for a few days?'

'No, not really.'

Edith Johnson was more than happy to look after Tamara. After living next door to Bill Reed for years, Tamara was like a breath of fresh air; she was like the daughter she never had.

'I must ring Marcus and tell him what's happened. Can I use your phone Edith?'

'Of course you can dear. Take as long as you like and don't worry about the cost.'

'I'll reimburse you. I couldn't possibly let you pay for a call to Hong Kong.'

'Marcus it's me, something terrible has happened. A body has been found in our back garden. I think it's Jane Birch.'

'What! I'll be home on the next flight.'

'I'm alright Marcus, you don't have to rush home.'

Marcus had already cut her off and was

booking the next available flight home.

'What will happen now?'

'I think a warrant will be issued for the arrest of Bill Reed.'

'Did you see how shocked and upset he looked when he saw you here? He didn't believe a word about revamping the garden. He looked really scared.'

'It didn't go unnoticed Tam. I was watching him all the time you were talking to his wife.'

'I wonder where he is now.'

'Probably trying to do a runner. We'll have all the airports and seaports watched; he won't get far.'

'Poor Jenny, she'll have a terrible shock. She idolizes him.'

'I know. I'm wondering which way she'll go when she finds out. Will she turn him in or help him get away?'

Bill and Jenny were at their Juniper Road home. Bill was frantically packing and asking Jenny to hurry up.

'Why Bill? We've plenty of time to get to the airport before our flights.'

Eventually they were both in the car. 'Look, as we couldn't get the pet passport in time and we can't leave Pepper behind I think the best bet is to head for the West Country.'

'Do you mean you didn't book the flights after all?'

'No, we'll go later on when we get the dog's paperwork.'

'Well really Bill, I can't see what all the rush is about. Why didn't you tell me sooner that we wouldn't be catching a flight?'

'I tried to but you were too busy prattling on about what you were going to take. I couldn't get a word in edgeways.'

'Let's have some music on the radio.'

'No, don't put that thing on.' His words were too late. Jenny had already switched on in time to hear a programme interruption for a news bulletin.

'*This morning the body of a woman was discovered in the back garden of a house in Marsden Road. The body is believed to be that of Jane Birch, although the body has not yet been formally identified. Miss Birch came from the London area and went missing two years ago. She was last seen in the vicinity of Marsden Road.*'

'Oh my God Bill. It's your old house there're talking about isn't it? That's what that policeman was doing there this morning with Tamara.'

Bill was deathly silent.

'Don't just sit there Bill — say something, please. What does all this mean? You killed her, didn't you, and buried her in the back garden? Answer me!'

They had now reached the New Forest and Jenny had stopped the car in a quiet spot, not knowing what to do next.

'I'm not driving any further until I get some answers from you.'

'Jenny my love, my darling.' He reached out and tried to kiss her. When he saw the cold look in her eyes he began to cry.

'Please help me, I didn't mean to do it. It was an accident and I was frightened that no one would believe me and I would be locked up away from you forever.'

'How could it be an accident?'

'She started to make advances towards me.'

'She did what! Stop lying to me Bill. If you want any help from me I'll need to know the truth. I want to know everything that went on that afternoon and no more lies please.'

'She came to the house that afternoon at two o'clock as arranged. She was very full of herself, a bit flighty if you ask me. She reminded me of Tamara, the type of woman that thinks she knows it all. I showed her around and she said she liked the place but the price was too high and perhaps she could persuade me to drop it. I said no, I couldn't afford to as we were buying another place and if I lowered the price any more we wouldn't be able to buy our holiday apartment. She was a very determined woman and wouldn't take no for an answer. We were in the kitchen doorway and she started rubbing her body up against mine, saying she was sure she could change my mind and perhaps we should go upstairs again to the bedroom. I was so disgusted I pushed her away quite roughly and she banged her head on the wall. I thought at first she was just knocked out but then I saw blood coming from her head and I realized she was dead. It was no good calling an ambulance, it was too late for that. Then I panicked and didn't know what to do. With all the trouble going on in Woodfield I thought the police wouldn't believe my story that it was an accident and they would blame everything that was happening on me. I came home to you, I wanted to tell you everything but I was afraid you wouldn't believe me either and I would lose you forever. That night I went back and buried her in the garden. You do believe me don't you darling? All I've ever wanted from life was you and dear little Pepper.'

'What I don't understand, Bill, is why a smart woman like Jane Birch would make advances towards you. If as you say she was a smart businesswoman like Tamara, then why on earth would she fancy someone like you?'

'Oh, thanks very much. It shows what you

think of me. It's a wonder I'm worthy to be your husband.'

'Now don't be silly, Bill, you know what I mean. The smart types like her and Tamara usually go for the good-looking rich men like Marcus. You and I are just ordinary people and we don't live in their sort of world.'

'She wasn't interested in me as a man. I could see through her straight away. All she wanted was my house at a cheap price and she thought she could get it by using her charms, but she was sadly mistaken and her actions cost her her life.'

'OK, I believe you Bill.' Inwardly he sighed with relief, yet again she believed every word he said. What a woman; I can't go wrong with her at my side, she'll back me in every possible way.

'This is what we're going to do.' She started the car and headed west. 'First of all we must disguise ourselves or we'll be picked up by the police the first time we stop. I'll buy us each a wig. A blonde one for me and one for you with a lot of hair totally different from the style you have now. You'd best stay in the car out of sight while I do the shopping. We'll stop at the next town that has a department store.'

★　★　★

319

The police had asked Tamara if she had any recent photos of Bill and Jenny. She supplied them with a wedding photo which Jenny had given to her on their return from Scotland.

That evening on the television news a photo of the pair was flashed across the screen. Also a description of the car they may be driving and Jenny's number plate. The police made a statement asking anyone who knew of their whereabouts to contact them immediately. The next move by the police was to gain entry to the Reeds' house and start digging in their back garden. The patio was the first place to be dug up, they worked all through the evening and into the early hours. Eventually the body of Joanne Thorn was discovered. There were tears in some of the policemen's eyes as they discovered the body of this young girl. Many had been part of the team searching for her when she was first reported missing. They all knew the story of how she left her young child with a friend while she tried to earn some extra money selling cosmetics, and was never seen again.

★   ★   ★

Tamara and Marcus couldn't believe how Jenny was still standing by Bill and they were hiding out somewhere.

320

'How could she stand by him knowing he's a rapist and serial killer Marcus? I've known her all my life and I still don't understand her.'

'Perhaps he's holding her against her will and she has no other choice but to help him. I'm sure at the first opportunity she'll turn him in.'

'Oh my God, I never thought of that. Her life could be in danger and we're just sitting here unable to do a damn thing.'

'Look love, the police are doing everything they can. With all the resources they have these days they'll soon pick them up. I'm sure Jenny will be alright, she's a sensible woman. From what I know of her she'll play along with him till it's safe to escape, you mark my words. Soon she'll be back with us unharmed.'

'Do you really think so Marcus?'

'Yes I do. She is more use to him alive than dead. He can't drive for one thing and he won't get very far on foot.'

★ ★ ★

Jenny, wearing her blonde wig, had approached a car dealer to part-exchange her small car for a large estate. She thought how lucky it was that she had all her car documents in the glove compartment. Tamara had told her so many times not to leave them in the car, but she kept forgetting to take them out. She told the car dealer they were about to purchase two very large German Shepherd dogs and needed the space in the back to accommodate them. What she was really thinking was that it would serve as somewhere to sleep if they couldn't find anywhere else, and that was exactly what they ended up doing. Jenny felt it unsafe to book into a hotel or bed and breakfast, so that night they huddled together in the back of the car with Pepper between them. It was a cold November night and Jenny couldn't sleep with the cold, she had never been so cold in all her life. She lay there for hours thinking how in a very short time her whole life had changed. Here they were, hiding like criminals on Dartmoor, like the convicts did when they escaped from the prison. Soon it would be Christmas and where would they find themselves then? Would they still be sleeping rough? She had planned such a lovely Christmas, seeing Marcus and Tamara and exchanging presents. Suddenly she thought of Tamara. What must she be thinking? She never really liked Bill. She would definitely think the worst of him, and it was her fault that all this started by getting the police around and digging up the garden. I don't think I'll ever forgive her for ruining my life.

17

After eventually falling asleep Jenny was woken by the sound of dogs barking in the distance. It was daylight and she had no idea how long she had been asleep; it felt like only minutes but it must have been a few hours.

'Bill, wake up, I can hear dogs barking. Come on, please move. They may be police dogs searching for us.' Bill was awake in an instant.

'Calm down Jenny, the police don't know we're here. It's probably just ordinary people walking their dogs.'

'We're going to have to move anyway. We need to get some breakfast somewhere, perhaps one of those little inns on the moor when they open.'

'I don't think any of them will be open early at this time of year, it's out of season.'

'Then we'll have to go to the nearest town and get breakfast somewhere and some dog food for Pepper. We have our wigs so we should be quite safe, we are completely unrecognizable with them on. Let's have a look at the map and see where the nearest big town is. Exeter . . . that looks big enough for us to wander around unnoticed.'

It didn't take them long to get to Exeter: it was a lot closer than they imagined. After parking the car with Pepper left in it they set off to get some breakfast.

'I feel quite guilty leaving poor little Pepper in the car. Did you see the sad look on his face when we left him?'

'Yes, but we'll bring him back something as soon as we've eaten. Besides, if the police have issued a description of a couple with a Yorkie dog, it will only draw attention to us even though we look completely different from our usual selves.'

'Yes, I suppose you're right.'

After they'd eaten breakfast it was decided Bill would go back to the car and take Pepper for a walk around the car park while Jenny did the shopping she wanted. She was passing an electrical shop which had televisions in the window. She was stopped in her tracks by the sight of her house on the television screen. She pressed her face against the glass trying to hear what was being said but it was impossible. She dashed into the shop just in time to catch the words: '*The police have now confirmed that the body recovered in Juniper Road in the early hours of Sunday morning is that of Joanne Thorn the missing cosmetics agent.*' Jenny felt sick; she thought she was going to faint with shock. A worried shop assistant who had been watching Jenny rushed over with a chair.'

'Are you feeling alright madam?'

'Yes thank you, I'll be alright in a minute.'

'Would you like a glass of water?'

'Yes please.'

She was glad when the assistant left her for a minute while she gathered her thoughts. Realization had dawned on her that Bill must be the Woodfield killer after all. What possible excuse could he have for Joanne Thorn being buried in their garden? What should she do now? Mad thoughts began to fill her mind. Should she kill them all by crashing the car? Should she confront him? Oh God, please help me, I don't know what to do. Tamara was right all along but I wouldn't listen to her. I was just a sad old maid glad to have any man and grabbed the first one to show any interest in me. The shop assistant returned with the water which gave her an excuse to sit there a bit longer. She still couldn't make up her mind what to do. I have no alternative. I'll have to go to the nearest police station and hand myself in. I could be sent to prison for helping a murderer escape even if he is my husband. She put the water down and thanked the shop assistant for his help and asked directions to the nearest police station.

As she stepped outside the shop Bill was walking up the road with Pepper.

'What on earth are you doing in that television shop Jenny?'

'I was walking by on the way to the pet shop when I felt faint and a kind young man ran out of the shop and offered me a chair and a glass of water.'

'My poor love, are you alright now?'

'Yes thank you. I think it was lack of food and then eating such a large breakfast, it all got too much for me. Anyway what are you doing here? I thought we agreed you'd stay in the car park with Pepper until I got back.'

'I know but you were gone so long I was worried and thought I'd come and find you.'

Now what am I going to do? No chance of getting to the police station now. She felt quite miserable and began to cry.

'Jenny darling, whatever's the matter? Why are you crying? We're safe for the moment, we'll soon sort something out. Please don't cry, people are looking at us.'

They got back to the car and Jenny sobbed even louder.

'I can't go on like this Bill. Just drifting around with no definite plan and nowhere permanent to stay. Perhaps you should give yourself up.'

'What! . . . Jenny, how could you even

think such a thing? I told you I'd sort something out and I will.'

'Yes, but what? What can we possibly do? Our lives are ruined. We'll be running for the rest of our lives.'

'There's a caravan park nearby. I thought we could stay there for a few days till we've had time to form a plan.'

Jenny reluctantly agreed and thought, at least there should be a lot of people there, perhaps I can enlist someone's help. Then a thought struck her: it's out of season and probably all closed down. Another thought struck her for the first time. Is my life in danger?

The caravan park was closed for the winter season but the manager lived on site and agreed they could stay there temporarily. Bill asked if they could rent one of the holiday bungalows. The manager agreed, saying officially no, but unofficially yes, and a sum of money changed hands and everyone was happy with the arrangement. Except Jenny, who was beginning to feel scared; she was alone with a serial killer with no conceivable help for miles around.

'Well, isn't this cosy Jenny, just me, you and Pepper with no one else around for miles and miles.' She shivered slightly at his words, she noticed that his eyes were cold and sinister and had a look that she had never seen before. She felt her days were numbered if she didn't get away from him soon.

'Shall we put the television on Bill?' As soon as she said it she knew it was the wrong thing to say. The news would be all about the murder, and then he would know that she knew he was a killer and her life would be in grave danger. 'On second thoughts let's not bother after all, we'd be taking advantage of the manager's generosity using even more electric watching the TV.'

'I believe, Jennifer, the electricity was included in the price of our stay. A nice little Christmas bonus for our friend.'

'I'm tired and ready for bed. I'll get some clean sheets out of the airing cupboard and make up the bed.'

Bill paid her no more attention and switched the television on. My God, that's our house; police have found the body of Joanne Thorn under the patio. A good job Jenny is in bed, I don't know what I'd have done if she'd been sat here watching the news with me. She would become murder victim number six. A thought then struck him, perhaps she does know. She has been a bit subdued since I found her in the shop with a dozen TVs on and probably blaring out all the details of the police's latest find. There is no other way out of this: she'll have to go and I'll have to make a run for it alone. He calmly walked to the kitchen and took a knife from the drawer, slipped it in his pocket and walked towards the bedroom with murder once more on his mind. He called softly to her as she lay in bed petrified.

'Jenny . . . . Jenny darling, are you awake?'

'Yes Bill, what is it?'

'Did you see any news while you were in the television shop today?'

'No. I told you I was feeling unwell and nearly passed out. The last thing I'd be doing is looking at television.'

'Liar!' He slapped her hard across the face. Jenny began to cry.

'Shut up woman, before you get much worse.'

Pepper began to bark loudly, snarling, trying to protect his mistress.

'Shut up you stupid little mutt.' He kicked the dog violently across the room. Pepper lay cowering in the corner whimpering in pain.

'Please Bill, don't hurt my Pepper, all he's ever done is loved you. You know he means everything to me.'

'Well he means nothing to me, I could put an end to his miserable life just like that.' He clicked his fingers. 'In fact I've had enough of his whining on and on all the time, seeking attention. It's time I put a stop to it.'

'No . . . Bill don't! Please, for pity's sake don't hurt him any more.'

Bill paid no attention to her words and walked across the room and picked the little dog up by his throat and throttled him.

'Oh no! No . . . you've killed him. How could you be so cruel?'

It was at that point Jenny realized that her life was going to come to an end. She began to pray, please God, let it be over quickly, don't let me suffer. Bill walked towards the bed and took the knife from his pocket. He held it against her throat, she closed her eyes thinking, this is it. He ran the knife softly across her neck and she began to bleed. Blood began to trickle down onto her white nightdress.

'Would you like to hear about all the other women I've killed before you die Jennifer?'

'No. No I wouldn't, if you're going to kill me, get on with it and spare me the details.'

'But Jennifer, wouldn't you like to hang onto your life for another few hours? I would really like to tell you how it was for the others. Up to now I've had no one to share my pleasure with.'

'You're sick. Totally deranged. Tamara was right all along. I should have listened to her.'

'Ah yes, Tamara, the one who got away.'

'What do you mean, got away?'

'Well you see, she was always top of my list. I would like her to have been my number one murder, but unfortunately the opportunity never arose and I had to make do with threatening letters and phone calls.'

'You! . . . It was you all the time, sending those terrible letters and frightening her half to death.'

'Who else my sweet, it was good to see her running scared a few times. As for that useless piece of rubbish Gary Stevens he was no help to her at all. I was so disappointed when they split up. I could have got to her if he'd stayed around, and then Marcus came along. Good old Marcus who saved me from an attempted murder charge. I wonder if he'd finance my trial this time if I get caught. Still, we'll never know as I don't intend to get caught.'

'If you think you can get away with all that you've done you're a fool.'

'Don't call me a fool.' He slashed out with the knife and caught her arm. 'All this blood is going to waste in here. We should be outside letting you bleed all over God's Carpet, then everyone will know I struck again.'

He began stabbing her with the knife, he seemed to get pleasure from more blood spurting from her body. She must try and get away and get help before she bled to death.

'You know, I only had the pleasure of using the knife on two of the woman. Jane Birch, now she was the one I had real fun with, she made up for not getting Tamara. She was even better than Tamara. I knocked her unconscious and then had sex with her while she was still alive, then I began cutting her body into pieces. Do you want to know which was the best bit?'

'No, stop! Stop, please stop.' Jenny put her hands over her ears to drown out the sound of his voice droning on about torture and rape. He slapped her hard and stabbed her again with the knife just below the neck. She was feeling weak and sick and wondered how long it was going to go on for.

'The other one I used the knife on was . . . Now, let me see, what was her name? Ah yes, I remember. Melanie Taylor. I managed to cut her throat only very slightly to begin with then some blasted dog walkers turned up and I couldn't finish the job. How I hate dogs, and their owners I hate even more.'

'Is there anyone you love Bill? I thought you truly loved me once. Did you ever have any feeling for me at all?'

'No, none. I used you to add a bit of respectability to my life.' He took pleasure at

332

the hurt look in her eyes. She was going to die never having been truly loved by any man. If she made a rush at him then surely he would stab her and finish her off, but he was too quick for her; it was as if he read her mind. He just pushed her back on the bed and laughed in her face.

'Not so fast, we haven't finished yet. Your time hasn't come. You must be patient my dear and indulge me a little longer. Now where were we? I know, let's start at the very beginning with the very first murder I committed. Well actually it wasn't murder because she died of natural causes. I felt thoroughly cheated over that one. Her name was Alice Jones, she was way before your time. She was small, petite like a little butterfly and oh so delicate, she seemed to just fade away in my arms. Then there was Jodie Bowden, now she was a real bonus. It wiped that smug look off Gary Stevens' face. He who knew it all, but he wasn't so clever when the police came and arrested him. I nearly died laughing, I could hardly contain myself. It even had repercussions on the stuck-up Tamara; she must have been on the police list of suspects for a while. The woman scorned, it was priceless. Come on Jenny, you can't die yet, you have to hear about my last two victims.'

Jenny was beginning to slowly slip away. She felt a coldness that was beginning to spread throughout her body and the room was growing dimmer. Bill threw a glass of cold water over her face.

'I'm dying, let me go now Bill, please.' He threw a blanket over her and laughed callously.

'Keep warm for a little bit longer, you simply must hear about Jessica Hale. What a little hellcat she was, arguing with her boyfriend, and using foul language. She put me in mind of Kendra Rickman. Unfortunately I haven't got time to tell you about all the rapes. Correction, you haven't got time before you join your beloved mother up above.'

He gave out another shrill laugh, making her shiver at the sound of it and feel even colder than she already was. His cruelty was beyond belief. He gave her another stab with the knife and she gave a small moan of pain.

'That's good, you're still with me for the last murdered girl Emma Dewey. That interfering copper tried to stop me but fell down dead on the grass with a heart attack, and then consequently was blamed for all the murders. I couldn't believe my luck, what a bungling lot of fools the police are.'

'Remember names.' Jenny's voice was just above a whisper.

'What was that Jenny? How did I remember all the names? As you well know I have a very good memory and as soon as the bodies were identified I used to sit and remember every little detail about them. I'd go over and over again in my mind, their names, faces and what they were wearing.' He gave a sigh and looked at Jenny. 'Why Jenny' I think you've left me at last. Death was the only way you would ever leave me. Till death us do part as we vowed on our wedding day. I'm sorry I won't be able to lay a wreath on your grave, but here take — your smelly little mutt and enjoy the afterlife together.'

He picked up the dead dog and placed him on her stomach. A loud banging on the door brought him back to reality. His clothes were covered in blood, so he quickly took them off and put on a dressing gown. The banging on the door continued, whoever it was wasn't going to go away.

'All right, all right, I'm coming.' He opened the door to Hank the site manager.

'You've got to get out of here and now. My governor will be here first thing in the morning and if he sees I've let you have one of the bungalows I'm done for.'

'Look here, we can't go tonight, it's too late.'

'It's only ten o'clock.'

'My wife isn't at all well and she has taken one of her sleeping pills, and nothing on earth will wake her once she's gone off to sleep.' He smiled to himself and thought, nothing will ever wake her again. 'What time is your boss due here tomorrow?'

'He'll be here nine o'clock sharp, he's one of those annoying people who's never late for anything.'

'I promise you we'll be gone by eight o'clock at the latest. How does that suit you?'

'Fine. Are you sure you'll be away by that time?'

'Yes, of course. You have my word.'

Bill closed the door and immediately made plans to leave. He collected all the cash they had between them, dressed in warm clothing and set off on foot.

Trevor Passell the site owner arrived the next day and burst into the office red and angry.

'What the hell do you think you're playing at Hank? Ripping me off again.'

'I don't know what you mean Mr. Passell.'

'As you know, from the top of the hill you can see all the bungalows and caravans and outside one of the bungalows is an estate car. What the hell is it doing there if you haven't let one of the bungalows again? I told you last time that if you did it again you were out.

336

Now get out, you're fired.'

'But Mr. Passell, I know nothing about anyone in the bungalows. If there is someone there they must be squatting. It could be someone dumped a car there.'

'How the hell did they get on site in a car without your knowledge?'

'Probably during the night when I was soundo.'

'And I suppose the reason you were soundo was because you'd been down the pub all evening and had a skinfull.'

'I don't know how you could think such a thing Mr. Passell.'

'Quite easily. Now get the keys and we'll check out what's going on, and if I find you've been lying to me, that's it — you're out.'

They approached the bungalow which was deathly quiet. Hank prayed they weren't there, then the car would appear to have been dumped as he had said. Hank put the key in the door and unlocked it.

'Hello . . . Anyone in there?' He sighed with relief when there was no answer. 'See, I told you no one was here. I bet one of the locals stole that car and dumped it here.' He turned to go.

'Just a minute, not so fast. We'd better check over the place in case they've been on a wrecking spree. I'll check the bedrooms, you check the kitchen and bathroom and make sure everything is in order.'

'Oh Christ, what the hell has been going on in here? Hank .... . Call the police for Christ's sake, some woman's been murdered.'

Hank called the police and within ten minutes they were cordoning off the area and asking questions. Hank was in two minds whether to come clean or to deny all knowledge of the couple he'd let the bungalow to. The police questioned the two men separately. The police officer asked Mr. Passell what made him visit the site on this particular morning.

'Well officer, it's my manager you see. I can't trust him — he lets the bungalows out in winter and pockets the money. I'd get rid of him if I could but nobody wants the job in winter, it's so lonely up here this time of year. Now summertime that's a different matter altogether, people are begging me for jobs. Everyone wants to be here in summer but not in winter, so you see I'm left to the mercy of that useless article outside. I have no other choice; I can't afford the site to be left unguarded, so Hank is better than no one at all.'

'Do you think he's capable of murder?'

'No, not him. Petty theft maybe but not murder.'

'What if the woman refused to pay him? Perhaps he got angry and killed her.'

'No, I don't think so. If I know Hank he would have demanded payment upfront or he wouldn't have given her the key.'

The police officer questioning Hank suspected he wasn't telling all he knew.

'You say you'd never seen the woman before you walked into the bungalow with your boss.'

'Yes that's right.'

'Then why are you so jumpy?'

'I'm not.'

'I say you are. You're hiding something and if you're not careful you'll be up on a murder charge.'

This last statement panicked Hank. Better to be sacked than charged with murder.

'Alright, I'll tell you what I know. This geezer and his woman came and asked if they could rent one of the bungalows for a few days. At first I said no and then I felt sorry for them. The woman looked so down as if she was upset about something, so I risked my job and gave in.'

'So it was pity that drove you to help this couple.'

'Yes that's right.'

'So money wasn't the motivation?'

Hank didn't bother to answer the last sarcastic comment.

Dog handlers were called in to track down the missing man. The police were confident that he wouldn't get far on foot and he would soon be apprehended. They couldn't understand why he didn't take the car but concluded he probably couldn't drive as the site manager said the woman was driving when they arrived.

★   ★   ★

Tamara was surprised to see DC Don Woods on Edith Johnson's doorstep.

'Can I come in Tam? I wasn't sure if you would still be here with Mrs. Johnson or if you'd moved somewhere else.'

'No, we haven't anywhere else to go except a hotel and Edith wouldn't hear of it, she insisted we stay with her for as long as we need to. Have you any news for me? Have you caught up with them yet?'

'Yes, we have — with Jenny, that is.'

'Oh thank God! How is she? Is she alright?'

'No Tam, I'm afraid she isn't. I have some really bad news. Your friend was found murdered at a caravan site in Devon this morning, but there was no sign of her husband Bill Reed. I wanted to tell you myself before you heard the news on television.'

'Oh no . . . no . . . no . . . not Jenny. He's killed Jenny. My lovely friend Jenny.' She began to scream and cry hysterically. Marcus and

Mrs. Johnson rushed into the room. 'I should have taken better care of her, it's all my fault.'

'Now Tam, there was nothing you could have done to save her. She made the choice herself in marrying him, and nothing you could have said would have dissuaded her, she was a very determined woman.'

'Yes, and look where it got her, Marcus.'

'I'd better leave you to it.'

'I'll see you out. Do you think they'll catch him soon?'

'Yes, he won't get far on foot. It's only a matter of time before he's picked up.'

'I'd better get back to my wife.'

'It may be best if you call a doctor to give her a sedative, she's had a really bad shock. I didn't realize they were such close friends, they are like chalk and cheese. Has your wife known her long?'

'Yes, they go back a long way — to school days in fact. Jenny was always being bullied at school because she was quite plain and Tam always jumped in and defended her.'

'We'll keep you informed of the situation as it progresses. Bye for now.'

★ ★ ★

The police found Bill Reed in some woodland close to the caravan park. He hadn't got very far, as they had predicted. He was protesting his innocence, saying he had nothing to do with his wife's death, he had gone for a walk and when he returned he found her dead. He was so upset and scared he didn't know what to do so he ran away to find help. He thought the murderer must have been Hank the site manager so he couldn't ask him for help as he might meet the same fate as his wife. He thought it best to head for the woods and seek help from the houses in the next village.

He was taken to the nearest police station for questioning and later charged with the murder of his wife Jennifer Reed. While in custody he asked if he could make a phone call to Marcus Wheeler-Osman regarding his legal representation. Marcus was very shocked when he received the call from Bill protesting his innocence and asking for his help in securing the services of Benjamin Walters to defend him again.

'No Bill, I'm afraid you're on your own this time. You must make your own arrangements for your defence, I won't make the same mistake twice.'

'What do you mean? I'm innocent, you must help me. I suppose your bitch of a wife Tamara put you up to this, she's never liked me.'

Marcus slammed the phone down, outraged at the cheek of the man.

18

Tamara was in a state of total shock and disbelief, her worst nightmares and fears had come true. Her dear friend of over forty years was killed at the hands of that fiend. It was the most terrible thing she had ever experienced and nothing would ever be as terrible as this.

'Tam, how about if we go back to Hong Kong for a while? I have unfinished business there.'

'You go if you like. I'm staying here till after the trial is over.'

'Look, nothing will happen before Christmas, I don't expect we'll even know when the trial will be until well into the New Year. The police said they'd keep us informed and I'm sure they will.'

'No, I'm not going anywhere.'

'Tam, we can't impose on Mrs. Johnson any longer. We have to go somewhere so it might as well be with people we know and care about. Lee and Mei will be only too happy to have us stay with them through Christmas and the New Year. You could experience a real Chinese New Year, you'll love it. Please Tam, say yes.' She remained silent. Marcus tried again.

'Look, I'll ring the police and find out when we're likely to hear the trial date. I'm pretty sure it won't be this side of Christmas. I've had a word with Mrs. Johnson and she's planned to go and stay with friends for Christmas so we can hardly remain in her house while she's gone. The police won't release our house to us for a while so we won't be able to go back home either.' This last statement released another outburst from Tamara.

'Home! How dare you call that place our home. I'll never set foot inside that house of death ever again.'

'But what about all your clothes?'

'I don't want them, you can burn them all, I'll buy new ones. I'll never touch anything from that house ever again. The place should be torched. How we were ever talked into buying that place I'll never know.'

Marcus sighed and went away to ring the police. He came back confirming what he had already said, there would be no trial date set this side of Christmas.

'You know, if we went to Hong Kong you could put Rosie's mind at rest about her nightmares and the lady dressed in white that she saw. You could tell her how right she was

344

and that no one listened to you either. She got in real trouble with her parents over what she was saying, Lee was very angry with her for a long time.'

Marcus sat down in despair; he just didn't know what else to say or do.

'Alright then, we'll go. You win, you're right.'

'I'm sure it's the right decision Tam, and when we get back you'll feel a lot stronger to face the trial.'

The Changs were pleased to have Marcus and Tamara spend Christmas with them and Tamara wasted no time in telling the family all that had happened. Rosie was delighted that she had been right all along, although she said she felt a great sadness for the lady in white and the terrible loss her family must be feeling. When Tamara was alone with Rosie she started asking questions about her psychic powers.

'Do you get into very much trouble with your parents about your wonderful gift?'

'No, not really, it was just over what I saw in your house that my father was cross with me. He said that I'd made the family look very ungrateful to you and Marcus, after the kindness you had shown us.'

'Have you had any other premonitions since you were in England?'

345

'A few but nothing as important as the lady in white at your house. She was so pretty and she was only asking to be found, but no one was listening to her except you and me. What I would really like to do — but my father won't hear of it — is to help the police solve crimes. He said I must go to university like my sisters and study a useful profession.'

'Have you any idea what you would like to do, Rosie?'

'No I haven't, but it would probably be something to do with the law. Then I would be able to experience my psychic feelings about people and places and no one would be any the wiser. My gift would be able to help me tell the difference between the good and bad people.'

Tamara smiled and thought, what a very intelligent child Rosie is. At sixteen she had a good grip on reality in spite of her gift, and seemed to know what she wanted from life.

The Christmas and New Year holiday went by quickly and now it was time to return home to the horror that they had left behind.

'Where will we stay when we get back Marcus? I think you're right, we can't keep imposing on Edith's hospitality any longer and besides I want to get as far away from Marsden Road as possible. Staying next door is not helping me in any way whatsoever.'

'I think we'll probably rent an apartment in Ocean Village in Southampton or anywhere else that's available. We'll just have to see. Don't worry about it now, just try and get some rest. We have another three hours before the plane lands.'

'Do you think the police will have released Jenny's body yet?'

'I don't know darling, we'll just have to wait and see.'

As soon as they had reached Southampton Marcus booked them into a hotel for the night. The next morning he contacted the police to see how things were progressing. He learned that the trial date was set for September and Jenny's body was due to be released shortly.

'Do you know, Tam, if Jenny wanted to be buried or cremated?'

'Buried I think, she talked of having a plot so her and Bill could be buried together; she never wanted to be parted from him, not even in death, but that's not going to happen now. If he died tomorrow I wouldn't let him within a mile of where she was buried. Perhaps we ought to have her cremated.'

'Not if she asked to be buried, Tam. Besides, if the police wanted to know anything else then cremation is pretty final.'

'The police are not going to keep digging

Jenny up just because they haven't done their job properly in the first place. I won't have it.' Tam began to sob uncontrollably. Marcus felt so helpless, all he could do was put his arms around her and try to comfort her as best he could. After a few minutes she stopped crying, then another upsetting thought struck her and she started to cry again.

'Marcus, I've just had a terrible thought, Jenny didn't really have any friends or relatives, we're the only ones who really cared about her. We'll be the only people at her funeral, that's so sad.'

Tamara couldn't have been more wrong. The whole of Juniper Road attended, even the Rickman family, who would never pass up a chance for free food or drink, or getting their faces on television. The police were also in attendance as well as the media. Tamara began to feel better in the knowledge that people did care enough about her friend to come to her funeral.

★ ★ ★

The date of the trial was scheduled for the beginning of September. Tamara could barely remember what she had done during the long nine months' wait for the trial. She had given up work and just drifted from day to day with

348

no conception of time or what day it was. On the first day of the trial she was in a terrible state. Marcus had begged her not to attend or put herself through the trauma of it all. He told her they would know all the details in the press but she insisted on being there from start to finish.

Initially Bill was charged with three counts of rape and six murders, but after legal argument the judge, Mr. Justice Tobutt, directed that there was insufficient evidence to suggest that he had anything to do with the rape of Tracey Sellwood in Moreton Park as he was being questioned by the police at the time the rape took place, so a formal not guilty verdict was entered against the count. This would be kept on police files as an unsolved case. The count regarding the first girl to die in Drayton Park, Alice Jones, was amended to rape and manslaughter as she had died of a heart attack brought on by the fear of what was happening to her. Bill Reed pleaded not guilty to all counts and had no objection to any of the jurors.

Tamara glanced at the jury, there were seven men and five women of mixed ages. Marcus commented they were a good mix of people and the judge was a top man not noted for his leniency in such serious cases.

'The barristers look so young Marcus.'

'Don't let that fool you Tam, they know what's what. Perhaps it's us getting old.' He squeezed her hand and smiled at her, but she didn't smile back.

'Which barrister is which?'

'The one nearest to us is for the prosecution and the one nearest the jury is the defence barrister.'

'Well at least the prosecution barrister looks the more dominant of the two. Bill's barrister looks like she's not long out of school.'

'I believe she's very good, her father is a High Court Judge, a very prominent man by all accounts.'

Kendra Rickman was first in the witness box to give her account of the night she was raped. She gave her evidence from behind screens and was not visible to the defendant or the public in the gallery. Tamara noticed that one of the older lady jurors was staring at the witness box with a look of disapproval on her face. Tamara thought Kendra was doing nothing to help the case against Bill, in fact she was probably making things worse. The defence barrister was on her feet to cross-examine Kendra.

'Did you recognize the man that attacked you, Miss Rickman?'

'No, but I reckon it was Bill Reed.' She was

warned by the judge to only answer the questions put to her.

'Miss Rickman, you failed to identify Mr. Reed at the time of the attack or any subsequent time since.'

'Well, he was wearing dark clothes and a balaclava so how could I, but I know the rapist was the same height as him.'

'Miss Rickman, if we arrested all men the same height as Mr. Reed the courts would be bursting at the seams. Was there ever animosity between you or your family and the Reeds?'

'What do you mean?'

'Was there ever any upset or quarrels between your family and the Reeds?'

'Well, he was always looking up at our bedroom window and watching me and my sister undress. One day my sister's boyfriend nearly smacked him in the mouth.'

'Did you ever think of closing your curtains when you undress?'

'No, why should we? Just because he's a dirty old perv who likes watching girls undress. It's his problem not ours.'

A ripple of laughter went around the courtroom. The judge called for silence or he would clear the courtroom.

'What did your parents think of the Reed family?'

351

Prosecution counsel Mr. Carpenter was on his feet in a flash.

'My lord, this question cannot be answered by the witness. My learned friend should put the question to the witness's parents.'

'Yes, I agree. Please keep to the questions in hand, Miss Campbell.'

'Did your family ever have any trouble from the Reed family?'

'No, we didn't have nothing to do with them. Mum thought she must have been really desperate to marry him, like it was her last chance. We all thought he was a bit of a creepy perv, always out after dark with their dog.'

'No further questions my lord.'

Bill Reed sat in the dock with a smug look on his face knowing that Kendra Rickman's evidence had done nothing to help the prosecution case against him. He even looked across at Tamara with a smirk on his face. She looked quickly at the jury and hoped that some of them might have noticed, especially the older lady juror, but unfortunately she was busy making notes and didn't even look in his direction.

'That wasn't very good, was it, Marcus.'

'No, but don't worry, she's only the first witness. I don't expect anyone else could be as bad as her.'

'Did you want to say anything further, Mr. Carpenter, before I dismiss this witness?'

'Yes my lord. Now Kendra, you said Mr. Reed was always out at night with the dog. Was he always alone or was Mrs. Reed ever with him when he walked the dog?'

'No, she was never with him. He was always on his own after dark, you'd only see her with the dog in the daytime.'

'Apart from the rapist's height being the same as Mr. Reed, did you notice anything else about him?'

'Yes, he smelt funny.'

'What do you mean, funny?'

'He smelt of a horrible dog smell.'

'No further questions. Thank you Kendra, that will be all.'

Due to the trauma of the incident the next witness was allowed to give her evidence via the TV link to the courtroom. Melanie Taylor was the exact opposite of Kendra Rickman: she was articulate and well spoken. She was dressed in a white blouse, dark suit and wore a scarf around her neck to hide the scar left from her throat wound. She told of the night she was attacked as she was walking through the park on the way to her friend's house.

'It had been raining earlier in the evening and I was hurrying before it started again. Suddenly I was grabbed from behind and dragged into the bushes by a man dressed in black. All I could see was two dark coloured eyes staring at me from the slits in his balaclava. He told me to be quiet or he would kill me. He held a knife to my throat, I was terrified. I was frantic to get away from him so I said the grass was wet and could we go somewhere else — I was hoping I could break free from him and make a run for it.'

Prosecuting counsel Joseph Carpenter asked for his response to her request.

'He said, shut up, that's the least of your worries, you'll be lying on God's carpet.'

'What happened next?'

'He began tearing at my clothes, I struggled and tried to scream then he cut my throat, blood was spurting everywhere. I was feeling very weak and then he raped me. I thought I was dying and then I heard dogs barking in the distance and he ran off. The people walking their dogs helped me; I owe my life to them.'

'Did you notice anything else about the rapist?'

'There was a funny sort of smell. I wasn't sure whether it came from the grass or his clothes. Sometimes when you walk through the park there is a terrible smell of dogs' pee — you can only smell it at certain times, usually when the weather is hot or very wet.'

'Thank you Melanie, there will be further questions for you to answer.'

Julia Campbell began her cross-examination via the TV link.

'Miss Taylor, you say the smell of dog's urine was very strong on the night you were attacked, and you couldn't tell if it came from the attacker or the grass you were rolling about on.'

'Yes, that's right.'

'So in fact your attacker may not have been a dog owner at all.'

'I suppose so.'

'No further questions.'

Mr. Justice Tobutt addressed Melanie Taylor, explaining that she could leave the court. She did not want to stay in the court building a minute longer than she had to, and besides, her parents were in the public gallery and would keep her informed of the proceedings.

Police statements were read out from the three dog walkers John and Jacky Curtis and David Kernan. They all said that Mrs. Curtis had stayed with Melanie Taylor while John Curtis and David Kernan gave chase to the rapist, unfortunately losing him in a nearby housing estate. They didn't get close enough to give any sort of description of the attacker.

The next count was of rape and the

attempted murder of Alice Jones. The prosecution had no evidence or witnesses to call in the case of Alice Jones and the defence barrister concluded there was no case to answer. Her client could not remember what he was doing on a particular day four years ago and probably no one in the court could remember what they were doing either.

'She's very good Marcus, you were right, looks are deceiving. If she comes from a family of lawyers no wonder she's doing so well, the law has been bred into her. You don't think she could get him off do you?'

'I don't know, strange verdicts have come out of the jury room in the past and we have a long way to go yet, but I think the most damning piece of evidence is Jenny's murder. I think that will probably clinch it.'

On the third day of the trial the first witness to be called was the taxi driver who dropped Jane Birch off at the corner of Marsden Road. He was asked by the defence if he could have been mistaken about the identity of his passenger. He was quite emphatic that the woman in his taxi was Jane Birch and not anyone else. He explained that she wore a gold chain around her neck. This was confirmed by the police to be on the body of the woman found in Marsden Road and had not been disclosed to the public at the time of the discovery of the body.

Next to the witness box was DC Don Woods. He was asked to read out the statement he made on the day the body of Jane Birch was dug up from the garden in Marsden Road.

'*I was asked by the occupant of 10 Marsden Road, a Mrs. Wheeler-Osman to help her dig up the rose bushes at the bottom of her garden as she believed the body of Jane Birch was buried there. She thought her friend's husband Mr. William Reed had murdered her.*'

Mr. Justice Tobutt asked, 'On what basis did she make her accusation?'

'She said she had dreamed of a lady in a white suit who had been buried at the bottom of her garden, and she had suspected Bill Reed was the Woodfield murderer for a long time but no one would believe her, not even her husband.

'Would you normally dig up a member of the public's back garden on the basis of a dream?'

'No, my lord, but I also had my own suspicions about Bill Reed.'

'Carry on reading your statement DC Woods.'

'*I applied for permission to dig up her back garden and permission was denied.*'

'So you went ahead anyway.'

'No, I mean yes, my lord. I conveyed to Mrs. Wheeler-Osman that the police were unable to help her as the case was now closed and they saw no reason to reopen it.'

'Please continue.'

'*Mrs. Wheeler-Osman asked if I could help her out as a friend, not as a policeman, in digging up the back garden. I agreed as I could see how distraught she was and she had been having nightmares since moving in, I thought if there was no body then I would have at least put her mind at rest. The first thing I dug up was a piece of white material and the remains of an arm, so I immediately called for assistance.*'

DC Woods then went on to outline the discovery of the next body by the police, that of Joanne Thorn.

'After the discovery of Jane Birch the police then proceeded to Juniper Road to question Mr. William Reed. On arriving at the property they discovered that Mr. and Mrs. Reed seemed to have left in rather a hurry. Dishes were left in the sink and food still on the table, and mail unopened on a hall table. After several hours of digging the body of Joanne Thorn was found buried under a newly laid patio in the Reeds back garden. Also recovered was some bloodstained clothing hidden under floorboards in a shed. An alert to all forces was put out for the arrest of William Reed, who was later apprehended at a caravan site just outside Exeter in Devon.'

The next witness to be called was Roy Rickman. Prosecution counsel Joseph Carpenter asked him to give an account of the last afternoon Joanne Thorn was seen alive, the day he helped Bill Reed with his patio.

'Well, I wasn't doing anything that day and Bill Reed asked me to give him a hand with his patio, so I agreed to help him out. I'm always willing to help a neighbour at anytime.'

'I doubt that very much, not without a backhander,' Tamara whispered to Marcus.

'Did you see Joanne Thorn during the lunchtime of that day?'

'Yeah. She called at Bill Reed's house to collect a make-up catalogue. He said, I'll be back in a minute, and went to get the catalogue for her.'

'Did she go with him or wait in the road outside your house?'

'She went with him.'

'Approximately how long was he gone?'

'I dunno, about half an hour, I s'pose.'

'What were you doing while waiting for Bill Reed to come back?'

'I had a can of beer with the lorry driver that delivered the paving slabs for the patio.'

'Did Bill Reed seem flustered at all when he came back?'

'A little bit. I says, you alright Bill? You look a bit hot, and he says, yes, I've just been burying some rubbish in the hole before we pour the concrete.'

'Did you find that a little strange — that someone was burying rubbish under the footings of a patio?'

'Nope, I never give it another thought.'

'Did you see Joanne Thorn leave Bill Reed's house on that afternoon?'

'Nope, I only sees her go in.'

'No further questions.'

Julia Campbell was ready to cross-examine Roy Rickman.

'You say you had one can of beer with the lorry driver and you think the time it took to drink a can of beer could have been up to half an hour.'

'Yeah.'

'Come now Mr. Rickman, you're a man of the world and used to handling a drink or two. I put it to you that you and the lorry driver downed a can of beer in about five minutes, ten at the most.'

Roy Rickman shrugged his shoulders. 'Dunno. I wasn't timing us.'

'And I would conclude that Bill Reed would not have had time to kill Joanne Thorn in the time it took you both to drink a can of beer, would he?'

'Dunno.'

Next witness called was Sarah Cawte, a friend of Joanne Thorn.

'Sarah, I know this is very distressing for you, but take your time and if you need a break we can stop.' The judge nodded his approval to Joseph Carpenter.

'Can you tell the court what happened on the last day you saw Joanne Thorn?'

'Yes, she said she had to collect one more of her cosmetic catalogues from Juniper Road.'

'Did she say which house she had to collect the catalogue from?'

'Yes the Reeds' house. She said Mrs. Reed was really nice but she thought Mr. Reed was a nasty piece of work and she wouldn't like to meet him on a dark night.'

'Did she say why she came to this conclusion?'

'Yes. She said every time he came to the door he stared at her in a funny way, almost as if he was undressing her. She always felt a little scared when he was around without Mrs. Reed.'

'When she didn't arrive home were you worried?'

361

'Yes, Jo always kept her word. If she said she wouldn't be gone long then she wouldn't. Besides, she loved her little girl so much she would never leave her for very long.'

Sarah Cawte began to cry. There were tears in the eyes of quite a few of the jurors as well as Tamara.

'Are you alright Tam? We can go outside for a bit if you want?'

'No I'm alright.' She dabbed at her eyes and cleared her throat. 'I cannot believe how much unhappiness he has caused to so many people, no punishment will ever be enough for what he's done.'

Joseph Carpenter had no further questions and Julie Campbell was ready to cross-examine. The judge asked Sarah if she could continue or if she needed a break; she said she would like to continue.

'Miss Cawte — it is Miss, not Mrs.?' Sarah nodded her agreement. 'Are you absolutely certain that Joanne Thorn said she felt uneasy in the presence of Mr. Reed? Could she not have referred to one of her other customers? I would imagine she delivered to a great many people.'

'Yes she did, she had a really large area she covered. I helped her sometimes because she had so many deliveries to make, but she definitely meant Mr. Reed.'

'How can you be so sure she meant him?'

'Because I was helping her one day and we were in Juniper Road. She said, I've got to deliver to the Reed's house next. I hope it's Mrs. Reed that answers the door, he's really creepy and frightens me. I waited by the gate for her to make sure she was alright.'

'Did she mention Mr. Reed at any other time or was that just a one-off?'

'No, she mentioned him every time she had to make a delivery to their house because she hated going there so much.'

'No further questions.'

The judge said the case would now be adjourned until Monday morning at 10.30 am. He warned the jurors not to discuss any of the details with their families or other jurors.

'Come on Tam, let's get back to the hotel, I could do with a stiff drink, I don't know about you.'

'I could do with a good sleep. I'm exhausted.'

19

The weekend seemed to fly by and Monday morning found Tamara sick with dread at another week or perhaps even longer listening to the horrible deaths of the young girls.

The court session resumed with the prosecution outlining the murder of Jodie Bowden. The first witness called was Lucy Apps, a friend of Jodie Bowden.

'Lucy, could you tell the court what happened on the night Jodie Bowden was murdered?'

'Jodie had just split up with her boyfriend Gary Stevens, she said she'd dumped him because he was too old, but we all knew he'd dumped her. She always put on this big show of toughness but underneath I knew she was quite upset, so to cheer her up I suggested we all go to a friend's in Woodfield who was holding a party.'

'What was the friend's name?'

'Janine Hewlett.'

'Did you go to the party with Jodie?'

'No. She said she would see us there. She was quite late arriving and a bit flustered. She said some old perv with a dog had followed her, but she soon got over it and started drinking quite a bit.'

'Would you say she was drunk?'

'Yes, very.'

'Why was she walking home alone very drunk and incapable?'

'Well, no one could get a taxi as something was on in town. Janine had called one earlier for Jodie as she wanted to get her out of the house in case she was sick. She said no one was sleeping over as her parents would be home in the morning and she had to clear the place up after the party.'

'Why did Jodie not get in her taxi and go home?' At this point Lucy began to cry uncontrollably. The judge asked her if she would like a break and she confirmed she would. The court was cleared and Marcus and Tamara managed to get a coffee before everyone was back in court again.

'Are you ready to continue Lucy?'

'Yes.'

'Try not to get upset, no one is blaming you for what happened to Jodie. Take your time in answering the questions. I'll repeat the question I asked you before the break. Why did Jodie not get in her taxi when it arrived?'

'Because my boyfriend Rob suggested we pinch her taxi as we couldn't get hold of one, and if we hadn't done that she would still be alive today — it's all our fault she's dead.' She began to cry again and the prosecution counsel asked her if she would like a glass of water before continuing; she nodded her head.

'How did your boyfriend think she was going to get home without a taxi?'

'I felt guilty at what we had done but he said, don't worry about her, Janine will let her stay she's a decent sort. She won't throw her out on the street in that state.'

Julia Campbell, cross-examining, asked: 'The man with the dog that she thought followed her, did she recognize him?'

'No, she said she'd never seen him before. Rob looked out the front door and said he couldn't see anyone, he's gone now.'

'So no one at the party actually saw this supposed man follow her. It could have been a figment of her imagination. Was she a girl given to exaggerate quite a lot? Perhaps you could even describe her as a bit of an attention-seeker.'

'Yes she did, we never knew when to believe her. It was really hard with her to know when she was lying or telling the truth.'

'Thank you, no further questions.'

Robert Quinton, Lucy's boyfriend, was called to the witness box and his evidence was identical to what Lucy had just given. Next Janine Hewlett was called as a prosecution witness and gave her account of what happened on the night of her party.

'Tell us Janine, why did you let Jodie Bowden leave your house in such a state?'

'I didn't know what to do with her at first, she was in such a state and I was really mad at Lucy and Rob for playing such a dirty trick on her. We were both stood at the gate then she got quite abusive with me when I said she couldn't stay the night and she decided to walk home. I could see the state she was in so I relented and called out to her, come back Jodie, you can stay if you want to. Then she yelled back at me over her shoulder, *up yours I don't need you, Gary Stevens or anyone, I can look after myself*. That was the last time I saw her.'

'Thank you Janine. Stay where you are, you may be asked some further questions.'

Julia Campbell asked, 'Did you think Jodie Bowden was capable of getting herself home in the state she was in?'

'No, I thought she should have stayed but she wouldn't come back. I couldn't force her so I went back into the house to clear up after the party.'

'So in fact anyone could have taken advantage of Jodie, the state she was in?'

'Yes, I suppose so.'

The only witness called in the murder of Jessica Hale was her boyfriend Tommy Shields. He told how the evening had started out well and then they quarrelled on the footpath through Drayton Park.

'She always wanted her own way, screaming, shouting and swearing at me if she didn't get it. When she said, you're dumped, I was quite relieved, I wanted to finish with her for a long time but I just hadn't got around to it.'

'Did you see anyone else in the park?' asked Joseph Carpenter.

'No.'

'Not even a dog walker?'

'I didn't see nobody. I thought we were the only ones in the park.'

Julia Campbell asked, 'Were you very angry with your girlfriend that evening?'

'Yes I was.'

'Angry enough to kill her?'

'No! No way! There would be no point, she'd dumped me anyway.'

'Did you see her killer attacking her and decided to leave him to it as you were mad at her?'

'No! . . . I didn't see nobody or hear anything. When I left the park she was still alive.'

'Did she have any enemies at school?'

'Yes, she upset a lot of people, girls and boys. Everyone hated her, my mates kept telling me to ditch, her she's poison. She even upset the teachers. She had a fight with another girl in the classroom and was excluded for a while.'

'So any one of a number of people could have been her killer?'

'Yep.'

Emma Dewey's father then gave his evidence telling of the night he found his daughter murdered in Drayton Park. He said that all evening he had been worried about her walking home alone through the park. She was a good girl but also very headstrong, she said the murderer had been caught and she would be perfectly safe taking the short cut home as she always had in the past before the murders started. He said he remonstrated with her not to take that route home but it was all to no avail, so he decided he would go to the park and meet up with her and see her home safely. As soon as he entered the park he had a bad feeling, he knew immediately she was in danger, he called her name several times but there was no answer and he began to feel very uneasy. He ran along the path and then came upon the horrific scene of his daughter lying dead with a man beside her who was also dead but with his hands around her throat.

Next the statements were read out, given by Tamara Wheeler-Osman and Mrs. Jennifer Reed, taken the following day after the murder of Emma Dewey. They described how they had been frightened by a man in the bushes who called them silly bitches when they started to run away. Mrs. Wheeler-Osman said he had a London accent and the description given by her exactly fitted ex-Chief Inspector Charles Mann.

'Oh hell Marcus! My statement and Jenny's seem to be helping Bill instead of convicting him.'

'There's still Jenny's murder, yet that will be the one to seal his fate.'

'How can you be so sure?'

'He's going to have a really hard time talking his way out of that one. I feel he'll be found guilty on all counts. Common sense dictates that he must be guilty. He is implicated in all the murders in some way or other, it can't just be coincidence that everywhere he goes a murder is committed and two of the victims just happen to be buried in the back gardens of two of his houses.'

'I wish I shared your confidence. I'm really scared he's going to get away with it all.'

It was Friday afternoon and the court was adjourned until Monday morning when the final murder, that of Jenny Reed, would be heard. Tamara felt restless all weekend and couldn't concentrate on anything.

'Would you like to go home Tam? It's a bit unsettling staying in a strange town, not knowing what to do next.'

'No, we have no home, one hotel is much the same as another, so we may as well stay put. When this is over I'd like to go and live in Hong Kong as you've always wanted me to.'

'Tam, do you really mean it?'

'Yes, there's nothing left for me in this country anymore, only bad memories.'

They arrived at the court early on Monday morning, making sure of a seat in the public gallery. Because it was such a high-profile case, and due to all the publicity it had received, it was hard to get a seat in the public gallery; so far they had been lucky but even more people had turned up wanting to be in court to hear the verdict.

Prosecution counsel Joseph Carpenter called Hank Summers as his next witness; he was the site manager of the caravan park.

'Will you please tell the court what happened on the 9th of December last year when Mr. & Mrs. Reed came to the caravan park?'

'Well, I was quite surprised to see them standing there asking if they could rent one of the bungalows. At first I said no because the governor had warned me if I let anyone stay out of season again I would lose my job.'

'Were you in the habit of letting people stay at the park off-season?'

'No, I only did it a few times.'

'Why did you let the Reeds stay when you were on a warning?'

''Cos the lady looked so down and ill. She was white as a sheet and hardly said a word. I felt sorry for her. The bloke did all the talking. I gave them a key to one of the bungalows and left them to settle in. Later on that evening I gets a call from the governor saying he was coming over first thing in the morning at nine o'clock, so I panicked a bit and goes over to the bungalow to tell them to leave.'

'Did you see Mrs. Reed?'

'Nope, only him.'

'How did he seem? Was he calm or flustered?'

'Normal, he came to the door in a dressing gown and said his wife was sound asleep and he wouldn't be able to wake her as she had taken one of her sleeping pills, and he promises they'd be gone by eight o'clock the next morning.'

'Did you see Mrs. Reed alive again?'

'Nope, next time I sees her she's covered in blood and dead as a doornail.'

'Thank you Mr. Summers.'

Julia Campbell was ready to cross-examine.

'When you called at the bungalow to tell the Reeds to leave you say everything seemed normal. Did Mr. Reed seem like a man who had just murdered his wife?'

'Don't know what a man who just murdered his wife would be like. He just seemed normal to me.'

'When the police brought him back to the site office how did he seem then?'

'He was arguing with the police and saying he was innocent and he didn't do nothin'.'

The next prosecution witness was Trevor Passell, the site owner. His evidence tied in with Hank Summers' and gave an almost identical version of events. When asked if he thought Hank Summers capable of murder he replied emphatically that he was not.

Statements were also read out by the police who attended the murder scene in Devon and who were present at the subsequent arrest of Bill Reed. The police statement read that William Reed was found hiding in some woods close to the caravan park. He had said he returned from a walk and found his wife's dead body, so he had ran away to get some help. He thought that the site manager had murdered her while he was out walking so he was too frightened to ask for his help in case he met the same fate as his wife

The officer in charge of the case was the last prosecution witness to be called. He read out transcripts of the police interviews with William Reed, which were a mixture of denials and 'no comment' replies.

Joseph Carpenter informed the judge and jury that the prosecution's case had closed; with that Julia Campbell rose to her feet and opened the defence case by calling William Reed. Flanked by two Dock Officers he was lead across the courtroom to the witness box.

In his defence he stated categorically that he had never raped or murdered anyone, why should he, he was a happily married man. He loved his poor departed wife and she was his only alibi. He even managed a tear or two at the mention of her name. Tamara was seething.

'Look at him Marcus, the hypocrite!'

'Shush darling, don't go upsetting yourself again.'

Regarding the murder of his wife he gave the same version of events that had taken place, as he had given to the police at the time of his arrest in Devon. He was unshakeable and adamant that he hadn't killed his dear wife who meant everything to him, and her lovely little dog Pepper who he spent hours taking for walks. He began to sob and said he couldn't imagine what sort of person would want to harm a defenceless woman and her dog.

Tamara was raging at the hypocrisy of the man and wanted to get up and kill him with her bare hands. Marcus saw the look of anger on her face: he squeezed her hand and said, 'It's nearly all over Tam, try to be brave for a bit longer. We only have the summing up to go, then the wait for the verdict. Then we can get on with the rest of our lives.'

The defence case concluded and the Judge adjourned for the day.

The next morning Joseph Carpenter began his closing speech for the prosecution. He turned and addressed the jury.

'Members of the jury, you have heard evidence that the accused was a decent and upstanding citizen, a married man, a pillar of society. Do not be fooled by this. Ask yourselves, is it at all conceivable that rape and murder was happening all around him, ending in the tragic death of his wife, and he had nothing at all to do with any of it? He was not just a victim of circumstance. Two bodies were found in the back gardens of two of the houses he owned. Eventually he changed his plea to guilty to the death of Jane Birch, claiming it was an accident after she had made advances towards him to gain a price reduction on the sale of his house. You must ask yourself, would a business lady of Jane Birch's calibre, in a highly-paid job, lower herself to have sex with Bill Reed — just to save a few thousand on the price of his house? I don't think so.

'Then there was the body of Joanne Thorn. He claims someone must have slipped into his back garden from the path that runs along the back of the property and threw it into the hole he had dug for the patio footings and covered it with earth, all in a short space of time. With all the other murders and rapes the only alibi he has to his whereabouts at the time they took place were given by his wife, the late Mrs. Reed.

'You may ask yourself why he found it necessary to torture and kill his loyal wife who believed in him totally and never doubted a word he said. I put it to you that Mrs. Reed went away with him willingly, believing him to be innocent of the crimes committed, and when she subsequently discovered he was not innocent after all, he had no further use for her and she became just another victim — but he couldn't even kill his wife mercifully. No, he had to torture her, keeping her alive for several hours, even killing her precious little dog just to taunt her and make her pain even more unbearable to the very last moment of her life.

'Owing to the overwhelming amount of evidence against the defendant that has been put before you during this trial, I say to you, members of the jury, that the only just verdicts you can return are guilty on all counts.' Joseph Carpenter sat down hoping he had done enough to get Bill Reed convicted of the atrocious crimes committed.

Tamara had been sobbing throughout the barrister's closing speech but she was determined to stay and see it through to the bitter end.

Julia Campbell rose to give her closing speech in defence of her client.

'I ask you, ladies and gentlemen of the jury, to look at my client in the dock and ask yourselves, does this respectable man look like a rapist and serial killer? I think not. He is a man that loved his wife, his home and their little dog. He has been a victim of terrible circumstances. He has told the truth about Jane Birch and how frightened he was of being blamed for the Woodfield murders because of her accidental death. He is just an ordinary man and knew that a clever barrister could tie him in knots and implicate him in these murders. After all, the police throughout the past five-year reign of terror have arrested the wrong people many times. If Mrs. Jennifer Reed was alive today she would be standing here protesting her husband's innocence. She was a well-educated lady who came from a good family who had high morals. Her father was an army Colonel who died very young, leaving Jennifer and her mother alone. Despite this hardship her mother managed to send Jennifer to a good private school, ensuring that with a good education behind her she would have a good start in life. A woman of Jennifer's intelligence would hardly fall in love with and marry a serial killer. I think we must credit Mrs. Reed with more intelligence than to do something like that. She saw in him wisdom and understanding, a gentle kindness, a love that not many of us are lucky enough to encounter during our lives. It was bad luck that she and her husband chose that particular caravan park in Devon to spend the night. Someone watched them arrive together and saw him leave alone to go for a walk. A few minutes later, knowing Jennifer was alone inside, the perpetrator got into the bungalow, took a knife from the kitchen and killed Mrs. Reed, also killing the dog, as presumably it was making too much noise. After all, Hampshire does not have the monopoly on murder. I'm sure the county of Devon must have its fair share of murderers.

'I can find no concrete evidence to link my client to the attempted murder of Alice Jones or the rapes of Kendra Rickman and Melanie Taylor; neither of the girls were able to identify their attacker. When the murders and rapes of Jodie Bowden, Jessica Hale and Emma Dewey took place, my client was at home with his wife. Police records show that Mrs. Reed confirmed at the time of their investigations that he was at home with her. So, members of the jury, I must ask you to find William Reed not guilty on all counts.'

'She was convincing, Marcus, I'll give her that. I'm beginning to worry the jury might think so too.'

'We have the judge to sum up yet and give his directions.'

Mr. Justice Tobutt gave his summing up, telling the jury to look at the evidence before them and not to make character judgements of any of the people involved in this trial. If there was any doubt in their mind whatsoever then they must return a verdict of not guilty.

The judge's summing up lasted two hours

before the jury retired to begin their deliberations. The first thing to be decided was who would be the foreman. A smart young man aged about thirty-eight volunteered, and in the absence of any other volunteers the jury were in agreement that he should chair their deliberations.

'To start the ball rolling, can we have a show of hands as to who thinks Bill Reed is guilty?'

The jurors were divided in their opinion: seven guilty, five not guilty.

'OK then, we'll go around the table and each one give their reasons for and against.'

He started with the older lady who had looked on Kendra Rickman in a disapproving manner when she was giving her evidence.

'Could you tell us why you think he is not guilty?'

'I feel he has been a victim of circumstances and has been really unlucky. For instance, the first victim Alice Jones, there was no evidence at all to suggest he was involved in her rape. I think she was just brought into this to clear police files. I feel this also applies to the murders of Jodie Bowden, Jessica Hale and Emma Dewey. The nearest the police came to evidence was the ex-Chief Inspector found at the scene with his hands around her throat. I think the police got it right in thinking one of their own was the killer all along. As for the two other rape victims, Melanie Taylor couldn't identify him; and as for that common Kendra Rickman, she would say anything to draw attention to herself. The only thing the poor man is guilty of is burying Jane Birch in his garden, and I believe what he said — that it was an accident.' Everyone started talking at once and the foreman had to ask for silence to let the lady finish what she had to say and point out they would all get their turn to put their views forward.

'What about Joanne Thorn buried in his other back garden? All I can say is, it's a good job he didn't own any more houses with back gardens.'

The members of the jury all laughed and the foreman had to ask for silence once more, and he asked the young man who had just made the comment to wait until his turn came before he spoke again.

'Please continue.'

'Well, I happen to believe what Mr. Reed said about he left the hole unattended while he went to join the Rickman layabout three doors down who was busy drinking with the lorry driver. No one seemed to know how long the three were at Rickman's house. Someone could quite easily have entered his back garden from the footpath at the back of his property and seen Joanne Thorn walking along the footpath, attacked and murdered her. Then buried her in the freshly dug hole and covered her over with earth.'

'Sounds very unlikely to me,' answered another juror.

'Look, we know that the killer is a local man, he could even be a neighbour of the Reeds and watched him walk down the road to the Rickmans' house and seized his opportunity to attack that poor girl.'

'No . . . no, I'm not having that.' There were shouts of disapproval from the jurors and the foreman called for order once again.

'And what about his wife then? Are you trying to say the man was unlucky yet again?'

'Yes I am, that's exactly what I'm saying. I believe what he said about going for a walk and coming back to the bungalow to find her murdered. Poor man, can you imagine how he felt?'

'If he was going for a walk why didn't he take their dog with him? That's what people usually do when they own a dog,' asked an irate grey haired man.

'I don't know, perhaps he was looking for a late night shop that was still open and he knew he wouldn't be able to take the dog inside. I think you are all too quick to jump to the wrong conclusions without studying all the facts.'

This last comment caused another outburst, and the foreman felt he was losing control of the situation and was glad when it was time to adjourn for the day.

★　★　★

Tamara and Marcus walked around aimlessly, wondering how long the jury would take to reach their verdicts.

'Why does it have to take so long Marcus? Surely anyone can see he's as guilty as hell.'

'Well they wouldn't be doing their job properly if they just rushed through verdicts; you must remember they have a lot to consider, there were so many victims. I still can't come to terms with the fact that Bill Reed was capable of such calculating evil.'

'Don't tell me you think he's innocent?'

'No, of course not. He's definitely guilty, you were right about him all along.'

'Will we ever get over all this or do you think it will haunt us for the rest of our lives?'

'I'm sure the jury will reach the right verdicts and as soon as you see justice done for your friend and all the other poor girls, then you'll be able to start putting all this behind you, especially when we start our new life in Hong Kong. There won't be anything there remotely connected with all this and soon it will be just a bad memory.'

★　★　★

The jury resumed their deliberations the next day. It was the turn of the other jurors to have their say. The younger impetuous members of the jury were quite adamant that he was guilty and nothing they had heard from the elderly lady juror could convince them otherwise. As the foreman went around the table asking each one to speak it was abundantly clear they were getting near to a guilty verdict. There was just the elderly lady sticking to a not guilty verdict. After many hours of deliberation the jury returned to Court and were told by the Judge that a majority verdict could be returned. They returned to their room and resumed their quizzing of the adamant lady. There was no way she would be budged from her decision and reluctantly the foreman pressed the bell for an usher and asked her to deliver a note to the judge asking if he would accept an eleven to one guilty verdict. The jury sat in silence waiting for the usher to return. It was the quietest the foreman had ever seen them. He was tapping his pencil on the table; it seemed like the usher had been gone for half an hour, but in fact it was only five minutes. She came back into the room and said the judge would accept the majority verdicts and requested they return to court.

Everyone was assembled in court awaiting the jury's return. There was a deathly silence across the courtroom; you could have heard a pin drop. Tamara noticed the press were packed into their seats and the whole place seemed to crackle with anticipation, it was like waiting for the next clap of thunder in a storm. Bill had been made to stand, he was gripping the edge of the dock so tightly his knuckles had turned white and the veins were bulging on the backs of his hands. You don't look so clever now, thought Tamara. The jury returned, led by the foreman. Tamara was gripping Marcus's hand tightly, her heart was beating fast. The Court Clerk asked the foreman if they had reached verdicts and he confirmed they had. The clerk went through the charges and the jury foreman returned eleven to one majority verdicts of guilty on all counts. The courtroom erupted; Bill was red-faced with rage and began to shout abuse at the jury. The judge silenced the courtroom and quickly thanked the jury so they could leave.

Tamara was overjoyed; she had only just stopped punching the air when the sentencing procedures began. After hearing some pathetic mitigations by the defence counsel which made Tamara furious, the judge sentenced Bill to life imprisonment. He went on to describe him as a dangerous psychopath who should never be released.

'Marcus, does this mean he really won't ever be free to kill again?'

'Yes darling. Justice has been done, now we can get on with the rest of our lives.'

Tears of relief rolled down Tamara's face and she took one last look at Bill Reed, the man who had caused her so much pain and grief, as he was led away from the dock down to the cells.

After he was gone Tamara tilted her head and looked towards the ceiling of the courtroom, held her hand against her heart and whispered, 'That's justice for you Jenny, rest in peace.' With that Tamara tilted her head forward again and as she did the image of the lady in white flashed before her eyes. Only this time the lady was smiling as if to thank Tamara for what she had done.

We do hope that you have enjoyed reading this large print book.

Did you know that all of our titles are available for purchase?

We publish a wide range of high quality large print books including:
Romances, Mysteries, Classics
General Fiction
Non Fiction and Westerns

Special interest titles available in large print are:
The Little Oxford Dictionary
Music Book
Song Book
Hymn Book
Service Book

Also available from us courtesy of Oxford University Press:
Young Readers' Dictionary
(large print edition)
Young Readers' Thesaurus
(large print edition)

For further information or a free brochure, please contact us at:
Ulverscroft Large Print Books Ltd.,
The Green, Bradgate Road, Anstey,
Leicester, LE7 7FU, England.
Tel: (00 44) 0116 236 4325
Fax: (00 44) 0116 234 0205

Other titles published by
The House of Ulverscroft:

INHERITED FEAR

Eileen de Lisle

Ellee Preston's worst fears were realized — her husband Lewis had inherited his mother's house in Betts Lane, the dreadful house that had seen so much tragedy since the start of the century. Would they ever be able to escape from it? As the activities of the IRA reached Southampton, the house remained the same — sinister, dark and foreboding. Certain members of the family still seemed plagued by bad luck. Adultery, suicide and murder were to blight their lives. Who was the ghost? What did he want? It wasn't until Ellee's daughter Katey decided to have the house exorcised that all was revealed.

NINE BETTS LANE

Eileen de Lisle

When Florence Preston first moved to the house in Betts Lane in 1900, she did not feel there was anything amiss until she became pregnant. This pregnancy was to be the start of a lifetime of unexplained happenings and bad luck. Florence's first child was stillborn. She then received a warning from a gypsy on her doorstep, to leave the house as soon as she could. However, circumstances always prevented her from leaving. Florence felt this sinister house was holding her back, laughing at her. Would she ever be able to leave? Or would the house eventually claim her life?

GUILTY MIND

Irene Marcuse

On Saturday night Anita and Benno Servi were on the steps of their Manhattan apartment building, necking like teenagers. By Monday afternoon Benno was prime suspect for the murder of their babysitter, Ellen Chapman. Benno had walked the young student home. But when she didn't arrive to collect little Clea on Monday, Anita went to Ellen's apartment — where she discovered her body, stabbed with a screwdriver bearing Benno's prints . . . Had there been an affair? And why would Anita refuse to believe the facts? With more to discover, answering the questions about Benno's possible guilt is only part of the problem . . .

RETRIBUTION

Angela Dracup

When businessman Jack Wells is found battered to death in his workshop, skeletons begin to rattle in the family cupboard as DCI Ed Swift investigates. Jack's widow Sheila, however, points the finger of suspicion at Tamzin Crowther, a self-styled white witch. Whilst Swift must act on the strength of the forensic evidence mounting against Tamzin, he senses that the real killer is still free. Things take a sinister turn when Swift is assaulted outside his home — an attack that sounds a warning against his continued probing into the dead man's family — and the chilling and unexpected motive is revealed.

BONES BURIED DEEP

Max Allan Collins

Tempe Brennan's expertise is called upon by Special Agent Seeley Booth, who is stalled on a case deposing a Chicago mob family. He needs assistance with a bizarre discovery: a skeleton, with its bones wired together — and a chilling note — left outside a Federal building. But Tempe determines that the bones are from different corpses, suggesting a serial killer's handiwork ... And as Booth's Mafia case heats up it seems that one of Chicago's most notorious killers is involved. Tempe must unravel the story of the bones — where the truth lies buried — in order to stay alive.